a novel

Imperfect
love

Books by Rebecca Talley

NOVELS:

Heaven Scent
Altared Plans
The Upside of Down
Aura

CHILDREN'S:

Grasshopper Pie
Gabby's Secret

NON-FICTION:

Hook Me: What to Include in Your First Chapter

a novel

Imperfect love

Rebecca Talley

DuBon Publishing

This is a work of fiction, and the views expressed herein are the sole responsibility of the author. Likewise, characters, places, and incidents are either the product of the author's imagination or are represented fictitiously, and any resemblance to actual persons, living or dead, or actual events or locales, is entirely coincidental.

Imperfect Love

Book design and layout copyright © 2014 by Rebecca Talley
Cover design copyright © 2014 by Rebecca Talley

ISBN-13: 978-0692204795
ISBN-10: 0692204792

Printed in the United States of America
Year of first printing: 2014

For my wonderful family.

Thank you for your love and support.

You are the BEST.

chapter 1

A plus sign.

Lauren Wilson blinked the hopeful tears back. Was she seeing it right? She flicked on the bathroom light for a better look and scrutinized the pregnancy test wand.

Definitely a plus sign.

She leaned against the wall.

A baby.

Some moments are milestones, and some milestones are moments. Lauren gazed at the wand again. *This is definitely both.*

After trying for over two years—well, she seemed to be more intent on conceiving than her husband, Paul, but that didn't matter now. The wondering, hoping, then crying, month after month, didn't matter. Nothing mattered now. She was pregnant. Excitement bubbled up inside her. She'd finally have a baby and the happily-ever-after she'd dreamed about since she was a little girl.

Lauren rested her hand across her stomach, her fingers tingling. After all this time, it was finally her turn.

Finally.

She rushed into the bedroom to find her cell phone and call Paul with the news. Her anxious fingers stumbled over the keypad, searching for his speed dial number. *What if he's in a meeting? What if he can't take the call? I don't want to leave this on his voicemail.*

She ended the call before it could go through and sat on the bed. This wasn't something she wanted to tell him over the phone. It was too momentous. Too amazing. Too wonderful.

A photo caught her eye. She handled the delicate metal frame, memories of her wedding flooding her mind. What a perfect day it had been at the church on Third Avenue in Durango, her hometown. It was such a beautiful beginning to their life together, and now they'd move to the next step—adding a baby to their family.

Ideas of how to tell Paul swirled around her head. She wanted to make it special for him, so she decided to take some time to come up with just the right way to let him know he was going to be a daddy. *Daddy.* The word felt sweet and satisfying on her tongue.

Lauren glanced at the clock on the light green wall opposite the bed. Seven thirty. She'd have to hurry—she didn't want to be late for her first class.

Her hands stroked her stomach. *I'm going to have a baby. I can't wait to tell Paul. He'll be as thrilled as I am.*

Lauren drove into the crowded faculty lot and parked under the bare limbs of a large tree. She grabbed her jacket and exited into the cool weather. It was a typical March day in Denver. Billowy gray clouds lined the sky while traces of snow from last week's storm lingered around the school grounds. She made her way to her classroom, trying to hide the smile that tickled her lips. *A new life is growing inside me.* She wanted to sing it out and tell everyone she saw, but she needed to wait to tell Paul first, even if it felt like she'd burst.

Lauren sat at her desk, drumming her fingers while eighth graders filed in and took their seats.

"Hey, Mrs. Wilson, you look happy today," Briana said, tucking her long black hair behind her ears.

"I do?"

"Definitely." Katie grinned, exposing her braces.

"It's a beautiful day, how could I not be happy?" she said, hoping to avert any more comments. The last thing she wanted to do was blurt out that she was pregnant. She needed to keep her excitement under control until she told Paul. Then she'd shout it to the world.

"Looks like it might snow," Katie said, watching her.

"Yes, yes it does. I love a big snow storm, though, don't you?"

"Seems like you're *extra* happy. Even your eyes are happy." Lexi smiled.

Not liking the direction of the conversation, Lauren stood and walked to the front of the class. The bell rang, and Charlie rushed inside, his strawberry blond hair windswept.

"You're late again, Mr. Newton."

"I know. I'm sorry, Mrs. Wilson. But—"

"I don't want to hear any excuses." Lauren suppressed her smirk. Charlie was the best excuse maker she'd had since she started teaching. "Like how Ellie was so hot this morning, and you had no other choice but to talk to her, because she was practicing mind control over you. Or that your mom's car broke down on the other side of town after you made breakfast at the homeless shelter, so you had to jog to school. Or how your locker combination didn't work, so you had to find the janitor, who was where? Oh, yes, he was out helping get a small kitten down from a very tall tree." She arched an eyebrow, anticipating his response.

"All true."

"Charlie, Charlie, Charlie." Lauren shook her head. She had to give him credit for his creativity.

He broke out into a crooked grin. "May I just say how stunning you look this morning, Mrs. Wilson?"

"No, you may not."

He tried again. "May I say you look radiant, Mrs. Wilson?"

Lauren felt the warmth reach her cheeks. Could her students tell she had a glorious secret—a secret that would change her life? "Uh, no. Please take your seat so we can get started."

Charlie sauntered to the back row and slid into his desk. He gave Lauren a slight nod.

She glanced around the classroom, trying to keep her focus on the students and the new unit she was about to introduce. "Good morning. Our next unit of study for this year will be on memoir."

"So, like, we'll be reading people's diaries?" Charlie laughed. "I wonder if they'll be as lame as my sister's."

Other students started laughing. Lauren shot Charlie a look to let him know he shouldn't say anything else. "Memoirs are written accounts of people's memories of events or people or situations. It's their personal recollections and their perspective on what happened. Group one will be reading *The Diary of a Young Girl* by Anne Frank, and group two will be reading *Night* by Elie Wiesel. Group three will read *Because of Romek* by David Faber. All of these memoirs are accounts of the Holocaust."

"Hitler was a maniac," Jeff said under a mass of bushy, dark hair.

Lauren nodded. "He did some terrible things. But we need a deeper understanding of what happened. We'll study the events as well as the use of persuasive speech and propaganda. You will be required to do a project related to the Holocaust that you can present to the class."

Sara raised her hand.

"Yes?"

"Why did he hate Jews so much?" Her deep brown eyes searched Lauren's. "Why did people in my family have to die?"

Taken aback by the sudden lump in her throat, Lauren drew in a breath. She'd only been teaching a few years, and she'd never had a student directly affected by the Holocaust. "He wanted to create a super race and he blamed Jews for Germany's problems. He decided to exterminate them along with others that he decided weren't fit to live, including the handicapped."

"He was crazy," Charlie said, tipping back on his chair.

"Maybe," Lauren said. "For some reason, he believed he had the right to decide who should live and who should die. And people allowed him to gain that power."

"I went to the Holocaust museum with my family last summer. It was really hard to see some of the things in there," Sara said. "Why did he think it was okay to kill millions of people like my family?"

Lauren pursed her lips while images of children being executed danced across her mind. How could anyone kill innocent kids? She touched her stomach, and an urgency to protect her baby coursed through her.

"Mrs. Wilson?" Briana said.

Lauren looked up, suddenly aware that she'd slipped into her own thoughts. "Oh." She tried to recall the last thing someone had said.

Seeming to sense her confusion, Sara said, "Why did Hitler think he could kill so many people?"

Forcing herself to concentrate on Sara, Lauren answered, "Why does anyone think he or she can kill someone else? What gives anyone that right?"

"My father said that Hitler didn't even see the Jews as real people," Sara said, tugging on the long brown braid that fell over her shoulder.

"Perhaps that's how he justified his actions to himself. But"—Lauren raised up her hands—"we're getting ahead of ourselves. We'll be spending the next few weeks on the Holocaust. Today, I'm going to hand out the books and I want you to start thinking about what kind of a project you'd like to present."

After the bell rang, Lauren sat in her chair, pondering the Holocaust and her emotional reaction. While it was impossible to grasp how someone could be so cruel and could so easily kill other human beings, she'd taught this unit before without being so disturbed. Did the knowledge that she'd finally be a mother amplify her senses and make her hypersensitive?

Lauren sat at one of the staff lunch tables looking forward to some quiet time while she considered different ways she could tell Paul the amazing news. She could write a poem or send him on a treasure hunt or give him a box with baby formula inside. She needed something creative.

"Mind if I sit with you?" JoAnn, one of the math teachers, asked.

Lauren mentally rolled her eyes. Everyone knew that JoAnn was a talker and shared intimate details of people's personal lives. The last person Lauren wanted to sit with was JoAnn, but she didn't want to be rude. Lauren motioned with her hand, convinced she'd regret it. "Sure."

JoAnn flopped onto the chair, making a loud creak. "I'm on a diet. Doctor said I need to lose 90 pounds. I don't agree, but my husband made me promise to eat this rabbit food." She started poking her small salad. "You're lucky to be so tiny. I bet you've never worried about having to lose weight."

"Running helps me stay in shape." She probably wouldn't be able to do much running in the coming months, though. The corners of her mouth lifted.

"Exercise? Yeah, the doctor said I needed to do that, too. I think he's trying to kill me instead of make me healthy. Besides, it's common knowledge that menopause makes you gain weight." She looked at Lauren. "But you've got years before you have to worry about that. Are you going to start having your family soon? I mean, it's none of my business, you see, but time keeps marching on. I had my babies back in my twenties. Course, they're all grown now. I keep hoping they'll make me a grandma soon. Kids these days don't like to get married or have kids 'til they're older." JoAnn finally stopped talking and took a bite of her salad.

Lauren hoped they could enjoy the rest of the lunch period in silence.

Several minutes later, JoAnn began again. "Did you hear about Mr. Thompson?" JoAnn leaned in closer. "His classroom computer was loaded with porn." JoAnn nodded. "Yep. He had all sorts of disgusting things on it. I hear he's going to be fired. And that new secretary in the front office—she has a stalker who keeps coming by the school. I heard he's left her flowers and candy and notes even after she told him to get lost."

Lauren didn't know Mr. Thompson well, but she was uncomfortable being involved in a conversation with such serious accusations. Besides, she didn't want to be associated with any disparaging remarks about her coworkers. She preferred to mind her own business and didn't want to be pulled into anyone else's. "How were your classes today?"

"The same as they always are."

Before JoAnn could launch into any other gossip, Lauren said, "We're beginning our study of the Holocaust."

"Oh. I'm glad I only have to teach numbers. I'd never be able to teach kids about why a madman killed so many people. Numbers I understand. People? Not so much."

"And numbers make my head implode." Lauren smiled.

"You know what else I heard about—"

"I'd love to stay and chat, but I need to prepare for my next class." Lauren stood. "It was good talking to you, JoAnn."

"You too. We should do it more often." JoAnn had a spot of ranch salad dressing on her chin, but Lauren was too embarrassed to tell her.

"Have a good day," Lauren said as she left.

Since the lunch period was almost over, Lauren would have to wait until after school to think of a special way to tell Paul.

chapter 2

After school ended, Lauren collected her things and headed out to her white Prius. The day had turned warm. She sat inside her car for a moment watching a few clouds draped across the blue sky. This time of year, it could be snowing in the morning and sunny in the afternoon. People often joked that if you didn't like the weather in Colorado, wait a few minutes and it'd change. She looked forward to summer weather and checking out local parks so she'd know where to take her baby. Outings with Paul and their baby—could it get any better?

Lauren drove over to the local grocery store and found a basket. She'd decided to make Paul a special dinner with steak, potatoes, rolls, steamed asparagus, a green salad, and Bunny Tracks ice cream for dessert. She wanted tonight to be wonderful.

Before Lauren made it to the back of the store to buy the ice cream, she meandered down the aisle with the baby food, cereal, diapers, and other baby items. She picked up a bottle and examined it. An idea sparked. She'd fill the bottle with Skittles, Paul's favorite candy, then give it to him after dinner with a note attached: *Congrats, Daddy*.

Perfect.

Tossing the bottle into her basket, she pushed it quickly down the aisle and almost collided with another basket.

"Lauren? Is that you?"

"Oh, Mrs. Afton, I'm sorry."

"You seem to be in quite a hurry, dear."

Lauren laughed it off. "It's nice to see you today."

The small, gray-haired lady glanced at Lauren's basket. "Steak? Oh, my Henry used to love a good, juicy steak."

Lauren nodded. "It's Paul's favorite, too."

"Are you planning a special dinner?"

"Um, yes." Lauren stepped in front of the basket, blocking Mrs. Afton's view.

"Anniversary?"

Lauren shook her head.

"Birthday?"

Lauren cleared her throat. "No."

"Something else?"

Lauren gave a slight nod, hoping her next-door neighbor didn't notice the baby bottle. While she was thrilled with the idea of having a baby, she didn't want anyone else to know until she could tell her husband. Lauren pushed her cart and said, "I'm sorry, but I'm in a hurry. Have a nice day." She rushed to a checkout line so she could get home and start on her plan.

After she unloaded her bag of groceries, she tried to find a nice tablecloth. "I know I have one somewhere." She looked through a few drawers in the kitchen. "If I were a tablecloth, where would I be?"

Her cell phone rang. "Hi, Mom."

"Hi. How was your day today?"

"Fine." She rummaged through the linen closet.

"It sounds like you're out of breath or something."

"I'm trying to find a tablecloth," Lauren said, balancing her phone between her head and her shoulder while she took out a few towels to see if a tablecloth was hidden behind them.

"Oh?"

She didn't want her mom to ask any probing questions. "I want to see if I can use it for a class presentation." She checked under her bed.

"Remember the beautiful lace one that the Hubbards gave you for your wedding?"

Lauren pulled the phone from her ear and looked at it. How could her mom remember a wedding gift from over five years ago?

"Lauren?"

"Yeah, Mom, I'm here. No, I don't remember that." She wished she had the memory her mom had. She stood on her tiptoes to see if a tablecloth was hiding at the top of her closet.

"I hope you haven't misplaced it. It was so delicate. Looked like it was handmade."

"Maybe it's in one of the boxes in the garage from our move last summer." Lauren had meant to unpack all the boxes, but school had started and she didn't have the time or energy to do it.

"You should get everything unpacked."

"I know, but I'm still hoping we can find a house. I'm tired of renting. Paul thinks we need to wait a while before we purchase a home." *Maybe he will change his mind when he finds out we're having a baby.* She smiled.

"Paul *is* very practical. He likes to make sure things make sense." She could hear the edge to her mom's voice.

"Yeah, he does." Lauren wished he weren't so practical all the time. She checked a cabinet in the laundry room, but still no tablecloth.

"I'm sure you'll get a house."

"I hope so. With all the long hours he's been working this past year, we should be able to afford a down payment." She tried to sound grateful.

"I thought the long hours were temporary? Isn't that what he said?"

"Yes, but I know there have been some big cases and his dad wants him to take on more responsibility at the firm, which is good." Why did she always feel like she had to defend Paul to her mom? "I'm hoping he'll cut back soon." Lauren wanted to justify his schedule to her mom, and to herself, and keep a positive attitude. She missed the time they used to spend together—before he started working with his dad. With a new baby on the way, Paul would reprioritize his time. Wouldn't he?

"I don't know why—"

"Mom, I need to get dinner ready." The last thing she wanted was another discussion about Paul and his lackluster husband skills, at least according to her mother.

"Okay. Love you."

"Love you too." Lauren ended the call. She gave up on finding a tablecloth and walked into the kitchen to begin dinner preparations.

She turned on her iPod and set Pandora to a romantic piano station while she tenderized the steaks.

After peeling the potatoes and placing them in a pot of boiling water, she started to make the green salad. A thrill rippled through her. She hoped Paul would love the dinner she was making, but even more, she hoped he'd love the news about the baby. A baby. *Their baby*. Inside her. Growing.

A vision of her holding a tiny baby in her arms and snuggling it close played across her mind. She didn't care if it was a boy or a girl. She just wanted to have a healthy, happy baby and live her perfect life.

Lauren took a break from dinner and surfed through Facebook. She stopped on her sister's status update and the photos of her niece and nephew, who by all accounts were the most adorable children on earth. They were both smiling while holding dripping ice cream cones. Kaylee was the oldest at four, and Jace had just turned two. Lauren gazed at the two kids with their big grins and bright eyes. Soon, she'd be able to post photos of her baby and be part of the elusive Mommy Club like Bethany.

Her phone vibrated. She checked it to see a text from Paul. *I'll be home late. Sorry. Another meeting with the Gilmores.* Was he serious? Tonight? She tossed her phone on the table while irritation sizzled inside her—her plans were ruined. It was bad enough when he missed dinner other nights, but tonight was important. Lauren let out a long, vocal breath. She should've known better than to plan on Paul being home for dinner. When would she learn?

Unshed tears burned behind her eyes. She wanted to blame her emotions on the pregnancy, but the real problem was Paul, once more, choosing work over her. *Will I ever be first again?*

Of course, Paul had no idea she'd planned this special meal or that she had such wonderful news to share with him, but why couldn't he come home for dinner? Was that too much to ask?

What will I do with this food now?

chapter 3

Lauren turned on the television in her bedroom. She flipped through channels until she came to a late night talk show. The young female guest was apparently some Hollywood celebrity that she didn't recognize. In fact, the girl annoyed her with her hair tossing and big-toothed smile. She tried a few other programs, including an episode of Monk she'd seen before, but nothing appealed to her, so she turned the TV off.

A romance novel on her night stand caught her eye. Lauren had been meaning to start it for a few weeks, but after rereading the first page several times, she put it back.

Even a trip to the kitchen was fruitless, because none of the food sounded remotely appetizing. After pacing the hallway a few times, she returned to her bedroom and tried to convince herself to go to sleep.

The minutes slowly ticked away while she stared at the ceiling, her fingers tapping against her chest. *Where is Paul?* It was almost eleven o'clock, and he hadn't texted her back or returned her phone call. Paul's meetings rarely went this late. What was taking so long? And tonight of all nights—the night she planned to tell him he was finally going to be a father. She scrunched up the blanket into her hands then reached over and flicked on the lamp by the bed

Eying the baby bottle filled with Skittles on her dresser, she stood and walked over to the bottle. She picked it up and caressed it, her vision blurry from the tears.

The garage door opener sounded, and Lauren jumped, her heart pounding in response. Paul was home. Should she tell him now or plan another special night? She bit her lip and decided to tuck the bottle into her dresser drawer. She returned to the bed, wiped at her eyes, and finger-combed her hair.

"Hey, sorry I'm so late," Paul said as he entered the bedroom, his blond hair mussed and his hazel eyes tired.

"It's okay."

He gave her a gentle kiss on the cheek.

"The Gilmores drive me crazy. I wish we could drop them. But you know my dad, always chasing after the big clients and bending over backwards to please them." He kicked off his Italian leather shoes then shrugged off his suit coat and laid it across the bed. "How was your day today?"

"Good. I started my unit on memoir and the Holocaust."

"Did you cry this time?" He smiled.

"I don't cry that easily."

"You cry when you watch commercials." He laughed. "I love that about you."

Lauren smiled. "So other than the Gilmores, how was your day?"

"Busy." He sat next to her on the bed. "Dad wants me to open an office for the firm in Littleton."

"Really?"

"He wants to expand into other areas." Paul rubbed the back of his neck.

"And?"

"I don't know. I told him I'd think about it and get back to him." He stood and unbuttoned his blue shirt. He removed his clothes and dropped them to the floor.

"What would it mean?" Lauren pushed the irritation down that, once again, Paul left his clothes in a heap. *Does he even know we have a laundry basket?*

"I'd have to invest a lot of time to get it going. Hire other attorneys. A lot of work, but I think it'd be worth it." He turned off the lamp and fell into bed. "I'm exhausted."

Lauren lay down next to him, arguing with herself whether to tell him the news or not. He deserved to know, and she was sure she'd erupt like Mount Vesuvius if she had to carry around this incredible secret any longer. It wasn't the way she'd planned to tell him, but maybe that didn't matter. Besides, knowing they were going to have a baby would influence his decision to open a new office. At least she hoped it would.

After a few minutes she said softly, "Something exciting happened today." A smile exploded across her face.

No response.

She rose up on one elbow. "Paul?"

Nothing but rhythmic breathing. He was asleep.

She dropped back down, disappointment churning inside. Paul was a good husband, she reminded herself. He was simply distracted right now. When he learned the news, things would be like they used to be, before work and ambition got in the way. This baby was *exactly* what their marriage needed.

chapter 4

The next morning, Lauren awoke to the sound of the garage door closing. It was only six fifteen but Paul had already left for work. *He didn't even say goodbye.* Did he really have to work so much? Was it her imagination or did he seem to be working more lately?

She pulled the covers up to her chin while thoughts circled her mind. Certainly, Paul wasn't deliberately avoiding her, but if she had to hang onto this secret much longer, she'd explode. This was way too exciting to hold in. For a moment, she considered calling her mom and telling her, but decided Paul deserved to know before anyone else. Even her mom.

Lauren rose from bed and gazed out the window. Morning was just beginning to break, and the neighborhood was bathed in a serene, purple haze. She loved the early morning when so many possibilities lay ahead. And today those possibilities were almost intoxicating. Once Paul knew she was pregnant, he'd be so ecstatic. They'd spend more time together, and Lauren would finally have her perfect life—just as she had imagined it.

Pulling on her robe, Lauren headed toward the kitchen. After school she'd drive over to Paul's office and kidnap him. She'd take him to a nearby park and after walking around, hand-in-hand, she'd present him with the baby bottle. The vision of his excitement was so real it almost felt as if his arms were already around her.

Today would be a good day.
A day that would change everything.

The hours dragged on, seeming as if time were moving backward. Every time Lauren glanced at the clock, only five minutes had passed.

At lunch, she checked her purse to make sure the baby bottle was still inside. She didn't want anything to get in the way of telling Paul today.

After school, as she was about to leave, one of her students approached her. "Hi, Mrs. Wilson."

"Hi, Calli."

"Can I talk to you for a minute?" Calli's deep blue eyes seemed troubled.

"Sure."

"I don't want to bother you, but I need someone to talk to." Calli twirled her straight blond hair around her index finger.

"You're no bother."

A tear snaked down Calli's cheek. "I just found out I'm adopted. My parents told me last night."

"Oh," Lauren eked out, unsure what else to say.

Calli's shoulders stooped. "I guess my birth mom did some drugs while she was pregnant with me and the doctors told her I'd have all sorts of problems." She wiped at her eyes with the back of her hand. "She didn't want me."

Lauren stepped closer to Calli and rested her hand on her student's arm for a moment. "I'm sorry."

"My parents were afraid to tell me, but finally decided I should know." She drew in a ragged breath. "I guess I always knew the truth. I don't look like my parents at all."

Lauren hadn't noticed any problems with Calli and hadn't seen an Individualized Education Program for her, either. In her estimation, Calli was like any other typical girl her age.

Calli looked at Lauren. "I guess they did lots of tests on me when I was a baby and I don't have any of those problems. So my real mom gave me away for"—she paused— "no reason."

"But you have parents now that love you and were willing to care for you even when they thought you might need extra help. It takes very special people to be willing to care for a child with a disability."

"Yeah, but my real mom didn't even care about me. I didn't matter to her." She started to sob.

Lauren reached over and pulled Calli close, caressing her back while Calli let the tears flow.

After several minutes, Calli pulled away. "I'm sorry. I didn't know who else to talk to. You're my favorite teacher."

Lauren smiled at the sweet, sincere comment. "You can always come to me, but I think you need to go home and work this out with your parents." Lauren smoothed Calli's hair. "They love you and they're probably worried about how you are feeling."

Calli glanced at her. "Would you mind taking me home? I don't feel like walking."

"Sure." She could spare a few extra minutes for this young girl without impacting her plans to tell Paul.

Lauren drove Calli home to a small yellow house with white shutters. She walked with Calli toward the front door. A thin woman with short black hair, who Lauren assumed was Calli's mom, stood in the doorway.

"Hi. Calli is one of my students," Lauren said as they approached.

Calli's mom gazed at Lauren with a solemn expression.

"Is there anything I can do?" Lauren asked.

"No. We'll be fine. We don't need your help." The woman reached for Calli's hand. "Come on inside." Calli stepped past her and went into the house. "Thank you." She shut the door.

Lauren turned and walked back to her car feeling like she'd been chastised for trying to do something nice. Two young boys on bikes rode past her on the sidewalk, almost knocking her down. She sat inside the warm car and watched some other kids playing basketball in the cul-de-sac. She hoped that Calli and her parents would be able to talk and work through all the feelings involved.

Lauren rested her hand on her stomach, thankful she didn't have any hard decisions to make about her baby. All she felt was unbelievable anticipation.

Lauren turned the ignition, and the engine roared to life. She headed toward Paul's office in downtown Denver. After fighting some traffic and finding a parking spot, she walked to the large brick building and went inside.

A woman in a tailored ivory pantsuit with long, dark brown hair stood at the reception desk speaking to Gretchen, the receptionist. The scent of expensive perfume wafted through the air.

Lauren didn't want to intrude, so she kept her distance. When the two women finished talking, the professional-looking woman disappeared down the hallway.

"Hi, Gretchen."

"Oh, hi, hon."

Looking in the direction of the hallway, Lauren said, "Is that a new employee?"

"Oh, yes. Raquel Ivanson. She's a new attorney that Mr. Wilson Senior hired last week. He's interviewing another one right now."

My father-in-law must be serious about expanding. Lauren turned her attention back to Gretchen. "I love your new hair. The blond highlights make your blue eyes pop."

"Oh, thanks. You were blessed with beautiful hair. If I had curly, thick hair like you, I wouldn't need to do a thing." She ran her fingers through her hair. "But I was cursed with this mousy brown, limp mess. I gotta do something with it."

"I love the change."

"You don't think I'm too old for it?"

"No. It makes you look so much younger."

"I'd believe you, but I see these wrinkles staring back at me every morning." Gretchen laughed.

"I think you look wonderful."

"Well, you made my day, hon. What can I do for you?"

"Is Paul in?" Lauren patted her purse.

"No, I'm sorry. He left about thirty minutes ago."

Trying to control the disappointment, Lauren said, "Oh. When will he be back?"

"He said he wouldn't be in for the rest of the day." Gretchen adjusted her glasses. "I'm sorry."

Lauren waved her hand, hoping to dissipate the frustration in the pit of her stomach. "It's okay. He didn't know I was coming. Kind of a surprise." She forced a smile. "I'll text him in a while and see when he's coming home."

Lauren left the building and decided to do a little window shopping. A crisp breeze filtered through her hair as she walked along the Sixteenth Street Mall.

She stopped at a children's store and stared at the brightly-colored clothing displayed in the window. Before she knew it, she was inside.

"Hi, can I help you find something?" a skinny, twenty-something girl with shaggy black hair asked.

"Oh, I'm just looking. Thanks."

"I'm Lacey. Let me know if you need any help." The girl turned to walk away.

Almost afraid to say it aloud, Lauren said, "Actually, um, do you carry newborn items?"

Lacey turned back to her with a smile. "Yes. All of our newborn things are in that far corner." She gestured toward the back of the store.

"Thanks."

Lauren was immediately drawn to a rack of the tiniest outfits she'd ever seen. She picked one up and held it. Pink giraffes adorned the front and the little feet had giraffe faces. On the back, ruffles lined the bottom area. A big pink bow sat in the middle of the ruffles. She could definitely imagine holding a baby in that outfit. *Her baby.*

Though it was tempting to purchase every newborn outfit she saw, Lauren decided to wait a bit, at least until Paul knew. Then she'd go on a spending splurge that would put Hollywood celebrities to shame.

On the way home, she envisioned all the cute little clothes she'd get and how she could decorate the nursery, including a crib with a canopy. She'd thought about this so many times before, but this time it was real. She could actually start planning for a baby. A shiver of excitement raced up her back.

When she arrived home, Lauren checked her phone. No text from Paul. Opening the refrigerator, she decided to try to resurrect the dinner from last night, even if she had to eat it by herself. No need to waste a perfectly good meal.

She reheated the steak and the potatoes, and just as she was setting them on the table, Paul opened the front door and came in with a bottle of champagne in his hands. "Guess what?"

"I don't know." Lauren was so happy to see him, she didn't care what he had to say. She'd finally be able to tell him.

"We won the Jackson case." He hugged her and picked her up off her feet.

She laughed. "That's great."

He set her down. "I'll say. It was a huge case too. And because of my investigations into the Durhams, we won the case." He grinned, his hazel eyes sparkling.

"I'm proud of you."

He opened the cupboard and found two wine glasses. "Let's celebrate."

Lauren bit her lip. "I want to celebrate, but I think I'll skip the champagne."

"Huh? Why?" He gave her a perplexed expression.

Lauren grabbed her purse and pulled out the bottle. Without a word, she handed it to Paul.

"What's this?" With a bewildered look, he read the card attached to the bottle. "Wait . . . what?"

Lauren nodded, her smile so wide it hurt her cheeks.

"We're going to . . . you're . . . we're having a . . ." The happy questions hung over them like a bouquet of fresh roses.

"Yes. We are." Her heart beat with rapture.

Paul collapsed onto a kitchen chair and raked his hand through his hair. "Wow. I don't know what to say."

Ignoring his body language, Lauren said, "That you're as thrilled as I am."

"Well, yeah. Of course." He sat back against the chair, looking as if he'd lost all the air in his lungs.

"But?"

"I didn't expect this. I'm surprised." He gazed at her, the baby bottle rotating in his hands.

"Surprised in a *good* way, right?" She held her breath, waiting for his answer.

"It's just that I'm so busy at work trying to open this new office and . . . but this is great news." He stood and pulled her in for a hug.

"Really?'

"Yes."

"You're sure?"

He looked at her, "Yeah."

Lauren tried not to let her disappointment in his reaction show. What had she expected, exactly? Cartwheels? Hollering at the top of his lungs? Dancing? Singing? Probably not, but at least a little more enthusiasm.

"Lauren?" Paul said.

"We've been trying for a while, and it's finally happened. I wanted you to be—"

"I'm totally happy about it." He embraced her again. Maybe she'd expected too much from him.

"I'm not sure of the date. I'll call tomorrow and make an appointment to see the doctor. Can you come with me?" She wanted Paul to be there with her every step of the way. This was their baby, and she wanted them to share everything together.

He stepped back from her. "I really want to, but we'll have to see what my schedule is like."

She nodded, trying to keep her emotions in check. "Okay. I'll let you know."

chapter 5

A few days later, Lauren and Paul were both getting ready for work. Already dressed in a navy blue skirt and cream-colored blouse, Lauren walked into the bathroom while Paul was shaving. "I think we should go see my mom and my sister and tell them in person."

Lauren's heartbeat intensified at the sight of her handsome husband wearing only a green towel and smelling of Irish Spring. Paul let the water from the bathroom faucet stream over his razor. "I don't know if I can make a trip to Durango right now, but you should go and tell her and Bethany." He began shaving under his chin.

Lauren reached out and touched his bare shoulder, his skin soft and warm under her fingers. "But I really want you to come with me. It's our baby. Our announcement." She gazed at him in the mirror. "It's really important to me that we both tell my family. Together."

Paul grabbed the hand towel and wiped at his face. "I'll see what I can do, but no promises." He smiled at her. "Maybe next weekend?"

Lauren clasped her hands together. "We can leave after work on Friday and drive back Monday morning. I can get a sub." Her mind worked, quickly figuring out details.

"Sometimes, you remind me of a little girl." Paul touched her on the nose.

"I'm so excited, I can hardly stand it." Lauren rose up and down on her toes a few times.

Paul walked out of the bathroom. Over his shoulder he said, "Don't forget, we need to tell my parents too."

She faced the bedroom and leaned against the door frame of the bathroom. "When?" Lauren was hoping he'd say in a few years or so, but knew she wouldn't be so lucky.

"Mom has been asking us to come to dinner for a couple of weeks," Paul said from his walk-in closet.

Lauren had successfully avoided her in-laws for over three weeks—three weeks, four days, and ten hours.

Wearing his charcoal suit pants and unbuttoned burgundy dress shirt, Paul said, "Did I forget to tell you?" He pulled out some socks from his drawer and sat on the bed then leaned over to put them on.

Lauren sat next to him. "Yeah." *Thank goodness for small favors.*

"Sorry. I have a lot on my mind." He sat up then stood to button his shirt.

"I know."

He grabbed a silver paisley tie and slung it around his neck. "Should I tell her we'll come over this weekend for Sunday dinner?"

"Sure." Lauren was so thrilled to be expecting a baby, even a dinner with the in-laws couldn't dampen it.

Paul turned and gazed at her. "You're beautiful today. Your big brown eyes are shining."

Shining? Lauren liked that image. "Thanks."

"And you'll be a great mommy."

"Mommy." She giggled. "I *love* how that sounds."

Paul put on his suit coat. "We better hurry or we'll both be late for work."

That Sunday afternoon, Lauren tried on at least five different outfits. Two dresses, a pantsuit, and two skirts with matching tops. She'd married into the Wilson family five years ago, but she still felt like she was an outsider eager for approval.

Paul walked into the bedroom in black slacks and a teal dress shirt. "It's getting late. You know how my mom is about being punctual." He stepped into the bathroom and combed his blond hair.

"Obsessive." Lauren said it softly enough that Paul didn't hear her. Or at least he didn't respond.

He turned and faced her. "Why aren't you dressed?"

"I can't find the right thing to wear."

"Just put on one of the dresses in your closet. My parents don't care."

If only that were true. Lauren had learned the first time she met Paul's parents that appearances were important. Actually, they were crucial. "I want to look right for dinner."

"You're way too worried about it."

I wish.

"Whatever you decide, we need to hurry. We don't want my mom to have a breakdown because the soup is cold."

During the drive over to the Wilson's home in Cherry Creek Estates, one of Denver's most exclusive neighborhoods, Lauren picked at threads on her dark green dress, wishing she'd chosen to wear her navy blue pantsuit instead. How would they react to the news? She hoped they'd be happy. Maybe the baby would bridge some gaps and make them a family. She gazed out the window at the luxurious homes passing by. *Probably not.*

Paul parked the car in the circular driveway, and they walked toward the stone pillars of the entryway. Lauren interlocked arms with Paul.

A petite woman with over-sized glasses opened the door. "Hello?"

"Hi." Paul extended his hand. "I'm Paul Wilson, and this is my wife, Lauren."

"Oh yes." She opened the door wider.

"You must be new," Paul said.

"Yes, sir. Mr. and Mrs. Wilson are waiting in the living room."

"Thank you."

Lauren's dress shoes clicked on the marble floor as they made their way to the expansive living room with the highly-polished, black grand piano in the corner.

Paul's parents both stood. His mother, with her blond, perfectly coiffed short hair, was dressed in a simple black dress with a large, gold brooch pinned on it.

"So good to see you, Paul," his mother said as she drew him in for a hug.

She turned to Lauren and dipped her head. "Nice to see you, dear."

"Hi, Georgia."

Paul's father, Robert, who was dressed in a blue pin-striped shirt and navy slacks, said, "Welcome to dinner. Nice to see you, Lauren. It's been a while." He smoothed his gray-streaked hair.

"Yes, it has." Lauren didn't know what else to say, so she stood next to Paul and locked her knees together.

"It is five thirty, exactly. Time for dinner. Let's move into the dining room," Georgia said.

The antique wooden table was set exquisitely. Each place had more dishes than Lauren used in a week. She hoped she'd remember which utensil to use, how to sip her soup properly, and how to place her napkin in her lap. No wiping her mouth on her sleeve at this house.

They exchanged small talk as they ate soup, salad, roast turkey with cranberry sauce, steamed broccoli, and strawberry cheesecake for dessert. Lauren was thankful the pregnancy hadn't made her too sick to eat. Other than some fatigue, she felt great.

"Let's go back into the living room to visit for a bit and have coffee," Georgia said.

They sat on the formal couches and endured silence for several minutes.

"I have some files I want you to read over."

"Sure, Dad," Paul said.

"How are things progressing for opening the new office in Littleton?" Georgia asked. "We're so proud of you for taking this on. Your father says you are doing very well. I tell him that's no surprise." She smiled.

Paul nodded. "Thanks, Mom. Things are good. Busy. Lots to do."

Lauren elbowed him so he'd say something about the baby. The sooner he told his parents, the sooner they could leave.

Georgia turned to Lauren. "You look very nice this evening. The forest green brings out the blush of your cheeks and complements your red hair."

"Thank you." *Oh no. Can Georgia tell I'm pregnant just by looking at me?*

"Have you thought about our last conversation about going back to get your master's?" Georgia sipped her coffee from a delicate china cup.

"I've been really busy with my classes."

"I'm sure you are an excellent teacher, which is admirable, of course, but the place to make an impact comes from administration. Don't you agree?"

Lauren shifted her weight. "I love teaching. I feel like that's where I can really make a difference."

"Yes, but as a principal, and eventually the superintendent, you could make a much bigger difference and make a mark for yourself at the same time."

Lauren nodded. She didn't have the aspirations her mother-in-law had for her. She loved being a teacher and interacting with students every day. She loved to watch them learn and grow. It wasn't worth trying to explain that again to Georgia.

"What do you think, Paul?" Georgia turned her attention to her son.

Lauren elbowed him again.

Paul cleared his throat. "We wanted to come over tonight so we could tell you something."

Both of his parents gazed at him intently.

"Are you finally buying a house?" Robert said. "It's about time with what I'm paying you." He laughed heartily.

"No, it's not that."

Paul was stalling. Was he afraid to tell his parents?

"Well, spit it out, Paul. Don't keep us in the dark," Georgia said. She set her cup down. "We're both wondering what this is."

"Well." He licked his lips. "We're going to have baby."

"A baby? Really?" Georgia said, shock evident in her tone.

"Yes." Paul put his arm around Lauren and pulled her close. "We're both very excited."

"That's great news, son." Robert clapped Paul on the shoulder.

Georgia smiled, but her eyes held something back. "Yes, it is. Very good news. We are surprised, though. We thought Lauren would be going back to school and that you'd be solely focused on the expansion and building up our client list over the next few years. We didn't anticipate you'd be having a baby so soon."

So soon? They definitely had a different view of time than Lauren did.

"Lauren isn't planning to do any more schooling right now, and I can still take on the extra work with the expansion. A baby won't change that."

"You're right. You can do anything you put your mind to. You will yet do great things." Georgia gazed at Lauren. "When is the baby due?"

"In November. We haven't seen the doctor yet." Lauren squeezed Paul's arm.

"What a lovely surprise. I'm sure he, or she, will be a delightful addition to our family," Georgia said.

"We can't wait," Lauren said, even though she wasn't quite sure that Paul felt the same way.

They continued to visit for another thirty minutes.

"Bye, Mom." Paul kissed Georgia on the cheek. "It was a delicious dinner."

"Don't be such a stranger. I know it's a bit of a drive from your condominium, but I miss seeing you."

"Okay, mom." He glanced at Lauren. "*We'll* try to come over more often."

Georgia gave Lauren a hug. "Congratulations. You'll make a wonderful mother."

"Thank you." Maybe this baby *would* bridge the gap between her and Georgia. Maybe.

Robert shook Paul's hand then said goodbye to Lauren.

As soon as they were in the car, Lauren let out a long breath, relieved it had gone better than she thought it would.

A wide grin broke out across Paul's face.

"What are you smiling at?"

"Can you see my mom as a grandma?"

The idea invoked a contradictory image in Lauren's mind. *Georgia* and *grandma* didn't go together. At all. She grabbed Paul's hand in both of hers. "I can hardly think of anything besides having our baby."

"I think you'll need to have patience. It's still months away."

"I know. I've just been wanting this for so long."

Paul glanced at her. "I'm sorry I've been so wrapped up in work. I promise to be better."

chapter 6

On Thursday, Lauren arrived at school and found Mr. Johnson, the principal, in her classroom. She hoped there wasn't anything wrong because he didn't usually come to her classroom simply to chat. "Hi," she said as she set her black leather bag on her desk.

"Lauren, something has come to my attention."

"Yes?" She had no idea what he meant.

"A parent called to complain that you'd taken her child home in your car."

"Yes, I did." Lauren nodded, not understanding the problem.

He rubbed his clean-shaven chin then peered at her through his dark-rimmed glasses. "That puts us in an awkward situation."

"Why?" Since when was it wrong to help a student?

He sat on the edge of a desk and clasped his hands together in his lap. "The parent claims you are interfering in a personal situation."

"Not at all." Lauren's face heated at the implication of wrong-doing. "Calli came to me and asked for my help."

"Not according to her mother. She wants you to leave Calli alone."

"I don't understand why Calli—"

"Just leave her alone, so we don't have any problems. Remember last year when Mr. Frasier was accused of—"

"Yes, but this is totally different." Lauren had done nothing wrong. Since when did helping a student become a crime?

He stood. "We don't want parents to have any reason to cause problems for our teachers." He adjusted his glasses.

"But—"

"Please." He held his hand up. "If Calli needs help or needs someone to talk to, we have the resources for that. We have counselors who can help her. I know your heart is in the right place, but it's better to not get personally involved, especially if a parent has expressed concern."

Lauren said nothing, but her anger bubbled. How dare someone, anyone, insinuate she was doing anything but caring about a student.

"Are we clear on this?" He waited for her answer.

She gave a slight nod. "Yes."

Mr. Johnson left, and Lauren plopped into her chair, shocked. Since when did talking to a student after school and giving her a ride home constitute a federal offense? Why was it so difficult to do something kind? Calli's mom completely overreacted.

Students began filing into her classroom. She put the Calli situation out of her mind so she could focus on teaching her lesson.

After the kids settled into their desks, and the early-morning hum of conversation died down, Lauren said, "We'll be seeing some images today that are pretty hard to watch. I want you to see what happened to these people, but if the images are too difficult, you may be excused to the library." The last thing she wanted was make anyone else feel uncomfortable.

She showed them images of a brick wall where prisoners were executed and chambers where they were gassed. She said nothing, letting the silence emphasize more than her words could.

"These people had no voice," she finally said. "They had no rights. Hitler wanted to exterminate all those he felt violated his idea of perfection. And he had an entire army that followed him and carried out his orders."

"I would've said something or stood up against Hitler," Brianne said, her long black hair falling over her shoulders.

"Would you?" Lauren looked at her, wondering if her student actually understood the implications of taking such a stand. "What if it meant completely changing your life? Or risking it? Would you do it then?"

"Yes." Brianne said it with conviction in her brown eyes.

"You don't understand what this world was like." Lauren took a few steps across the classroom. "Here, in the United States, you can say what you want. You have freedom of speech. But back then, in Germany, those who said anything were punished. Germans were just as afraid of Hitler as the Jews were. He was merciless in executing his plan to create his perfect nation."

"But people helped," Brianne said.

"Yes. There were courageous people, but they had to be very careful. They couldn't voice their opposition. They had to help in secret."

They continued to discuss how a whole nation could have allowed such atrocities when the bell rang, interrupting their discussion.

"Please read the assigned pages in your books tonight and be ready to discuss them in your groups tomorrow."

That afternoon, Lauren drove home in silence. She was lost in her thoughts about her lesson. The images of death and destruction lingered in her mind. Would she have been strong enough to stand up against something so wrong? Would she have been able to say she wouldn't participate?

Her thoughts went back to Calli. Lauren didn't know why her mom had reacted the way she did. She was careful not to speak to Calli in class today and hoped Calli's mom would mellow out.

Lauren pulled her car into the garage then went into the empty house.

In her bedroom, she eyed her closet. "Where is my suitcase?"

She and Paul planned to leave tomorrow after work and make the seven hour drive to southwestern Colorado. Early April in Durango meant the days might be warm, but the nights would be chilly.

Her phone rang. "Hi, Mom."

"Still planning to come, right?"

"Yes."

"Why this special trip?"

Lauren rummaged through her clothes. "Can't I come home to visit because I want to see my mom?"

"Of course, but you don't do it very often. Is everything okay?" Her mom was fishing for the reason, but Lauren had no intention of giving her any bait.

"Everything is fine. I can't wait to see you and Bethany and the kids." The anticipation was almost too much.

"I'm surprised Paul can leave for the *whole* weekend."

"Mom, don't start." She pulled a couple of shirts from her closet.

"What time will you be here?"

Lauren switched the phone to her other ear. "Close to midnight."

"And when will you be leaving?"

"I'm hoping to talk Paul into staying until Monday. I've already called for a sub."

"I wish you could stay longer. Or even better, move back to Durango."

"Mom, you know Paul's career is here. Our life is here in Denver."

"I know, but you can't blame me for trying. I miss you."

"I miss you too." Lauren found her brown leather jacket and laid it across the bed.

"I already have the meals planned, and your sister and the kids will be here most of the weekend. Matt has a training, so he won't be here."

"That's too bad, but I'm glad I'll get to see Bethany and the kids. It's been way too long."

"See you tomorrow night. Drive safe, especially over Wolf Creek. There may be snow. You know how these spring storms can be."

"Thanks, Mom. I'll text you when we're leaving."

They said their goodbyes, and Lauren tossed her phone on the unmade bed. She grabbed a couple of pairs of shoes and began searching for her suitcase.

chapter 7

The next day at school, Lauren set her papers on the right side of her desk and opened the bottom drawer to retrieve her lunch. She snuck a few of the red grapes she'd packed in the fruit salad, the sweetness of the grapes exploding in her mouth. She looked forward to her lunch break so she could eat more.

"Excuse me?" a female voice carried from the doorway. "I'm Amy Norris."

Lauren looked up to see Calli's mom.

Oh great. She's probably here to yell at me. Lauren steeled herself and rose from her desk. "Yes?" The last thing she wanted was a confrontation with a student's mother.

The small woman with deep brown eyes and olive skin said, "May I speak with your for a few minutes?"

"Sure." Lauren's nerves crackled. She didn't want to say the wrong thing and make the situation worse.

Mrs. Norris shuffled toward her. "I'm sorry about speaking with the principal. It's just that . . ."

Lauren waited for her to continue, squelching her desire to ask the woman to leave.

Calli's mom made eye contact briefly. "We didn't want Calli to know she was adopted. We thought we were protecting her that way."

Lauren nodded, her heart slightly softening.

"She started asking us questions for a biology assignment on genetics. We tried to answer them, but we didn't do a very good job." Her eyes saddened, and Lauren's anger melted away.

Mrs. Norris sat on one of the chairs and stared at the floor.

Lauren wasn't sure what to say or do while the heavy silence hung over them. Finally she said, "I'm sure you did what you thought best." She sat in a chair next to Mrs. Norris wanting to comfort her, but afraid to try.

"I really wanted to be a mom. That's all I've ever wanted to be." She picked at some lint on her bulky pink sweater. "My friends were having babies. Seemed like everyone I saw had children." She paused. "Except me." Lauren could definitely relate to that feeling, and she began to see Calli's mom through new eyes.

"When the opportunity came up to adopt Calli, we jumped at it. Even though the doctors said she'd be disabled because her birth mom had been on so many drugs, I didn't care. I wanted her anyway." Her eyes glistened.

"I think you were very courageous to take on a baby with disabilities." Lauren wished she were that brave.

"I'm not sure it was courageous, I just wanted her." She wiped at her eyes. "And the doctors were wrong. She's perfect."

Lauren wanted to throw her arms around this woman, but she refrained because it wouldn't be appropriate. "Calli is a wonderful girl. She's very sweet, and she works hard in my class."

"She talks about you." Calli's mom smiled slightly. "You're her favorite teacher." She sniffed. "When I realized you'd brought her home, I felt threatened."

"Threatened?" Lauren realized why Mrs. Norris had acted the way she did. It wasn't because Lauren had done anything wrong, but because she was trying to protect herself and her relationship with her daughter.

"Probably sounds ridiculous to you, but after we told her the truth she was so upset. She said things—"

"I'm sure she didn't mean them." Lauren couldn't begin to understand the anguish this woman had gone through. It was a reminder that even though she saw these kids every day in school, she had no idea what the dynamics were at home.

"I was scared. So I overreacted. I'm sorry. It's just been difficult."

"No need to apologize." Lauren reached out and touched Calli's mom on the shoulder. "I'm sorry if I overstepped."

"You didn't. She came to you because she likes you, and she's trying to make sense of everything. Maybe we were wrong to keep this from her." She rubbed her arms. "I didn't want her to feel bad because her mother gave her up for adoption—to feel like she was unwanted. She's been a gift to us."

"She knows that." Lauren peered at her wishing she could do something more than offer a few words.

"I guess adoption isn't easy on anyone." She paused. "I sometimes wonder if her birth mother ever thinks about her, if she regrets her decision, and if she'd known Calli was going to be fine, if she would've kept her." She shook her head. "Then I tell myself to stop thinking about it because Calli is everything to me. I don't know what I'd do without her."

"She is a wonderful girl."

Mrs. Norris nodded. "Yes, she is." She went on to share some stories about Calli and Lauren listened without interrupting, hoping that this would help Calli's mom feel better.

The bell rang, and Mrs. Norris glanced at the large clock on the wall. "I'm sorry. I took up your whole lunch break."

Lauren wanted to tell this courageous woman how deeply their conversation had touched her and how she hoped she'd be the same kind of mother someday, but she didn't want to make things awkward. "Not a problem. I appreciate you coming by."

Mrs. Norris stood then reached her hand out to shake Lauren's. "Thank you for listening. And thank you for caring about Calli."

Lauren smiled and watched Calli's mom leave the classroom. Her stomach growled, but the warm feeling that enveloped her compensated for her hunger. Students began walking in, and she prepared to teach her next class.

During her last class of the day, Lauren said, "Have a good weekend everyone. I'll be out of town on Monday, so please be nice to the substitute teacher."

"I hope it's Miss Grayson," Adam said. He raised his dark eyebrows up and down. "She is hot." He whistled.

Lauren pointed at Adam. "No more of that, Mr. Colson. I don't want to hear that you've proposed to her again."

The class broke out in laughter.

"You should've seen him, Mrs. Wilson. All down on one knee and everything," Carlos yelled.

"I know. I heard all about it." Lauren shook her head and kept her smile to herself. Imagining her student proposing to a substitute teacher, during class, was so ridiculous it was humorous. "None of that while I'm gone. Best behavior please."

"She would've said yes," Adam said, nodding vigorously.

"Hopefully you'll get a different sub this time."

"Aw, Mrs. Wilson, you're no fun." Adam frowned.

"Yeah, I know. I've crushed your dreams."

"Exactly. Miss Grayson is my soul mate," Adam said, clutching at his chest.

"Seriously, Adam. You're a chubby 8th grader with stringy hair and a big zit on your chin," Camry Jones said from her desk toward the back. Several girls joined in laughing with her.

"Hey—" Adam started.

"That's enough." Lauren held her hands up. "Please read the assignment over the weekend."

"Homework? Over the weekend?" Landon, a quiet boy with glasses, said.

Lauren nodded.

"You're killin' us," Carlos said above the groans of the other students.

"I'm sure you'll survive."

The students left the classroom, and Lauren rushed out to her car. She was anxious to go home and get on the road. She hadn't been to Durango in months, and she couldn't wait to have a break from school and to tell her mom that she was finally going to give her a grandchild.

Her stomach reminded her that she hadn't eaten, so Lauren grabbed items out of her lunch sack and munched on them while she drove back to her condo.

Lauren finished packing her toiletries and set the suitcase by the front door. She called Paul to see where he was, but it went straight to his voicemail, so she texted him.

A few minutes later, he texted her back. *I'm sorry. I can't make it to Durango this weekend.*

What? Why not?

Emergency conference with the Gilmores tomorrow.

Her heart beat rapidly. She wanted to slap the Gilmores. *Saturday?*

Yeah.

Paul knew how important this trip was to her. How could he cancel on her at the last minute? *What about our trip?*

I made a reservation for you.

To fly?

Yes.

When?

7:20 tonight on United.

Too expensive.

I've already paid for it.

Tears built in the corners of her eyes. *I don't want to go without you. I can't.*

I wanted you to be with me.

Meeting is about to start. Flight 4920. Return on Monday.

She turned her phone over in her hand a few times. She desperately wanted to share the news with her family, but just as desperately wanted Paul to be there. It was *their* news. Together. If that meant they had to wait then so be it. *We can go another time.*

She waited for a response, but after ten minutes realized he wasn't going to text her anymore. The disappointment stung. She wanted to share her news in person with her family, and she wanted Paul to be there with her. Why did it have to be so difficult?

If she didn't go to Durango, her mom would be so upset. She didn't want to be responsible for ruining her mom's weekend like Paul had ruined hers, but she didn't want to go alone either. It wasn't fair that Paul was making her choose.

Lauren paced in the kitchen, her shoes clacking against the ceramic tile. What should she do?

Her phone rang, and she hoped it was Paul. Instead, it was Bethany.

"Hey."

"Can't wait to see you. Have you left yet?" Bethany said.

"No." She walked into the living room.

"Mom said you'd be leaving soon."

Lauren heard the kids in the background. "Change of plans."

"What?"

"Paul can't get away." She crumpled onto the loveseat, the large cushions practically swallowing her.

"Oh no. We were all really looking forward to seeing you. Especially Mom. I think she's been cooking for three days."

"I don't know what to do." Why did she have to make such a hard choice?

"Can you come without him?"

"He said he made a reservation for me to fly into Durango tonight."

"Then come. Oh, wait . . . hang on . . . Kaylee, please stop bugging your brother . . . Sorry. What time should I pick you up at the airport?"

"I don't know." Lauren paused. "I wanted him to come with me."

"But if he can't, you should come anyway. He can come next time."

Bethany had no idea how important it was for Paul to be there, because she had no clue what Lauren was about to tell them. "Maybe."

"You don't want Mom all upset, do you?"

"No." Lauren didn't want to disappoint her family, but she didn't feel quite right about sharing such important news without Paul.

"Just come."

Lauren leaned back against the loveseat and stared at the ceiling. She desperately wanted to tell her mom and sister about the baby so they could all share the experience. Logically, she knew Paul hadn't purposely planned the conflict, but she couldn't stop the frustration and resentment that simmered inside her. His job was more important than coming with her to Durango. "Okay. I'll come."

"Awesome!"

"I'll text you the time when I get to the airport here. I better hurry if I want to make it."

"We haven't seen you in months."

"I know. I'm looking forward to plenty of time with the kids." She stood and walked into her bathroom to check for anything she might have forgotten.

"They're both excited."

"Me too."

Lauren hung up the phone. She was eager to see her family, but upset that Paul wasn't coming along. He'd been choosing work over her for far too long. His ambition was charming when they met, even appealing, but now it seemed to get in the way of their relationship. Worse, it was getting in the way of sharing the most exciting news she'd had in years. She wanted to see her family and revel in the news that she was going to be a mom, so she planned to tell them without Paul. It'd serve him right for bailing out at the last minute.

Lauren made it to Denver International Airport on time and boarded the small plane bound for Durango. While on the plane, she tried to read a book, but her mind kept wandering back to the life growing inside her. A boy? Girl? She didn't care. She'd need to make a list of names, buy cute little clothes, figure out how to decorate a nursery, study parenting books. She couldn't wait to get started.

After a bit of turbulence, the plane finally touched down. Her stomach was a tangle of nerves. She'd contemplated a clever way to tell her family, but the last time she tried to do that, it bombed. A simple "I'm going to have a baby," would have to suffice.

Lauren walked across the tarmac, into the building, and through the doors. Immediately, she spotted Bethany wearing a big smile.

"Hey, sis," Bethany said as she hugged her. "You look amazing. Been working out or something?"

Something. "Look at you. You don't look like a mom of two small kids."

"They keep me running. All. The. Time." She laughed. "I feel like all I do is chase after them."

Lauren looked forward to the same thing in a few years.

"Glad you got here safe."

"Me too." Lauren touched her sister's silky hair. "Your hair is so long. I've always wished mine was straight and smooth like yours."

"And I've always wanted curly hair like you."

They both laughed.

"At least we both have the same color, right?" Lauren lifted a strand of her hair.

"What color did we decide our hair is?"

"Deep auburn with burgundy highlights." Lauren said it with a British accent.

"Oh yeah." Bethany laughed again. "Because we hated people telling us our hair was red. That's too boring."

"Exactly."

They walked over to the baggage area and Lauren picked up her small gray suitcase. "Where are the kids?"

"At Mom's. She thought it'd be easier to get you without them."

They headed toward the glass double doors to exit. "Guess we're both husbandless this weekend." Lauren tried to make light of it, but her heart hurt.

"We're going to party it up. Our men will be sorry they missed all the fun."

"It's so good to see you, Beth." Lauren slung her arm around Bethany's shoulders.

"You too, Lor."

They found Bethany's dark green, four-door Subaru and got in. Bethany started up the car and pulled out onto the road that was lined with native brush.

"Feels like I haven't been home forever." Lauren gazed out the window at the darkened sky sporting millions of twinkling lights. She couldn't see stars like this in Denver because of all the city lights.

"If you listen to Mom, it *has* been forever."

Lauren looked at her sister. "She's still pretty lonely?"

"We try to visit as much as we can, but, yeah, she misses Daddy."

"We all do. I can't believe it's been four years already." A pang of sadness shot through her. She wished her dad were still alive to hear her news. He would've been so excited. He was such a great dad.

"So tell me how the big city is."

"You should come visit. There's so much to do in Denver. The kids would love the zoo and the museum. Oh, and the aquarium. There are lots of parks. And, of course, Elitch Gardens."

"Maybe." Bethany shrugged. "I'm not sure I'll ever talk the hubs into leaving Durango, even for a trip. He hates the city traffic and congestion. He loves the big, wide open space here."

"Can't blame him. I miss it too. Sometimes, Denver gets to me, and I wish I were back here in small town, USA."

"Never changes much." Bethany smiled. "That can be good. And bad."

"How's the house renovation coming?"

"Um, you know. Kind of a money pit, but it's been fun."

"I can't wait to have a house, so I can do all the things I watch on HGTV. Paul keeps saying it'll be soon, but he's been saying that for a long time. I'm so anxious to do projects and really make a house a home."

"Maybe if you started a family . . ."

The tips of Lauren's ears heated, and she was sure her expression would betray her secret. Thankfully, it was dark, and Bethany didn't notice. At least she didn't say anything.

After a few moments of silence, Lauren said, "All the houses still look the same on our street."

"Remember the Beaumonts?"

"Yeah."

"Mrs. Beaumont up and left last week. She's divorcing Mr. Beaumont."

"No way. Why?"

"Mom doesn't know, but Mr. Beaumont is pretty torn up about it."

"Wow." Lauren shook her head. Mr. Beaumont was such a nice guy. Why would his wife leave him? That was something Lauren vowed would never happen. Even though she resented Paul's work schedule, and she was still upset he hadn't come with her, nothing would compel her to get a divorce. "I thought Mom and Mrs. Beaumont were good friends."

"Guess they weren't as close as Mom thought."

They pulled into the driveway, and the same porch light that had been on every night Lauren went out on a date was still on, waiting for her. Memories of her dad standing at the front door flooded in.

She usually kept them tucked away because that was the best way for her to deal with her grief, but seeing her childhood home brought them all back.

The front door opened before they reached it.

"Aunt Lauren," Kaylee shrieked. She jumped into Lauren's arms.

"Hey, baby girl. Have you missed me?"

Kaylee nodded, her blond hair bouncing. "Thanks for the presents you send me. Do you have one now?"

"Maybe." She hugged her niece, inhaling the apple scent of her hair. "There might be something special in my suitcase."

Kaylee giggled. "Yay! I love presents." She wiggled out of Lauren's grasp and disappeared into the house.

"Hi, Mom," Lauren gave her mom a hug, noticing that her mom was a little more fluffy around the edges than the last time she'd seen her. "I've missed you."

"Not enough to come see me more often."

Lauren pulled away and gazed into her mom's brown eyes. "Mom."

Bethany brought Jace over. "Say hi to your Aunt Lauren."

Jace buried his head in his mom's neck.

Lauren reached out and caressed the soft, light brown hair that now covered his head. "He has so much hair now, and he's gotten so big. Last time I saw him—"

"That's what happens—"

"Mom," Bethany said.

"Okay. I'm just glad you're here now. Even if it's only for a few days."

Lauren sat on the familiar beige couch that had been in the living room for at least fifteen years.

"Do you want something to eat or drink? I can make you a sandwich. Or there's some soda in the refrigerator."

"No, thanks. I'm not hungry." In fact, her stomach was queasy.

Her mom sat on the couch next to her. "How was the flight?"

"A little bumpy."

"Why didn't Paul come again?"

Lauren gave her mom a look. It was no secret that her mom didn't adore Paul. She tolerated him, but that was about it. "He had to meet with some clients."

"Is he working on the weekends now?"

"Sometimes. His dad wants him to open another office in Littleton, so Paul's been working a lot."

Her mom's silence said volumes.

"I know what you're thinking," Lauren said.

"Then I won't need to say it." She tucked her bobbed red hair behind her ears.

"Can we not argue about Paul this weekend?"

"I just wish—"

"Mom, really."

As much as Lauren wanted to tell her family right then and there, her stomach was still unsettled, and she didn't want to share the news with her mom's attitude about Paul. She'd tell them all about it in the morning.

chapter 8

Lauren awoke to the smell of bacon filtering through the house. She pulled on a pair of comfortable gray sweats and a lavender t-shirt and made her way to the kitchen, thankful she was feeling better from the flight.

"Mmm, I love bacon."

"I know." Her mom smiled.

She inspected the electric griddle. "And you're making chocolate chip pancakes?"

"I sure am."

She hugged her mom from behind. "You're the best, Mom."

"I miss cooking." She flipped some pancakes onto a plate. "I'm here alone most of the time and it's no fun to cook for one."

"I thought Bethany and the kids came over a lot." Lauren snatched a piece of bacon and sat at the round kitchen table. The salty taste danced on her tongue as she chewed. It had been too long since she'd enjoyed some bacon.

"They do come over, but it's not the same as when your dad was alive. They go home after a while, and I'm all alone again." Her mom poured some orange juice into a glass.

"I'm sorry. I miss Daddy. He was always so cheerful and told the corniest jokes. He could make me laugh even after a lame date or when I had a fight with one of my friends."

"That reminds me. I heard that Shanna is expecting their second baby."

"That's great news." And Lauren meant it. For the first time in over two years, hearing someone else was pregnant didn't bother her and make her feel self-conscious, because she was going to have a baby and finally earn membership into the Mommy Club.

"They live in Portland, Oregon now."

"I should look her up on Facebook and get back in touch."

Her mom handed her a plate piled with bacon and pancakes. "You two were such good friends in high school."

Lauren eyed the deliciousness on her plate while she waited for her mom to sit down and join her. "I guess we drifted away from each other. That happens when everyone goes in different directions."

Lauren's mom checked the oven.

"Are you baking something else?"

"A cake for Suzanne."

"Mrs. Campbell down the street?"

"Yes." She sat at the table across from Lauren.

"Why?"

"She was diagnosed with pancreatic cancer some months back. I wanted to bring her my special cake to let her know I'm thinking about her."

"That's nice of you." Lauren took a big bite of the chocolatey pancakes.

"Why don't you come with me after I finish the cake, and we can visit with her for a bit?"

Mrs. Campbell had always been so nice when Lauren was a kid. "I haven't seen her since I moved away from home."

Her mom sipped some orange juice. "Ethan travels a lot and he lives in Boulder, so he doesn't make it back here very often."

"Ethan Campbell. Wow. I haven't heard his name in years. I used to have such a crush on him back in the day, with his black hair, green eyes, and killer smile. We nicknamed him Adonis." She shoveled some more pancakes into her mouth, realizing she was acting like a starving teenager again, but not caring.

"He and your brother were such good friends."

"He used to tease me when he'd come over. I lived for those days. He was so good-looking."

"And such a nice, well-mannered boy." Her mom pointed to Lauren's mouth. "You have a little chocolate on your chin."

Lauren wiped at her face.

"I wonder if he and Justin would still be good friends now." A sad expression crossed her mom's face.

Lauren shrugged. "Who knows? We've all changed so much. High school was a long time ago."

"Sometimes I wonder what Justin would be like. Would he be married? What would he be doing for a career?" Her mom's voice broke.

"Me, too, Mom." She placed her hand over her mom's.

The doorbell interrupted them.

"I'll get it." Lauren made her way to the front door and opened it to Bethany and the kids.

"I don't know why Mom keeps the door locked. We live in the safest town in the world," Bethany said as she put Jace down on the floor.

Jace squealed and headed for the kitchen.

Kaylee was dressed in a purple tutu. "I'm a ballerina today."

"I see that. Maybe you can give us a little performance later," Lauren said.

"I been practicing." Kaylee did a few twirls with her hands raised above her head.

"Mmm, something smells de-lish," Bethany said. "I shouldn't eat it, but I'm going to anyway."

After breakfast, they sat in the living room, the morning light streaming in through the windows.

Lauren's stomach quivered while she mentally prepared to share her wonderfully happy secret.

"You look like the cat that swallowed a canary," her mom said.

"You do seem to be hiding something," Bethany said. "Are things okay with Paul?"

Lauren nodded. "Yes."

"So, what gives?" Bethany smoothed her long hair into a ponytail.

Lauren drew in a breath. "Paul really wanted to come, but he had a meeting he couldn't get out of. We wanted to tell you together."

"You're moving back to Durango?" her mom said with a bright smile.

"No, Mom. We're staying in Denver."

"Something exciting at school?" Bethany watched her.

"No." She took another breath. "Actually, Mom, you are going to be a grandma. Again."

Her mom gazed at her then glanced at Bethany. "Are you saying . . ."

"Yes," Lauren said, clapping her hands.

"You're pregnant?" Bethany said.

"I am."

Bethany squealed. "That's so awesome."

"Have you been to the doctor?" her mom asked, wearing such a big smile Lauren wondered if her mom's face might crack.

"Not yet. I'm barely pregnant. Only seven or eight weeks."

"What does Paul think?" Bethany said.

"He's happy."

"Really?"

Lauren looked at her sister, trying to read her body language. "Bethany, what are you trying to say?"

Bethany shook her head. "Nothing."

"It's something." Lauren wasn't about to let it go at that. Her sister had something to say and she wanted to hear it.

Bethany held up a hand. "Don't worry about it."

"No. I want you to spit it out." Lauren's heartbeat sped up. She was growing tired of the innuendos about Paul. Sure, he wasn't perfect, but her family seemed to see the worst in him.

"Why don't we get ready for some fun today?" her mom said, obviously trying to change the subject.

"No, I want to hear what Bethany thinks about Paul." Lauren stared at her sister, waiting.

Bethany glanced at her mom then back to Lauren. "Fine. I'll tell you, but I don't want you to be mad."

"Why would I be mad? I'm not mad. I never get mad." Lauren drummed her fingers on her thigh. "Why should this make me mad?"

"You're already getting all . . ."

"All what?" Lauren stared at her, waiting for her to say what was on her mind.

"Maybe we should get the kids and go do something fun?" Her mom said, again trying to diffuse the situation.

"No, Mom." She looked at her sister. "I get all *what?*"

"Defensive."

"What is that supposed to mean?" Lauren furrowed her brows.

"You get this way about him."

"You mean about my *husband*?" Lauren tried to control the irritation flaring up inside her.

"See, this is going to end in a fight."

"No, it's not. Just tell me what the problem is."

"It's not that there's a problem, exactly." Bethany picked at her fingernails, a habit she'd had since they were kids.

"Well then, what?"

"Bethany, let's not get into this," her mom said, giving Bethany a hard look.

Lauren glanced between the two of them. "Wait. You two have been discussing me and Paul?"

Her mom gazed at the ground.

"What is going on here?" Lauren sat up, her heart thumping against her ribs. Why were her mom and sister talking about her marriage? What was going on?

"It seems like Paul doesn't make you very happy," Bethany said.

"What? I never said that." *What is she talking about?*

Bethany raised her eyebrows. "It's what you haven't said."

"What does that mean?"

"It seems like you aren't that happy, that's all."

"I completely disagree with you." Lauren's face burned. She wasn't sure if it was because she was mad that Bethany put her on the spot or because she voiced what had been in Lauren's own thoughts. Paul had seemed a bit distant over the last several months, but now that she was pregnant it would change things back to where they once were. She'd have her life back on track.

Bethany shook her head. "I'm sorry. I didn't mean to upset you."

"Is this what you think too, Mom?"

"I think we shouldn't talk about it. It's really none of our business. Right, Bethany?" She shot a look at Bethany. "I'm sure Paul is thrilled with the news."

"He is. He's very excited." Was she trying to convince them or herself?

"Let's go out and do some shopping. There's a new baby store on Main," her mom said. She hugged Lauren. "I'm so happy for you."

"Thanks, Mom." She inhaled the familiar floral scent her mom always wore. She had hoped for a better reaction from her mom and sister about her pregnancy, instead of focusing the discussion on

Paul, but she was determined not to let anything ruin her blissfully happy news.

"I'll run home and get the stroller," Bethany said. "It'll be nice to get out in the fresh air while we walk around downtown. There are a few new stores since you were here last." Bethany jumped to her feet and left.

Lauren put on her jeans and gazed at herself in the mirror. How much longer would she be able to wear these? She pulled her shirt away from her body and tried to imagine herself with a protruding belly. A smile ran across her lips. No longer would she have to envy the pregnant women she saw. Her body would shout to the world that she would soon be a mother.

Bethany and her mom were wrong. Things between Paul and her were fine, and they'd only get better. She was happy. Really happy. And she'd prove to her family this weekend how happy she was.

Lauren tried to tame her unruly waves and put her hair into a loose ponytail. Some days she wished her hair were like Bethany's then it wouldn't be such a chore to fix it.

Her phone caught her eye, so she checked it for any texts or voicemails from Paul. None. *He must be busy in his meeting.* He was a hard worker and she appreciated it. Really, she did. Because they were happy. Very happy.

Grabbing her brown leather jacket, she headed out to the living room.

"You look nice," her mom said, rummaging through her purse.

"Thanks."

"You won't be able to wear those pants for long. Maybe we should buy you a maternity outfit." Her mom's whole face smiled.

A warm, joyous feeling encompassed Lauren. *Maternity clothes.* "That'd be great."

"Are you feeling okay?"

"I feel awesome." Lauren reached into her mom's purse and pulled out a pack of gum. "No nausea or anything."

"Help yourself."

Chewing, Lauren said, "Thanks. If there's one thing that will never change, it's that you have wintergreen gum in your purse. Always."

Her mom leaned against the doorjamb. "You know, I didn't get very sick while I carried you or your sister. Your brother, on the other hand, made me so sick I could hardly move for three months. I hope you don't get that sick."

"Me too." Lauren gathered her brown flats from the floor by the front door and put them on. "I still have the rest of this semester at school. I can't get sick."

"When are you due?"

"The middle of November, I think. I'm going to make an appointment with the doctor when I get back, and we'll know more."

Bethany pulled up in her Subaru, so they went outside.

Downtown hadn't changed much since the last time Lauren was in town, or when she used to frequent it during her high school years for that matter. She missed the small town charm of Durango with its western flare and old brick buildings.

They walked into a store with displays of the most adorable children's clothing.

"Oh, look at this little dress. So many ruffles." Her mom handled a pink dress with layers and layers of lace.

Lauren covered her mouth. If she had a little girl, she definitely wanted to dress her in something like that.

"Isn't this sweet?" Bethany showed her a pajama set with pale yellow ducks.

"I feel like I'm in heaven," Lauren said. "So many cute little outfits."

"Maybe you should wait until you find out what sex it is," Bethany said. "You don't want to get a bunch of clothes you can't use."

Bethany sounded like Paul—always so sensible. Lauren, on the other hand, wanted to buy lots of frilly dresses and an equal number of boy outfits. She couldn't get enough.

"Whether it's a boy or a girl, the baby will need some little newborn pajamas." Her mom handed her a few unisex, all-in-one outfits in yellow and green. "Not too girly and not too boyish. Perfect for a newborn. What do you think?"

"I love them. They're so soft. And so small." Lauren ran her fingers over the outfits, imagining her baby in each and every one. She pulled tiny, green pajamas with cat faces up to her nose and inhaled the new clothes' scent. In about seven months' time she'd have a baby to fill pajamas like these. She could hardly believe it.

"My first gifts for my new grandbaby."

"Really?" Having these outfits would make Lauren's dream feel so real.

Her mom nodded.

"Oh, thank you, Mom." Lauren hugged her. "These are perfect."

"Mom-my. I'm hungry. I'm so hungry," Kaylee whined and yanked on Bethany's shirt.

"I know, sweetie." Bethany caressed Kaylee's head.

"I want to eat now."

"Just a minute," Bethany said.

"No, I want to go now," Kaylee yelled.

Lauren watched the exchange between mother and daughter. Though it was drawing attention from other customers in the store, Lauren looked forward to the same kind of experience.

"I'll take the kids and wait outside. Shopping plus my two kids equals a big headache." Bethany shuttled the kids out of the store.

Lauren smiled.

"Why the smile?" her mom asked.

"I didn't know if I'd ever have that to look forward to."

Her mom wrinkled her nose. "I'm not sure a whining kid is something to look forward to, exactly."

"It is, believe me. I wondered if I'd ever have a baby."

"Have you been trying for very long?"

Lauren raised two fingers. "Over two years."

"Really?"

Lauren nodded as she thumbed through some receiving blankets.

"I thought you were focusing on your career and waiting to start a family."

Lauren moved over to a rack of socks, headbands, and hats. "Paul wanted to keep waiting, but after being married for three years, I wanted to start having kids."

Her mom followed her. "And Paul?"

"He said we could start a family. But month after month passed and turned into a year. Then two years. I was about to go see a specialist." She looked at her mom. "But then I finally saw that elusive plus sign."

"What was Paul's reaction?" Her mom showed her a gray outfit with elephants.

Lauren shrugged. "He was surprised."

"In a good way?"

Lauren moved to another rack, hoping her mom would stop asking so many questions.

After a minute or so, her mom said, "Paul is happy about this, right?"

"He's under a lot of stress right now, and he didn't expect it." She looked directly at her mom. "But he's happy about it. He wants kids."

She reached out and touched Lauren's arm. "You'll make good parents." She paused. "It wasn't so long ago that *you* were *my* baby."

"Like thirty years ago."

"Feels like yesterday."

Lauren put her arm around her mom. "Let's go find Bethany and the kids."

chapter 9

The next morning, Lauren awoke with a wave of nausea. She got up and went in to the kitchen to get a drink of water. She leaned over the kitchen sink. The thought of eating anything for breakfast turned her stomach. Morning sickness? She had *morning sickness*. A ribbon of glee shot through her. Not that she wanted to be sick, but this confirmed that there really was a life inside her, and it wasn't her imagination.

Several minutes later, her mom walked in. "Uh, oh."

Lauren smiled. "Yep. Guess I spoke too soon."

"I have some crackers in the cupboard."

"I think I'll pass." Lauren leaned her head down and inhaled deeply.

"Why don't you go back to bed and rest?"

"Sounds like a great idea."

After a few hours of sleep, Lauren felt better. She found her mom in the kitchen putting the finishing touches on a cake. "I love your angel food cake with fresh strawberries all over it, but right now it isn't very appetizing. Sorry."

"Good thing I didn't make it for you." Her mom smiled.

"Oh, yeah. For Mrs. Campbell, right?"

"Yes. I wish I could do more." Her mom licked her fingers then put the knife and other dishes in the sink.

"I'm sure she appreciates your friendship." Lauren sat at the kitchen table, the wooden chair feeling hard and uncomfortable.

She watched the soap suds mushroom in the sink as her mom ran water over the dishes.

"Since you aren't feeling well, I'll just take the cake over to her and be back soon."

"I'd like to go," Lauren said, wanting to visit with her old neighbor.

"Will you feel up to it?"

Lauren wiped at her face. "Give me fifteen minutes."

The fresh, cool air helped as Lauren walked with her mom toward Mrs. Campbell's brown ranch-style house. "I almost feel like I'm a kid again. The neighborhood is still pretty much the same." She pointed to a driveway. "I remember crashing my bike right there. I still have the scar on my knee."

"You were all banged up."

"So was my bike."

"And you cried and cried and cried. I thought you'd never stop crying."

"Well, it hurt." Lauren made a pouty face then pointed to the white house with a tall blue spruce in the front yard. "Do the Cooks still live there?"

"No. They sold it a few years ago when George got sick. Went to live by their son and his family in Arizona. I thought I told you."

They turned and walked up toward Mrs. Campbell's red front door. Her mom rang the door bell. The door opened, and Mrs. Campbell, at least fifty pounds lighter than Lauren remembered her and wearing a scarf tied around her head, said, "Come in."

"Hi, Suzanne. How are you feeling?"

"I have good days and bad days." She smiled slightly as if it were too much effort to smile fully.

"I know you love cake." Her mom set the platter on the kitchen counter.

"Thank you, Emily. Your strawberry cake is one of my great weaknesses." Mrs. Campbell made her way slowly over to a beige easy chair. "Please, sit down."

"I wanted to let you know I was thinking about you."

Lauren and her mom sat on the floral-patterned couch.

The frail woman gazed at Lauren. "This can't be little Lauren."

"Yes, it is." Lauren's mom patted Lauren on the leg. "She came to visit for the weekend."

"Hi, Mrs. Campbell."

"You're all grown up. And still with all that natural beauty."

"Thank you." Lauren appreciated the kind words.

With effort, Mrs. Campbell leaned back in her chair. "Your mom's face lights up whenever she talks about you."

"I might be a little proud of her."

The door out to the garage opened into the dining area. "Mom, I can't find the—"

"Ethan, come in here," Mrs. Campbell said with a strained voice.

Ethan stepped into the house. His black hair was a bit longer and his shoulders were broader since the last time Lauren saw him. He still easily earned the nickname of Adonis. Ethan smiled and said, "Hello," as he strode across the room.

"You remember Emily and—"

"Lauren." Lauren was surprised he remembered. "Yes, of course I do." He stuck out his hand. "Mrs. Van Allen. You are looking very well. How are you?"

Lauren's mom shook his hand. "I'm good. How are you? It's been years."

"Yes, it has." He turned to Lauren and extended his hand. For a moment, she wasn't sure if she should shake it, because it was if she'd fallen into a time warp, and she was still the awkward teenager who couldn't string two words together in front of him. She then reminded herself that she was a mature adult, and her silly crush was a lifetime ago. She reciprocated and shook his hand. "How are you, Lauren?"

She was struck by the sincerity in his tone, as if he actually cared how she was. "I'm great. You?"

"Doing well."

"Ethan's here for a few days to help me with some things around the house." Mrs. Campbell's pride was evident.

"I'm not really the handyman she thinks I am." He smiled the same million-dollar smile that had driven the girls at Durango High

School crazy. Ethan had been a celebrity back then, and girls talked about him all the time.

Ethan sat in a chair next to his mom. He laid his hand across hers. In a tender voice he asked, "Can I get you anything, Mom?"

"They brought us a delicious cake."

Ethan glanced over at the counter. "I remember eating lots of great food at your house, Mrs. Van Allen."

"If memory serves, I think you and Justin ate anything and everything. I don't think I ever served a meal that you boys didn't wolf down."

Ethan laughed. "Well, you always made us such good food, especially the desserts."

"Your mom says you live in Boulder now," Lauren's mom said.

"I moved there a few years ago. I lived in New York for a few years then L.A. and San Francisco, but I got tired of the rat race and wanted to come back to Colorado. I travel a lot and Boulder is close enough to the airport in Denver, but still far enough away to have a more relaxed feel. Kinda like Durango on a bigger scale."

"Do you travel for work?" Lauren asked.

"He's a photographer. Takes photos all over the world for magazines." Mrs. Campbell patted Ethan's hand. "He's quite good."

"And she's my biggest cheerleader." Ethan drew his mom's hand up to his lips and gave it a kiss.

"I'm proud. I just wish you'd find a nice girl and settle down." Mrs. Campbell looked at Lauren with a smile. "Are you married?"

Lauren's cheeks warmed. "Uh, yes. Five years. I live in Denver. With Paul. My husband."

"I go to Denver pretty often during baseball season. One of my buddies from college lives there, and we go to the Rockies games. Do you like Denver?" Ethan asked.

Grateful that Ethan had redirected the conversation, Lauren said, "It's a lot different than Durango, but it's a good place. Paul, my husband, is an attorney. He's in a practice with his father." She laced her fingers together, reminding herself that years had passed since high school, and she was capable of carrying on a normal conversation with the man who once held her heart captive.

"What do you do?" Ethan gazed at her, seeming to be genuinely interested in her answer.

"I teach English at a middle school. We're just starting our unit on memoir and the Holocaust."

"Really?" He raised his eyebrows. "Some years back, I did a photo shoot for a reunion between a Holocaust survivor and one of her rescuers. It was for an article in *Time*. A pretty powerful read." He smiled. "And the photos weren't too bad."

"Don't be so humble. Those photos were breathtaking," Mrs. Campbell said in a quiet voice.

Feeling more at ease in the conversation, Lauren said, "Wow, I'd love to see them. Can I find them online or get a copy of the magazine?"

"I can send you a copy. I have a few back at my apartment." He grinned and that famous dimple appeared.

"That would be awesome to share with my classes."

"I'll be in Denver next week for a Rockies' game. I could drop off some other prints that didn't make it into the spread. "

A crazy idea sparked. "Maybe this is too much to ask, but would you be willing to come in and show the photos yourself to a couple of my classes and talk to them about the reunion?"

"A group of middle schoolers might be a tough crowd." He smiled then sobered. "It was an incredible experience meeting these women. Milda's family hid Eva and her mother for three years. I'll never forget them. You meet people with that kind of courage and it makes an impact."

"I think the kids in my class would love to hear about your experience. It'd be something different for them. You know, kinda outside the box."

"Why don't you give me your number and we can set it up."

Lauren laughed. How many times had she fantasized that he'd "ask for her number" when they were teenagers?

"What?" he asked with a puzzled expression.

"Oh, nothing." She gave him her number, and they continued chatting for a few more minutes when Lauren's mom said, "We better let you get your rest, Suzanne."

"Thank you. Good to see you, Lauren. Your mom has been very good to me." She paused and took a few breaths. "We widows have to stick together."

"I hope that you feel better soon," Lauren said.

Ethan walked them to the door and stepped outside with them onto the porch. "Thanks for stopping by and bringing one of your cakes. That was very nice of you."

"Suzanne has always been such a dear. I wish there were more I could do," Lauren's mom said.

Ethan nodded. "I know. I wish the same thing. I've talked to her about me moving back to help her. She doesn't want to be a burden, but I worry about her."

"I'll try to come visit more often," Lauren's mom said.

"Thank you." He turned to Lauren. "I'll be in touch."

Lauren and her mom walked back to the house.

They spent the rest of the afternoon visiting and going through old photos. Bethany came over with the kids and stayed for a couple of hours.

chapter 10

Monday morning came too soon. Though Lauren missed Paul, she loved being cocooned in her childhood home, surrounded by her family. She missed the daily interaction with her mom and sister when she was in Denver.

"These visits are too short," her mom said as Lauren emerged from her bedroom.

"I know. I wish I could stay longer, but we're right in the middle of our Holocaust unit, and tomorrow begins the project presentations." Besides, Lauren needed to get back to her husband.

Lauren passed on eating breakfast even though her mom kept insisting—her stomach couldn't take it.

Bethany stopped by with the kids, and they said their goodbyes. Lauren wasn't sure when she'd see her family again, and at the rate the kids were growing, they'd change drastically by her next visit. She wished she lived closer so she could be a part of their lives on a regular basis.

Lauren and her mom stood inside the airport, right outside the security area.

"Tell Paul we missed him," her mom said graciously.

"I will."

"Take care of yourself." Her mom pointed at her. "Get plenty of rest and fluids so you can take care of that baby."

Lauren nodded, her throat swelling. She hated saying goodbye to her mom.

"Let me know what happens at your doctor's appointment. I can't wait to find out if it's a boy or a girl." She clasped her hands together like a child waiting for a Christmas gift.

Lauren hugged her mom goodbye twice then went through the security area.

The plane ride to Durango hadn't bothered Lauren, but the return trip made her stomach feel like it was on a rollercoaster ride—the kind with the upside down loops. She grabbed one of the small white bags just in case.

At the Denver airport, she found her car and drove home.

She flung the front door open and left her suitcase in the entryway. Dishes filled the sink and the milk jug still sat on the counter in the kitchen. *Why is Paul such a slob? The least he could've done is clean up after himself after ditching me for the weekend.*

Paul wouldn't be home from work for a few hours, so she made her way back to the bedroom and lay on the unmade bed.

After almost an hour, she rose and found her planner with the name of an obstetrician another teacher at school had recommended. She dialed the number and made an appointment.

It was official.

"I made an appointment with the doctor," Lauren said as Paul sat down for dinner.

"What day?"

"Thursday." She sipped some water, hoping to calm the nausea. "Can you come with me?"

"Paul checked the calendar on his phone. "What time?"

"Four o'clock."

"I have a meeting that starts at two thirty. It might be over by four. I'll try to make it."

Lauren handed him the pan of lasagna, trying to ignore its aroma. "I'd really like you to be there."

"I can't promise anything, but I'll try." He took a bite. "This is delicious."

"Thanks. It's my mom's recipe."

"Aren't you going to eat any?"

"Not right now. Maybe later." The idea of eating anything made her even more nauseated.

"How was the visit?" Paul shoveled another fork full of lasagna into his mouth.

"Good." She got up and went into the other room. When she returned, she had a bag in her hand. "Look what we got." She pulled out the newborn outfits her mother had bought.

Paul smiled.

"Isn't it adorable? Can you believe we'll have a tiny baby that will fit in this?" She cradled the small, green pajamas in the crook of her elbow.

"I've never seen you so excited." He reached over and grabbed her hand.

"I can't wait to find out if it's a girl or a boy. Then we can start buying all sorts of clothes. And we'll need a car seat, a high chair, a little bathtub. And a crib, of course. I want to decorate the nursery with cute little baby stuff. We'll need powder and baby shampoo and little washcloths. Oh, and bunkies—I mean binkies." Her mouth worked so much faster than her brain, and her words started to trip on her tongue.

"Whoa, you're getting way ahead of yourself." Paul leaned back in his chair.

"I want to be prepared. That's all. A little preparation goes a long way." She stroked the newborn outfit in her lap, imagining her son or daughter inside.

Paul laughed. "This baby will be so spoiled."

"You better believe it."

Paul glanced at his watch. "Uh, oh."

"What?"

"My dad wants me to come over and look through a file for a new case."

"Tonight?" Disappointment welled up. "I just got home from Durango."

"I know." He nodded. "But we need to go over these files tonight. Do you want to come with me?"

The last thing Lauren wanted to do was spend another evening with her in-laws wondering if she'd ever measure up to their expectations. She wanted to spend the night with Paul talking about all of their plans for the baby, including buying a house with a swing set in the backyard and a flower garden full of purple petunias, but she'd learned that when his dad called, Paul jumped. "I have some work to do here to prepare for class tomorrow." She tried to smile, but it was flat.

"Are you sure?"

She let out a frustrated breath. "Yeah." There'd be plenty of time to talk about their future plans.

The next morning, Lauren introduced the first student. "Please be courteous and attentive during Sara's presentation."

Sara held a poster with a map of Europe, some photos of concentration camps, and names listed down the middle.

Sara turned toward the poster. "These are the names of my relatives that died." She pointed to a photo of a young girl with dark hair. "Ruth was a little older than me. I don't know much about her. As I've looked at her name, I've wondered what her favorite color was, what food she liked to eat, if she liked to sing or dance or paint." Sara faced the class, her eyes misty. "She was a real person. Just like me. But she never got to grow up. I'm always going to remember her as I grow up. I will remember to be happy to do and see things that she never got to."

Lauren's throat ached thinking about the little girl—a real person that was part of Sara's family—whose light was extinguished for no reason.

"I want to share a poem I wrote about Ruth."

Sara licked her lips then began.

I Will Not Forget

A cold, chilly night
A nameless girl
Ripped from her home

From her family
Because she was a Jew.

Sentenced to suffer
To cry alone
To wonder why
She must die
Because she was a Jew

Did she sing? Dance?
Read books by the moonlight?
A life cut short
A girl like me, dead
Because she was a Jew

Ruth, I will not forget
I will not pretend
You did not exist
Or erase your life
Just because you were a Jew.

Lauren wiped at the emotion slipping down her cheeks. She'd presented this unit on the Holocaust for the last four years, but she'd never had someone personally affected by it give a presentation. The effect was chilling. The Holocaust was more than a subject of study for this family. Except for a few sniffles by some girls in the back, the room was silent.

Lauren hesitated to disrupt the reverent feeling that encompassed the class, but she knew other students had prepared presentations. Finally in control of her quivering lips, she said, "Thank you so much Sara."

Without thinking, she brushed her hand against her stomach. She had so many plans for her child, so many dreams—probably many of the same dreams Ruth's mother had for Ruth. But Ruth never had a chance. She never reached adulthood simply because someone decided she didn't deserve to live. What a tragic and unnecessary loss. Sadness for so many lost hopes and dreams wound itself around Lauren.

Lauren struggled to clear her head and get back to the presentations. She called Jason to the front, and he proceeded to share his project.

Over the next few days, the students shared their projects. Somehow, the presentations this year struck a chord deep within Lauren. The lives that were lost seemed to affect her more deeply, and the callous disregard for human life penetrated her with more intensity.

Perhaps it was because she carried a life within her now, but these presentations affected her in a way she didn't quite understand, and her appreciation for all life grew.

chapter *11*

A few days later, Lauren sat in the waiting room of the doctor's office. Several wooden chairs lined the pale yellow wall, and a large glass table held various magazines. She glanced at her watch—four ten. She'd been waiting since three forty for both the doctor and Paul. Ten minutes later, a nurse with short black hair called her back.

No sign of Paul. He *knew* it was important to her for him to be there. She wanted to have this experience together, but once again, he was absent. How could he miss this appointment?

She sat at the nurse's station, gritting her teeth while anger built inside her. She wanted to call Paul and yell at him, but she forced herself to focus on the questions the nurse asked her.

She waited in the exam room for about fifteen minutes, stewing over Paul's absence when a tall, trim man in his sixties entered.

"Hello, I'm Dr. Maestas."

"Lauren Wilson."

He shook her hand. "Nice to meet you."

"You too."

He asked her about her last menstrual cycle and gave her an approximate due date of November 21st. It fit that her baby would be born near Thanksgiving, and her eyes moistened at the thought of having a new baby for Christmas—what better gift?

"How are you feeling?"

"I was doing fine until last weekend when I started feeling sick to my stomach. Food isn't appetizing at all."

"You'll need to keep yourself hydrated even if you don't feel like it. Popsicles seem to help." He smiled and wrinkle lines appeared near his small brown eyes. "I can prescribe some medication for the nausea if you'd like."

"I'll think about it. I'm not a big fan of medicine, and I don't want to cause any harm to my baby." Her sense of responsibility to protect her child was in full swing.

He smiled. "This medication is perfectly safe." He took a few steps toward the sink area. "We also need to schedule your prenatal testing."

"When?"

He opened a drawer under the counter and pulled out a brochure with a bald, chunky baby on front. "This lists all the prenatal tests. You can take this home and read it. I recommend the maternal serum screening, which we'll need to do between 10 and 13 weeks gestation. It's a simple blood test, and when combined with an ultrasound, we can make sure your baby is healthy."

Baby. This is real.

She laid back and the doctor spread some cool gel on her stomach then placed a hand-held heart monitor on it. Lauren heard a soft *choo, choo, choo.* A tingling sensation traveled up her spine and spread through her limbs, enveloping her in joy. "Is that the heartbeat?"

"Yes," Dr. Maestas nodded. "Sounds great."

Her heart swelled. There was a miniature human being living inside her—a life that depended on her. She closed her eyes and sent a silent prayer heavenward.

"My nurse will schedule the ultrasound and your next appointment."

"Thank you." The words didn't seem adequate enough to convey her feelings. She wanted to throw her arms around his neck, jump up and down with happiness, and shower him with gratitude, but she kept her emotions under control, so the doctor didn't think she was crazy.

Lauren left the office and slowly walked to her car. The air smelled fresher, the sky looked bluer, and the sun rays felt warmer. She reveled in the beauty of the moment. Nothing could ruin the blissful anticipation that wrapped around her.

Life was good.

That evening, Lauren sat in the living room, tapping her hands on her legs while she waited for Paul to come home. Despite his absence, she wanted to share her experience with him and discuss the prenatal testing. Being mad at him wouldn't change the fact that he missed the appointment, it would only alienate him, and she desperately wanted him to be a part of everything. She especially wanted to tell him how she'd heard the heartbeat of their baby.

Several minutes later, the door opened. Lauren chewed the inside of her cheek as she waited for him to come inside.

"Hey, Lauren," he said as he set his briefcase on the table.

She approached the kitchen, expecting Paul to apologize for missing the appointment, but he didn't. Instead, he opened the refrigerator and leaned down to look inside. "What's for dinner?" *Is that all he has to say?* She bit her lip. *Don't get mad. Remember how wonderful it was to hear the heartbeat.*

"Lauren?"

Trying to keep her anger in check, she repeated, "What's for dinner?"

"Yeah. I'm starving." He stood and loosened his blue striped tie. "Why isn't it ready?"

"Seriously?" She clenched her fists.

He wrinkled his forehead, as if completely dumbfounded by her question. "What are you talking about?"

"Today." How could he act so nonchalant? As if the appointment was nothing more than visiting the dentist for a cleaning.

"Yeah?" He finally looked at her.

She took a step toward him. Keeping her voice even, she said, "The appointment with the doctor."

"Oh." He nodded. "I had a meeting, and I couldn't leave." He brushed past her and reached into the cabinet for a glass.

She turned and stared at him, her shoulders tensing. "That's it?" He had a meeting and didn't even give the missed appointment another thought?

"Did you want something else?" He filled his glass with water and drank it in two gulps.

"An apology would be nice."

He spun around. "Okay. I'm sorry. Is that better?"

The insincerity in his voice made her want to scream. "What's wrong with you?"

He set the glass down hard on the counter. "I'm under a lot of pressure right now. I don't need you harping on me about missing this appointment."

"Paul, this wasn't some insignificant appointment," she said, her voice rising. "It was about our baby and—"

"I know what it was, and I'm aware that I missed it." A distressed expression crossed his face.

She glanced at the ground, suddenly infused with guilt. Paul *was* working hard for them with insane hours, and he felt incredible pressure from his dad. He didn't need more pressure from her, especially if it led to a big fight. The last thing she wanted was an argument today—the day she'd heard her baby's heartbeat.

Maybe she was being too demanding. There would be more appointments that he could come to. She didn't need to make a big deal out of this one and make things worse. Her gaze settled on him. "I'm sorry."

His face softened. "I'm sorry I missed it. I just have so much going on at work."

"I know, but I want you to be there with me, through all of this."

He raked his fingers through his limp hair. "I want to be there, but you have to understand that my dad is piling a lot on my shoulders. I can't disappoint him."

Paul grabbed his briefcase from the table and walked back to the bedroom, leaving Lauren alone, and lonely, in the kitchen. "No, but you can disappoint me." Her whispered words echoed in the empty room.

Lauren and Paul shared a bed that night, but they might as well have been in separate rooms. She hadn't meant to upset him. She simply wanted him to share this experience with her. More than that, she wanted him to *want* to be part of it, to feel the way she did about it, to be as desperately in love with the idea of having a baby as she was.

chapter 12

Lauren received a text from Ethan on Monday afternoon confirming that he'd be in Denver the next day. They made arrangements for him to come during lunch to go over his presentation for the classes afterwards.

Lauren was putting some papers away when Ethan arrived in her classroom. She glanced up and saw him with a large, black leather portfolio in his hands. "Hi," she said. "Come in."

"So this is where you work?" He looked around at the walls adorned with posters about parts of speech and quotes from Lauren's favorite books. "I haven't been in a middle school for years."

"Not much different than when we went to Miller." Lauren stood. "You know, a few years back."

"A few more for me than you."

"I appreciate you doing this. I think my students will really enjoy it."

"I've never done a presentation like this before, so I'm not exactly sure what you want." He set his portfolio on the desk and proceeded to open it.

Lauren gazed at a black and white photo of a small, hunched woman with silver hair looking out a window with sunlight illuminating her face. A single tear reflected on her wrinkled cheek. Ethan had captured so much emotion in that single shot.

Softly, he said, "I took that while Eva spoke of the day that her brother and father were taken from their home in Lithuania and murdered by the Nazis."

Lauren covered her mouth.

"Eva and her mother immediately went into hiding. They lived in a tiny room that was accessible only through a kitchen cabinet in the house where Milda lived. Milda's family was Catholic, so they were safe."

Lauren pulled the portfolio closer, studying the woman in more detail. "I can't imagine what Eva endured."

"I don't think any of us can. Eva and her mother had to hide for three years. Milda couldn't have any friends over because her parents didn't want anyone to know they were hiding Jews. Once, when Milda was alone at the house, some soldiers came to the door and wanted to search it. They threatened to shoot Milda, but she finally convinced them that there were no Jews in her house."

"She must have been so scared, but she still risked her life to save Eva. A true hero."

Ethan nodded. "Eva said that because of the bravery of Milda and her family, Eva was able to live and have her own family. "

Ethan showed Lauren a photo of the two women hugging each other. "This was the first time they'd seen each other since the war ended. Eva came to the United States with her mother, and she'd lost touch with Milda. A foundation in New York reunites survivors with their rescuers. Milda was the only member of her family that was still alive for the reunion. She came all the way from Lithuania."

"They look so happy to see each other."

Ethan smiled. "They talked and hugged and cried and hugged some more. Like two long-lost sisters."

Lauren could see the love between them in the photo.

"This is my favorite." He turned to a photo of two gnarled hands, fingers intertwined. "Even though Eva and Milda hadn't seen each other in over sixty years, they had an unbreakable bond between them, and it was like no time had passed. If not for the courage of Milda, and others like her, many more Jews would have died. Eva would have died." He paused. "That's what really struck me."

"What?"

"Eva was thrust into the conflict and suffered horrible things, but Milda and her family *chose* to protect her. They didn't have to. They chose to." Ethan cleared his throat. "To me, that is true courage—to choose to do something for someone else in the face of fear and uncertainty and with no thought of personal gain or reward. Milda protected Eva because she valued her as a human being and cared about what happened to her." Ethan licked his lips. "I know it isn't very manly to admit this, but when they looked at each other and said they loved one another, I got all choked up. I could feel their love."

Lauren studied him. "That's what I want."

Ethan looked at her.

"I want you to tell the kids about Milda's courage and bravery. Inspire them the way she inspired you. Give them a vision of what you saw in Milda, and in Eva, so they can see the Holocaust in a different light—how something good can come from something bad. And how we can each make a difference." She took a breath. "Imagine what the world would be like if we had more people like Milda who were brave enough to stand up against injustice and cruelty. Then people like Eva wouldn't have to live in fear. We need more Mildas, so we can have fewer Evas."

Ethan gazed at her while he sat on the edge of the table..

Lauren held her hands up. "I'm sorry. I know I'm too passionate about this subject, and sometimes I get carried away."

"There's nothing wrong with feeling passionate about what's important to you. That's how I feel about photography. It's more than taking photos. It's capturing moments that would otherwise be lost. It's finding the beauty in everything. Seeing the world from a different perspective. "

"May I look at more of your portfolio?"

They spent the rest of the lunch period going through Ethan's photos.

Lauren took time in each class to talk about the effects of the Holocaust before introducing Ethan. During the last class of the day, Lauren said, "This is Ethan Campbell. He was a neighbor and a good friend of my older brother when we lived in Durango. He's now a world-class photographer and had the opportunity to photograph a reunion between a Holocaust survivor and her rescuer. I've asked him to share his experience and show you some of his photos. Please be courteous to our guest."

Lauren sat in the back of the classroom and listened intently to Ethan talk about meeting Eva and Milda and how he wanted to honor them in his photos. She was impressed with his candor in sharing his feelings about his experience. He showed the kids a photo of Eva and Milda, surrounded by photos of Eva's children, grandchildren, and great-grandchildren. "I think this is a powerful reminder of what one person can do." He looked out over the class. "Because of Milda, all of these people had lives."

Ethan shared a few more shots before class ended. After the students left the room, Lauren thanked him for sharing his experiences and for allowing the students to see his photos. "I think you're a natural with kids. They were mesmerized. If you ever want a different career, you should think about teaching."

"Thanks. I think I'll stick with my camera, but I really enjoyed this. I'm glad you asked me."

She smiled. "I'm glad you agreed."

"It's been great seeing you, Lauren." He gathered up his portfolio. "You remind me of Justin."

"Really?"

"Yeah." Ethan paused. "You have the same enthusiasm he had."

Lauren liked that.

"He was a very good friend."

"He was a very good brother." Lauren nodded. "Thanks again for coming."

Lauren watched Ethan walk out of her classroom. He was a genuinely nice guy. Back in high school, she salivated over him and admired his good looks, but now she saw beyond that. He was a kind, caring person. Back then, she would never have imagined having such an easy conversation with him, either. Actually, she wouldn't have imagined having any conversation with him besides the unintelligible murmurings of a love struck teenager. She was grateful times had changed

Over the next week or so, Lauren and Paul spent very little time together. He worked long hours and she focused on teaching her

classes. She wrapped up the unit on the Holocaust, grateful to be done with this emotional subject, and moved on to her next unit on poetry.

The doctor's office had called and set up an appointment for an ultrasound at the end of the week. Before Paul left for work she said, "The ultrasound is today. Three thirty."

He gazed at her, then closed the gap between them and surprised her with a hug. "I'm sorry I've been gone so much."

"I know you're working hard."

"I have a meeting, but I'm planning to go with you to the ultrasound."

"Really?" Excitement built inside her. Maybe this would be the beginning of Paul being involved in the pregnancy.

He nodded. "I'll be there."

That afternoon, Lauren waited in the small ultrasound office, her nerves burning. Would Paul actually show up? He'd promised, but that didn't seem to matter much anymore.

Lauren turned toward the door in time to see Paul come in. She let out a breath of relief. He hadn't let her down this time. Thrilled he'd made it, she reached for his hand. He reciprocated and sat next to her.

A few minutes later, the technician called them back.

An older woman, with a round face and long nose, smoothed warm jelly on Lauren's stomach. "My name is Mary. Have you had an ultrasound before?"

"No. First one." Lauren smiled.

Rose guided the instrument on Lauren's belly. "According to your chart, you are eleven weeks and six days pregnant."

"I think that's right."

"We can pinpoint it through measurements. After we finish, I'll send the results to your doctor."

"Can we find out if it's a boy or a girl?" Paul asked, gazing at the screen with a strange, almost distorted, black and white image.

"We usually do that after eighteen weeks. We're doing this ultrasound because you've chosen the maternal serum screening. This ultrasound, paired with the blood test results, will tell us if there are any genetic conditions."

"That's not very likely though, right?" Paul said.

"Most babies are completely fine. I wouldn't worry about it."

Lauren could feel the pressure of the device as the technician moved it across her stomach. She suddenly had the urge to use the restroom.

"There's the baby."

Lauren watched a small image moving around, almost as if it were jumping up and down on a trampoline. "That's our baby?"

Mary nodded.

Lauren's eyes misted while the baby moved around inside her. She couldn't actually feel any of the movement, but she could see it on the screen.

"Lively little thing, isn't it?" Paul laughed. He squeezed Lauren's shoulder.

"I can't believe I'm seeing my baby. Right there. Moving around. It's surreal." She was unable to tear her gaze from the screen.

Paul rubbed her hand. "This is amazing."

Mary did some measurements and finished the ultrasound. "I'll send these right over to the doctor."

"My appointment is tomorrow."

Lauren and Paul left the office and stood in the parking lot. A sudden breeze lifted Paul's hair on top of his head, making it wave. Lauren laughed.

"What?" he asked.

"I think you need a haircut."

He patted down his hair with his hand. "So that was pretty cool."

"I'm glad you came." A surge of happiness rushed through her. She was grateful Paul had been there.

"Me too. You have a little person inside there, jumping all around." He caressed her tummy then gazed at her. "Look, I'm really sorry for everything lately. I feel so much pressure from my dad. I want to be there—"

She put her finger to his lips. "I know."

He kissed her fingers gently, studying her. "I really am excited about this baby. And today made it feel so real."

"Yeah, it did."

"I want to be a part of this from now on. I'm going to tell my dad—"

"Don't make your dad mad. We can figure this all out. As long as I know you're in it with me, it'll be fine."

He brushed a wisp of hair from her face. "You know I love you, right?" He rested his forehead against hers.

"I love you too."

After school the next day, Lauren drove to the doctor's office. The sun showered her with bright rays as she walked into the waiting room. Two articles in *Parenting Today* and twenty minutes later, Lauren sat in the exam room, waiting for the doctor.

Dr. Maestas walked in, and they exchanged small talk. Lauren lay back on the table and he checked the baby's heartbeat with a handheld monitor. "Sounds good." He measured her stomach.

"I had the ultrasound yesterday."

He nodded. "I haven't gotten the results yet. We'll send off your blood work to the lab."

"How long will that take?" She sat up.

"Results will be back in about a week. We can talk about them at your next appointment. Everything looks fine." He adjusted his glasses. "Do you have any questions?"

"Like a million." She laughed. "I'm just so excited to have a baby."

After a question and answer session, Lauren left the doctor's office and headed home to grade some papers so she could free up the weekend.

When Paul got home, she handed him a real estate catalog. He turned it over and asked, "What's this for?"

"I think your dad had a great idea."

"Huh?"

"You know, when we were at dinner and he thought we were announcing that we'd bought a house. I don't think we should disappoint him."

"Hmm. I don't know." He set the catalog on the kitchen table.

"Why not?"

"A house is a huge commitment, and I'm not sure we're ready." He sat on the couch in the living room and removed his tie.

"Ready?"

"Yeah. Financially—"

"We've been saving for years. We have plenty of money for a down payment, and the interest rates are great right now." Lauren sat next to him and massaged his neck. Using her most convincing tone she said, "Wouldn't you like to have a real home for our baby? A house that belongs to us? I'd love to find a house and be able to decorate it before the baby comes."

"I knew your addiction to those home improvement shows would be bad." He laughed.

"Our own home. With our new baby. How could life get any better?"

"Maybe you're right." He reached over and kissed her.

"We could go look at a few tomorrow."

He shook his head. "Sorry. I can't. I'm meeting with a client for breakfast and then I have to work on a motion."

"But I thought—"

"Last weekend meeting." He held up his hand. "I promise."

As much as Lauren wanted to believe him, she didn't, but she wasn't going to dwell on it and let it dampen her excitement.

chapter 13

At the end of the next week, Lauren checked her phone after she dismissed her first class. There was a voicemail, so she listened to it. A nurse from Dr. Maestas's office asked her to call back. Since the kids from her next class were coming in, Lauren had to put her phone away and wait.

After she finished teaching the next class, she slipped out and found a private spot to call.

"Hi, this is Sherry. Dr. Maestas would like to schedule an appointment with you and your husband. Today, if possible."

Lauren's heart fell into her stomach. Why did the doctor want to see them so soon? What was going on? "Okay. Why?"

"He didn't say. He just asked me to call and schedule an appointment. Can you come in at two o'clock?"

"Uh, no. I teach school and can't make an appointment before three thirty."

"Four fifteen?"

"Yeah." Lauren ended the call and cradled her head in her hands. Why did the doctor want to see them so soon? *Must be the test results.*

Her eyes burned, and her nerves sizzled while she dialed Paul's number. It went directly to voicemail. She dialed again, but the same thing happened. She paced back and forth a few times when her phone started to vibrate.

"The doctor called and wants us to come to his office," Lauren said into the phone.

"Why?"

"I don't know, but he wants to see us today." She blinked the tears back. "What if—"

"I'm sure everything is fine." His tone was calm and reassuring. "Don't get all worked up."

"But why is he asking us to come in now?"

"We won't know that until we see him."

"Can you make it at four fifteen?"

"Yes."

"You're sure?" She needed Paul to be there.

"Yes."

"Nothing will get in the way?"

"You say that like I plan for things to happen," he said with a defensive tone.

"I'm sorry."

"I'll meet you at the doctor's office this afternoon. I have to go."

Lauren held the phone in her trembling hand. What if there was something wrong with the baby? What if the test results showed something terrible? She tried to calm the worry tumbling inside her.

The bell rang, and Lauren had to return to her class. She wiped at her eyes and took a deep, cleansing breath. She was overreacting— wasn't she? After all, she was young and healthy and so was their baby. The doctor probably met with all new parents after the testing results came back. *I'm overthinking it and creating a problem where there isn't one. I'm stressing out for no reason. Right?*

Somehow, the more she struggled to convince herself that everything was fine, the more a sinking feeling enveloped her. Something was wrong. And she'd have to wait until four fifteen to find out exactly what it was.

chapter *14*

After an afternoon that felt more like a month, Paul and Lauren sat in brown leather wingback chairs in the doctor's private office. Lauren had been convinced she wanted to know any and all information about their baby, but suddenly she wanted to bolt before the doctor could say anything to destroy her dream. Perspiration collected at the base of her neck while she watched the doctor open the folder. *Please don't let anything be wrong with the baby. Please, please, please.*

"We have the test results back from the maternal serum screening. Keep in mind this test does not diagnose anything."

Lauren gripped her hands together, her heart sprinting.

"Your test results came back screen positive, which means you are in a higher risk category for your baby having Trisomy 21, more commonly known as Down syndrome, or Trisomy 18, an even rarer condition called Edwards syndrome. Again, this does not mean your baby has either condition, only that you are in a higher risk group." The doctor rested his hands on his desk.

"How do we find out for sure?" Paul asked, worry lines forming around his eyes.

"Since you are still in the first trimester, you can have chorionic villus sampling right away or wait and have an amniocentesis."

"Are those safe?" Lauren asked, tears building behind her eyes.

"Both the CVS test and amniocentesis can cause cramping and bleeding and pose a small threat of miscarriage. Both tests are highly accurate and can determine the sex of the baby. CVS can be done now, but we'd need to wait for about 6 weeks or so for an amnio. Results from the CVS are also quicker. If you decide to do further testing, choosing one test over the other really has the most to do with timing. That's why I called you to come in, so you can decide if you want to do the CVS."

Struggling to find her voice, Lauren softly asked, "What is involved in the CVS?"

"A long needle is inserted through the cervix, or through the abdomen, to collect a sample from the placenta." The doctor paused. "An ultrasound helps us guide the needle to the chorionic villi, which are delicate projections that make up the placenta and contain the baby's genetic makeup."

"Let's schedule it as soon as possible," Paul said with an anxious edge to his voice.

Lauren laid her trembling hand on Paul's. Did she want to risk this test? What if it harmed the baby? Was this the right thing to do?

Paul turned to her, his eyes searching hers. "We need to know."

He was right. They needed to know. Whatever it was, they needed to know. After a few moments, Lauren closed her eyes and said, "Okay, let's schedule it."

"My nurse will give you the appointment. Remember, this is a preliminary result and more than likely, everything will be fine. "Most pregnancies are completely normal. Don't worry needlessly," the doctor said with a gentle voice.

Without saying anything to each other, Lauren and Paul left in their separate cars. Anxiety laced her thoughts while she drove home. What if the baby has Down syndrome? Or the other thing—trisomy something? What would that mean?

She parked her car in the garage and dragged herself into the house. Paul was at the kitchen sink filling a glass with water.

"What if—" she started.

"I don't want to go there." He handed Lauren the glass. "We don't know anything yet and it's a waste of time and effort to worry about something that may never happen."

"But these test results—"

"Can be wrong. I'm sure our baby is fine." He walked out of the kitchen.

"But what if it's not?" she whispered.

That evening, Paul left to go back to the office and finish up some work. Lauren sat on the couch and vacantly stared at the flat screen TV. Finally, she got up and found the remote.

"Maybe I can find something to take my mind off this whole thing."

She surfed past the news stations because she didn't want to see any reports of crimes or deaths. She settled on one of her favorite shows on HGTV where the host transforms a drab room into something beautiful using very little money.

"No, no, don't choose that color for the walls," she said to the TV during the next show. "You need a neutral color so you can coordinate the curtains and the couch." She pointed at the tall woman with extremely short hair. "Do the travertine tile in the entryway, not that porcelain tile. Ew."

She lost herself in the home improvement shows and temporarily forgot about the weight of the upcoming testing on her shoulders. Her phone rang.

"Hi, Mom."

"Hi, sweetie. How are you feeling?"

"Today wasn't a good day."

"Feeling pretty sick?"

"Not exactly."

"What does that mean?"

With a trembling voice, Lauren said, "My prenatal screening came back positive for the baby possibly having a birth defect."

"What?" She could hear the concern in her mom's voice.

"Yeah." Her throat tightened. "I have to do more testing. My baby might have Down syndrome or some other thing I can't remember." She rubbed her eye with the heel of her hand.

"Oh, honey. Don't worry. I know plenty of women who've had false positives with those tests. I think they do more harm than good myself."

"But, mom—"

"Really, Lauren, I'm sure everything will be fine." Her mom sounded so certain and she wanted to believe her more than anything.

"That's what Paul said."

"I know you like to worry, but you shouldn't. Paul's right. And worrying isn't good for the baby," her mom said with a firm voice.

"The doctor said most pregnancies are completely normal," Lauren said, trying to reassure herself.

"See, everything will be fine."

They continued to chat for another half hour. Lauren ended the call feeling better. She made her way back to her bedroom and snuggled between the covers. She hoped that Paul would be home soon, but her eyelids wouldn't let her stay awake.

chapter 15

Lauren entered the perinatal center, a red brick building with a large wooden door. After signing in, she was escorted by a woman with gray hair and pink scrubs to a quiet, pale blue room with dim lights. Though the atmosphere was meant to be relaxing, that was the last thing she felt.

She'd practically begged Paul to come with her, but he had a lunch meeting he couldn't miss. Sometimes Lauren wondered if he really couldn't miss meetings or if he used them as an excuse so he didn't have to deal with hard things.

A tall, lanky woman with bleached-blond hair entered the room. "Hi, my name is LeAnne. I'll be the ultrasound technician that helps the doctor do the procedure."

"I'm Lauren." She licked her parched lips while a wave of nerves crested in her stomach. She wanted to be anywhere but in *this* room, undergoing *this* test.

"Try to relax." The woman gave her a smile. "The procedure may be uncomfortable. You should expect some cramping and even some bleeding."

Lauren nodded, her lower lip tucked under her front teeth to keep it from quivering.

The door opened, and a thin man with a shiny bald head and a black goatee stepped inside. "I'm Dr. Jeppersin. I'll try to do this quickly."

Lauren cleared her throat. "When will the results be back?"

"Usually seven to ten days. We'll send them to your doctor as soon as they are available, and his office will call you," Dr. Jeppersin said.

Lauren laid back and clenched her teeth as the doctor performed the test. She tried to imagine herself as a young girl, walking along the river, collecting wildflowers, and bringing them back to her mom so her mind wouldn't be so focused on this procedure and the impending results. Who was she kidding? No amount of imagination could persuade her to forget where she was or what she was doing. The results from this procedure would be definitive and had the power to change her life forever.

About thirty minutes later, Lauren sat in her car feeling alone and dejected. Fear of the results was palpable. All she wanted was to have a healthy baby. It seemed so unfair that after waiting so long, her baby might have some kind of genetic problem. Why was this happening to her? What had she done to deserve this?

Her chin trembled and warm tears leaked from the corners of her eyes. She texted Paul that the test was over and now the waiting began.

Lauren had taken the rest of the afternoon off so she could recover from the test. Since it was Friday, she figured by Monday she'd be able to return to school.

In the hall linen closet, she found a blanket Grandma Van Allen had quilted for her when she was a teenager. Lying on the couch, she tucked the edges of the blanket around her. The room wasn't cold, but the quilt seemed to offer the comfort she needed.

Her phone rang. *Mom.* She didn't feel like talking to her so she let it go to her voicemail.

Absently, she picked up a book and started to read. The letters all ran together and her eyelids grew heavy.

She awoke to Paul standing over the couch. It startled her, making her heart skip a few beats. "You scared me."

"Sorry. I brought home some Chinese." He gestured to the kitchen.

She lifted herself up on an elbow and Paul sat next to her. "Thanks."

"I'm sorry I missed being there. I ended up in a long meeting all afternoon that I couldn't leave."

"That's okay." She pasted on a smile. What else could she say? That he deserted her when she needed him? That he kept letting her down? That this was his baby too?

"How was it?" He seemed like he wanted to know.

"Uncomfortable. I've been having cramps."

"Is that normal?"

"I guess." She reached over and took a swig from her water bottle, allowing the cool liquid to slide down her dry throat.

"When will we know?"

"Maybe next week." She shrugged. "I don't know for sure."

"Everything will be fine."

"You really think so?" She wanted to believe him, wanted him to be right more than anything else she'd ever wanted.

He caressed her cheek with his fingers. "Yeah. The odds are that everything is normal. You'll see."

"And if the baby isn't—"

"Why be so pessimistic?"

She hated it when he accused her of being negative. "I'm not. I'm being realistic."

He got up and walked over to the kitchen. Over his shoulder he said, "Do you want the sweet and sour pork or the sesame chicken?"

Apparently, he was done talking and Lauren didn't have the energy to goad him into it. She'd carry the worry of the possible results herself. Alone. Something she'd learned to do over the last year or so anyway.

chapter *16*

Lauren struggled to keep her fatigue, nausea, and emotional stress under control the next week at school, but her heart wasn't in teaching. She was so anxious about the test results she could barely put a lesson together, let alone teach it. Each day droned on for what seemed like an eternity. Her stress level increased exponentially when the head of her department came in to observe one of her classes on Thursday morning. She hoped that Ms. Russell was satisfied, but decided she had more than enough to worry about at the moment.

The next day, the principal called Lauren into his office during lunch. *Ms. Russell must have talked to Mr. Johnson and now I'm in trouble.* Lauren fidgeted in the stiff chair across from the principal's desk and tried to stay calm.

"You seem to be having some difficulty with your classes." He leaned back in his chair, studying her.

"Everything is fine." She kept eye contact while pushing down the anxiety that climbed up her chest.

"Are you sure?"

"Yes." She hadn't told anyone at school about her pregnancy yet, because she didn't want it to affect their perception of her job performance.

"Remember, we have a faculty meeting this afternoon." The chair groaned as he sat forward. "You missed the one last week."

"I plan to be there."

"Very well."

Mr. Johnson didn't say anything else, so she took that as a good sign. Maybe she wasn't in trouble after all. She left his office and returned to her classroom. Resting her head on her desk, she told herself to find the energy to teach her next class and attend the faculty meeting. *I can do this.*

After her class was over, she rifled through some papers to see how many she needed to grade. School would be over for the summer in less than six weeks, and she was counting down the days. Some days, like today, she was even counting down the hours.

Lauren entered the stuffy staff room and took a seat by JoAnn.

"You look pale. Are you feeling ill?" JoAnn asked.

"No. Just the end of a long winter and not having a chance to get outside in the sunshine." She hoped her lame explanation would suffice. She didn't need JoAnn making things worse.

Mr. Johnson got up and talked about the absence rate. "We're having more students miss school. We need to enforce the attendance policy and encourage the kids to keep coming. I know the weather is getting warmer and the kids are anxious for summer break, but we need to make sure students are attending regularly."

He went on to talk about some specific ways teachers could help, but Lauren's mind was as far away as Mars. All week, she'd been trying to convince herself that everything would be normal and that her baby was fine. With the test results due back any day, her heart flip-flopped every time her phone rang. If it was good news, she wanted the doctor's office to call right away so she could stop worrying, but if it was bad news, she wanted a few more days of hope.

The faculty meeting went on way too long and by the time it was over, Lauren felt faint. Her skin was clammy and hot flashes assaulted her. She hurried to her car so she wouldn't embarrass herself by passing out in front of her colleagues. Once inside, she blasted the air conditioner and leaned her head against the seat, closing her eyes for a few minutes.

Her phone rang and sent her heart into a spasm for a moment until she saw it was her mom. "Hi."

"Hi, honey. I haven't talked to you for several days. How are you doing?"

"Okay. A little sick." She wiped at the perspiration along her hairline.

"I'm sorry. Did you decide to take that medicine for nausea?"

"No. I'm trying to deal with it."

"I wanted to tell you that I finished a quilt for the baby."

"That was fast."

"I've worked on it every night after work. It turned out pretty cute if I do say so myself. And I do say so." She laughed. Lauren wanted to join her, but the weight of the impending test results prevented her.

"I'm sure it's beautiful."

"What happened with the testing?"

"No results yet."

"That's a good sign. No news is good news." Her mother sounded hopeful.

"I hope you're right."

"Haven't you learned by now, moms are always right. You'll tell your kids the same thing."

"I probably will."

"You'll call me when you get the results?"

"Yes." Lauren's call waiting beeped. "Mom, there's another call. Probably Paul. I'll talk to you later."

Lauren answered the call without looking at the caller ID. "Hello" She expected to hear Paul's voice.

"Hi, this is Dr. Maestas."

Lauren's heartbeat thudded in her ears. "Yes?"

"We have the results from the CVS test."

"And?" Lauren's chest constricted and her teeth chattered in anticipation.

"The results are positive for Trisomy 21."

Lauren's mouth went dry and a pounding began in her temples. She felt like there wasn't enough air in the car."What?"

"Down syndrome."

"Are you sure? Could there be a mistake?" *Please let him say there could be a mistake.*

"The results are 98% accurate." He paused. "I'd like you to come in for a consultation about your next step."

"Next step?"

She couldn't think. She couldn't move. *Down syndrome?* How could her baby have that? She was young. Healthy. This happened to other people, not to her.

"Can you come in Monday afternoon?"

Her swollen tongue wouldn't form any words.

"Hello?"

"I'm here," she said, finally.

"I know this is a shock."

"Yes." It was all Lauren could mutter.

After making an appointment, Lauren ended the call. She stared out the windshield, too stunned to even cry. How would she tell Paul? Her mom? The baby she carried was defective. Damaged. Her carefully planned life was unraveling in front of her and she was powerless to stop it.

Numbly, she drove back home and waited for Paul. Her insides were twisted in double and triple knots. Her mind was on overload. She curled up on the couch, tucking her feet underneath her, and stared at the floor. Why her? Why did this have to happen? She'd done nothing to deserve this.

No more hoping that everything was fine. No more hoping that she'd have a normal baby. The results were in. Nothing was fine and her baby was not normal.

She barely heard Paul come home and had no idea how long she'd sat in the now dark room.

"Lauren? Why are all the lights off?" He flipped the light on, the sudden brightness stinging her eyes.

She said nothing.

Paul came and sat next to her. "What's wrong?"

Her still numb body didn't react.

"Lauren?"

After a few moments, she said, "Dr. Maestas called." She didn't look at Paul.

"And?"

"Test results are positive and highly accurate. Our baby has Down syndrome." The bitter words tripped on her tongue. They sounded wrong. Harsh. She wanted to take them all back. But she couldn't. She couldn't deny the results and what they meant.

"We should get another test. I'm sure this one isn't as accurate as they say." Paul stood and walked over to the kitchen."We'll get another test."

"Why?"

"Because we want to know for sure."

Frustrated with his unwillingness to accept the results, Lauren said in a loud voice, "We do. We know for sure."

"I don't think—"

"How many tests will we need to have before you admit that our baby has Down syndrome? Before you accept it?"

Paul pointed at her. "And you're ready to accept the first test results we get. I want a second opinion."

Too weary to continue arguing, Lauren buried her head in her hands.

Paul came to her and put his hand on her back. She leaned into him, desperate to feel his arms around her. "Everything will be fine," he said.

If only she could believe that.

Lauren spent the weekend in a daze, and Paul spent it at work. Late Sunday night, after Paul had gone to bed, Lauren checked the internet to learn more about Down syndrome. Page after page listed possible health problems. There were support groups and positive messages, but she couldn't help but focus on all of the problems— delays in speech and cognitive abilities, inability to live on their own, distinctive facial features that made it obvious they weren't normal, heart defects, hearing and vision problems, feeding issues. It was all too much.

Much too much.

chapter *17*

Lauren called for a substitute teacher for her classes on Monday. In the afternoon, she and Paul sat in the doctor's private office again, waiting to talk about the diagnosis. Though they'd hardly spoken over the weekend—Paul's usual reaction to stress—Lauren was grateful he was here with her.

Dr. Maestas walked in and sat across from them. "How are you?"

Lauren's cheeks throbbed. How did he think she was? He'd just told her that her baby had a birth defect and would never be normal. In a single sentence, he'd destroyed all the hopes and dreams she'd had for her baby. It wasn't supposed to be this way.

"We're in shock." Paul leaned forward in his chair. "Can we have another test?"

The doctor nodded. "But this one is highly accurate. Another test would simply echo the results of this one. I wouldn't recommend further testing for the diagnosis."

Paul sat back against his chair with a thud.

"Let's discuss some options," Dr. Maestas said.

Lauren gazed at him, wishing she would wake from this nightmare. She didn't want to be in his office talking about this. She wanted to be somewhere, anywhere, else.

"Trisomy 21 is the most common chromosomal abnormality. About one baby in seven hundred live births is born with it, and three hundred and fifty thousand Americans have the condition. With proper medical care and a loving home environment, children with Down syndrome can do very well. They can go to school, even college. They can work, get married, and be active in their communities. The outlook is good."

Good? Lauren couldn't see anything *good* about any of this.

"What other options?" Paul said.

"You can give the baby up for adoption. Hundreds of couples are on waiting lists to adopt a baby with Down syndrome."

"People actually want to adopt a baby with . . ." Paul didn't finish his sentence.

Dr. Maestas nodded. "Or, since the pregnancy is less than 20 weeks, you can also elect to terminate."

"An abortion," Lauren whispered, the air knocked from her lungs.

"Yes. Though most women in your situation choose to terminate the pregnancy, that is only one of the options."

"What do you recommend?" Paul clasped his hands together.

"That's a very personal decision. I recommend you take into consideration your emotional and mental well-being, your ability to care for a child with special needs, your finances, and your health." He paused. "People with Down syndrome can often have independent lives as adults, but you do need to consider that caring for your child may be a lifelong commitment. There are also many associated health issues with Down syndrome."

"What is it?" Lauren blurted out.

"I'm sorry?" Dr. Maestas said, a confused expression on his face.

"A boy or a girl?" She wanted—needed—to know.

"A boy."

Lauren rested her hand on her stomach. A little boy.

Paul stood, signaling that he was done with the conversation. "Thank you, doctor, we'll be in touch."

Lauren followed Paul out to the parking lot without saying a word. So many thoughts, fears, and questions collided in her mind.

On the way home, Lauren felt deflated, like someone had drained the life out of her. She'd wanted a baby so fiercely, but now it was an imperfect baby, not the one she'd dreamed about. Why would she have a baby with something that only happened to old women?

In the car, Paul asked, "What do you think?"

Lauren squeezed her eyes shut. What did she think? That life was cruel. Unmarried, teenage girls who didn't even want a baby gave birth to normal children all the time. She could provide a home and had plenty of love and desire for a child, but hers was abnormal.

"Lauren?"

"Why? Why us?" A sharp pain emanated from her chest, as if her heart were shattering into a million pieces.

"I don't know."

"I never thought this would happen. I thought we'd have a normal baby and live a regular life." Her throat grew so thick she thought she might choke.

"Me too." He caressed her cold fingers as he grasped her hand in his.

"What should we do?" A war of emotions raged in her. Anger, disappointment, and fear all converged on her. She wanted to scream, cry, yell, throw something.

"I'm not sure that we're prepared to have a baby with special needs. I'm not even sure it's fair to bring a baby into the world that will have problems. What kind of life will it have?"

Lauren closed her blistering, aching eyes. "He," she said softly.

"What?"

She glanced at Paul, his face ashen and his chin trembling. "Our baby is a he."

Paul gripped the steering wheel. "I don't know if I can handle this."

chapter 18

The next day, Lauren struggled to get through her classes. It wasn't fair to her students to be so distracted, but she couldn't help it. Her life had suddenly taken a detour she wasn't prepared to take, and she wasn't sure what to do. Talking to the doctor made it all too real. Too horrible.

After school, she drove to a nearby park. The late April air was warm and the sky a brilliant blue. She found a bench and sat there watching children playing on the brightly painted equipment. A little girl with black braids squealed as she swung higher and higher.

"It's my turn to swing," a boy with curly black hair shouted.

"I just got on the swing," the girl yelled back.

"You always hog the swing."

"No, I don't."

"Yes you do."

They continued to argue while a woman with a stroller and a small dog on a leash walked past. Inside the stroller, a baby dressed in pink with only a tuft of dark hair on her head held a bottle tightly in her chubby hands.

Children's laughter rang through the air as a group of kids chased each other around the park equipment.

Lauren watched them with interest, but her heart began to ache. A profound ache. Dull and deep. Her dream of having a healthy, normal baby had been stolen from her in a test result. She knew nothing about parenting, much less taking care of a child with a debilitating condition. How would she ever manage? She'd have to quit her job—give up her career—and devote her life full-time to raising this baby. There was no possibility of having another child with all the time she'd have to spend with this one

And what if he had catastrophic health issues? What if she spent all of her time in the hospital because he was sick all the time? And how would they afford to pay for that?

As Paul had said, was it really fair to bring a child into the world that would constantly be struggling? A child that would never know a real, normal life? Did she want a baby so much that she was willing to doom him to a low-quality of life?

She closed her eyes and faced the sun, allowing its rays to bathe her face in warmth. Why did it have to be this way? Why couldn't her baby be normal? What had she done to deserve this?

Lauren stopped by the grocery store to pick up a few things. Mechanically, she pushed the cart down the aisles, picking out familiar items without thinking about them.

"Hi, Mrs. Wilson."

Lauren turned to see Calli. "Hi."

"You look sad. Are you okay?"

She cleared her throat. "Oh, yes. I'm fine. How are you?" She willed herself to smile.

Calli didn't say anything, but she wore a melancholy expression.

"Something wrong?"

Calli glanced at the ground. "Some kids were making fun of me today. Teasing me that I'm adopted. Saying that my real mom didn't want me because I'm a loser."

Lauren's cheeks grew hot. How dare kids make Calli feel bad. How dare they be so mean. "Who?"

Calli shrugged as if trying to make it less hurtful to her than it was. "Some boys in seventh grade."

"I'm so sorry." She wanted to reach out and hug her, but was afraid her mom wouldn't like it. "That's wrong. I need to know their names so I can report them."

"I don't want anyone to get in trouble." Calli's blue eyes filled with tears. "Why can't people just be nice?"

"I don't know, Calli. I wish I did."

Calli's shoulders drooped. "I wish I weren't adopted."

"Why do you say that?" Lauren glanced around trying to see where Calli's mom might be.

"It makes me different. I don't like being different." She kicked at the floor.

Trying to comfort her, Lauren said, "Different isn't bad."

"It is to me." Calli glanced at Lauren underneath a crooked set of bangs.

Nervous that her mom would be upset that they were talking, Lauren said, "Is your mom here?"

"No, I came with my cousin. Well, I guess technically she really isn't my cousin." She plunged her hands into her pockets. "She's over in the cosmetics. I saw you and wanted to say hi."

"I'm sorry you're upset about this whole thing, but I think you're lucky to have such good parents."

Calli nodded. Someone called out her name. "That's my cousin. I better go. Thanks for talking to me."

Lauren watched her shuffle away. Finding out she was adopted seemed to have changed her. Lauren imagined Calli had too many questions and not enough answers about the why of it all. Maybe some questions simply didn't have any answers.

Lauren grabbed some toilet paper and proceeded to the checkout line.

That night after a silent dinner of spaghetti, Paul sat next to Lauren on the couch. He reached for the remote and turned off the TV. "I want to talk about this pregnancy."

Lauren folded her arms across her chest and sat back. "Okay." *It's about time.* He'd been avoiding her, as if that would do anything but make her feel frustrated and upset. Their baby had Down syndrome and dodging the subject was not going to change that fact.

"I've been doing a lot of thinking."

That was good because he sure hadn't been doing a lot of talking. "And?" Why was it like pulling teeth to get him to talk to her? This was the most important thing that had happened in their marriage and he'd gone mute.

"I met my parents for lunch and talked to them."

"About the baby?"

He nodded.

Seriously? He talked to his *parents*. Behind her back? A sense of betrayal wound around her.

"And?" She pushed down the angry words that begged for freedom.

He drew his brows together. "After a lot of thought and some research and talking to my parents, I think the best option is to terminate."

Terminate? Lauren had never noticed how ugly that word was. She sucked in her lips and clamped down on them. Her heart beat rapidly. If she said anything right now, she'd regret it. How could he talk to his parents and come to this momentous decision before discussing it with her? This was *their* decision, not his parents'. Truth be told, she didn't want his parents involved at all, but he'd chosen to involve them without her permission.

"I think we should set up the appointment and have it taken care of as soon as possible." He set his hand on his thigh. "There are less complications for you if we do it earlier."

She clenched her fists, digging her nails into her palms. He'd already made up his mind without so much as a conversation with her. How could he be so cruel and selfish?

"Aren't you going to say anything?"

She jerked her head back and stared at Paul. "You actually want *me* to talk about it? Sounds like you've already decided what to do with your parents. Why even ask me?" Her heartbeat rumbled in her ears.

"Why are you so mad?"

"Why?" She raised her hands up over her head and looked at the ceiling. Was he serious? "I'll tell you why. This is not your parents' decision. It's ours."

"I know."

She stood abruptly. "No, you don't. It's none of your parents' business." She shot him a look. "You talk to your parents more than you talk to me. And you spend more time with them, than with me. You choose them over me all the time." She pushed out a breath. "And now you've shared something with them that's none of their business." Her resentment toward his parents was out and relief washed over her. Even if she wanted to call the jagged words back, which she didn't, she couldn't.

"That's not true." He stood, his eyes hard. "I'm working with my dad."

"Are you? I don't even know anymore. You're never home. And now, when we need to make the most important decision of our marriage, you go to your parents."

"You're being totally unfair." He paused. "And childish."

She narrowed her eyes at him. "Childish?"

"Yes."

She pointed at him. "You never wanted this baby. You weren't even happy when I told you."

He held his hands out in front of him. "I was surprised."

"And now you want to abort it without even discussing it with me?"

"I think you need to calm down."

"I don't want to calm down." She grabbed a glass from the table and threw it to the ground. It shattered and made her jump back. "I want to scream. I want to . . ." She collapsed into a heap of sobs. "Why? Why did this happen?" She buried her face in her hands.

Paul knelt next to her on the floor and rubbed her back. After a few minutes, he took her by the hand and led her to the couch.

She rested her head on his shoulder, exhausted from the emotional turmoil. "It's so unfair."

He reached over and wiped a tear from her cheek. "I know having a baby is really important to you. We can try again."

"I don't know." Her body began to shake.

"We aren't prepared for a baby with a birth defect. I know nothing about being a father, let alone trying to take care of a baby with special needs. The whole idea overwhelms me."

"It overwhelms me too, but I don't know that abortion is the answer."

"What do you think the answer is?"

"I'm not sure." She'd never been so unsure in her life.

chapter *19*

That night Lauren stared at the ceiling hoping to get some answers. Maybe Paul was right. Maybe the best idea was to let this baby go and try again. It had taken a while for her to get pregnant this time, but it was possible it'd take less time for the next baby—a baby without the deck stacked against it, a baby that could have a normal, decent life.

She'd seen the statistics. Ninety percent of all pregnancies diagnosed with Down syndrome were terminated. The people who made the decision to abort weren't monsters, they were simply trying to make the best decision they could. Isn't that what Lauren wanted? To make the best decision she could?

Paul seemed so sure the right decision was to terminate. Maybe he didn't want a baby as fiercely as she did, but he wasn't a horrible person. He was her husband, and even though he'd discussed their private business with his parents, it wasn't with malice. He was as scared as she was.

And that was it. The idea of having a child with Down syndrome, or any disability, terrified her. Of course, Lauren was sad and disappointed, but the biggest factor was her fear of the unknown. Thinking about having a baby with this life-long condition paralyzed her. She had no idea what the future would bring, and the uncertainty ate a hole through her stomach.

Lauren tossed and turned all night, trying to make the right decision—a decision she could live with. Could she abort this baby? Never think about it again? Could she give birth to him and watch him struggle all of his life and not feel guilty? What was the most humane thing to do?

Morning light began to fill their bedroom. Paul's phone alarm went off. He rose from the bed and went into the bathroom. She'd been awake most of the night, wrestling with her choices. Why was it so cut-and-dried for Paul? He was so sure of his decision. Why couldn't it be the same for her? Maybe she needed to trust his judgment and follow his lead. Perhaps she was too emotional to see the reality of the situation and understand the implications of having a child with special needs. Maybe she was so intent on having a baby she couldn't clearly see what Paul could. He was her husband, and she loved him. She needed to trust him, because he was right. They were young and could try again.

After almost thirty minutes, Paul came out of the bathroom.

"I've made a decision," she said, sitting up.

"What is it?" He stepped toward her and sat on the edge of the bed.

Drawing in a deep breath, she said softly, "I'm going to call and make an appointment to have the abortion."

He stroked her shoulder. "I think this is the right thing to do."

She nodded. How could having a baby seem so simple one day and so horribly complicated the next?

Over the next few days, Lauren felt like her world had been shattered. Destroyed. All she thought about was the baby she'd wanted and lost, even though it still lived inside her. Would she be able to have another baby, and would that baby be able to replace this one?

The morning of the procedure came with an unexpected spring storm. Heavy clouds drooped from the sky as she and Paul drove in silence toward the clinic.

Lauren took unsteady steps toward the front door, her heart smacking against her lungs. She licked her burning lips. *I can do this. It's the right choice for everyone.* With each heavy step, she convinced herself to move forward, justifying the decision to terminate the pregnancy.

"We're doing the right thing. This baby would never be happy." Paul caressed her fingers as he held her hand.

She stopped and gazed at Paul. "But how do we really know that?" What proof was there that their son wouldn't be happy? No one could see into the future and say unequivocally that their son's life would be doomed.

"Because we can make that determination based on what we do know and what we think is best."

Lauren placed her trembling fingers across her abdomen. "But who are we to say that our son won't have a good life? Who are we to decide that for him?" Doubts about her decision began to circle her like vultures.

"We're the adults. Besides, it's your decision because it's your body."

Looking out at the gray horizon, she said, "And yet, I know he's in there. I've seen him on the ultrasound screen, jumping up and down. I've heard his heartbeat. Shouldn't I do all I can to protect him and keep him safe?" Lauren looked directly at Paul. "Isn't that what mothers do?"

Paul studied her. "I thought we'd agreed that an abortion was the right thing to do."

Thunder clapped in the distance. Lauren stared at the building in front of her, unable to move. Once she went inside, she'd come out a different person. When the abortion was completed, the life growing inside her would be gone. No more heartbeat, no more movement, no more baby. Could she live with that or would this decision forever haunt her?

She tried to swallow the growing lump in her throat and gather her courage. This decision would change her life, and she needed to be absolutely certain it was the right one. She needed to be sure she could live with the consequences and have no nagging doubts. But that's exactly what she had—doubts. "I don't think I can go through with it. It feels wrong."

"I'll be with you through the whole thing. I promise. I'll be right here. It'll all be over soon, and we can move on." Paul's eyes pleaded with hers.

She shook her head. "You aren't listening to me."

"But—"

Squaring her shoulders she said, "I want to go home."

"You're just nervous." He took her gently by the arm. "You'll feel better once we're inside."

Her feet stayed planted. "No, I don't think so." The more she thought about going through with the abortion, the more she knew, deep within herself, that it was the wrong decision.

"Lauren—"

"I can't do this. Please, take me home."

"Are you sure?"

"Positive."

They drove back to their condo without saying a word to each other. Rain fell from the bulging clouds, the wipers working in a steady rhythm to clear the windshield. Lightning streaked across the sky as the storm continued to build. Though the weather was in turmoil, a quiet peace encompassed Lauren. For the first time since the diagnosis, she felt calm.

The baby inside her had an extra chromosome, but he was still her son.

A part of her.

And in her very core, she loved him.

Truly.

Deeply.

Unapologetically.

The tension between her and Paul crackled like the lightning outside and Lauren didn't have enough emotional energy to initiate a discussion, so they spent the rest of the evening avoiding each other. Paul slept on the couch, a sure sign he was angry. By the time Lauren awoke, Paul was gone. She assumed he went to the office even though it was the weekend.

She spent the day catching up on the cleaning and laundry. After putting away the last load of clothes, her phone rang. "Hi, Mom." She sat on the bed, the muted afternoon light filtering through the blinds.

"How are you? I haven't talked to you in days."

Lauren was well aware of that. She had purposely avoided calling, because she didn't want to involve her mom. This was between her and Paul. At least *she'd* thought it was. "I'm okay."

"What's wrong?"

"Why do you think there's something wrong?" Sometimes she hated that her mom knew her so well.

"I can always tell by the tone of your voice when something is wrong. What is it?"

Lauren tried to form the words to tell her mom about the events of the last few days.

"Lauren?"

"We found out that we're having a boy." She tried to sound light.

"That's wonderful. Why didn't you tell me? You know I've been waiting to buy the stores out down here. I can't wait to get started."

Lauren smiled. "We also found out . . ."

"What?"

"He has Down syndrome."

"Oh." Lauren imagined the expression on her mom's face—a mix of disappointment, pity, and fear—an expression she was sure she'd become intimately familiar with now.

Rolling the edge of her shirt between her fingers, she said, "I didn't tell you because I wasn't sure *how* to tell you."

"Because you think I won't love him?" Her mom sounded offended, almost angry.

"No," Lauren said, trying to defend herself.

"Then why?"

"The doctor talked to us about options." Lauren rubbed her forehead.

"You mean abortion?"

"Yes."

"And?"

"Paul and I talked about it. I made an appointment at a clinic."

Her mom gasped and Lauren's eyes filled with tears. "So you're not pregnant anymore?"

"I couldn't go through with it." She flicked a tear from her cheek. "He's my baby."

After letting out a breath, her mom asked, "How did Paul react?"

"Not great."

"He wanted you to get the abortion?"

"Yeah. He thinks we aren't prepared for a baby with special needs and he feels like it isn't fair to bring a baby into the world who will struggle." She didn't want to dismiss Paul's concerns, but wasn't prepared to end her baby's life because of them.

"And you?"

Lauren gazed at her stomach. "He's my baby. I love him." She paused. "I want him, even if he's imperfect." That was the bottom line. She loved her son, despite his defect.

"Is Paul okay with that?"

"Honestly, I don't know. He hasn't talked to me much since I decided against it." Make that not at all.

"How dare he—"

"Mom, please don't." The last thing Lauren needed was her mom on a rampage against Paul. Things were too shaky as it was, and Lauren's emotions were too raw.

After a moment of silence, her mom said, "You need to work things out."

"I know."

She finished talking to her mom then pulled out some school papers, hoping the mundane task of grading would keep her mind focused on something besides her personal life.

A couple of hours later, she finished the last test and went into the kitchen to get a drink of water. She had no idea when Paul would come home.

Or *if* he'd come home.

chapter 20

The sun had dipped below the horizon when Paul finally came through the door.

"Hi," said Lauren.

"Hi." He set his briefcase on the kitchen table.

"I didn't know you'd have to go in today." She said it as casually as possible as she leaned against the doorjamb.

"Yeah," he responded without making eye contact.

In a light tone she asked, "Are you hungry?"

"No."

Lauren took a few steps toward him, her heartbeat quickening. "Do you want to go do something? See a movie?"

Going out was the last thing she wanted, but somehow she had to reach him. They needed to talk and work through this. Surely they could find some common ground and go forward.

"No. I'm tired." He grabbed the jug of orange juice from the refrigerator and filled a glass.

Facing the situation head on, Lauren said, "Are you going to keep ignoring me?"

"What do you mean?" He didn't even turn around to face her.

"You've hardly spoken to me since we got back from the clinic."

He shrugged and set his glass down.

"We need to talk about this."

She moved closer to him, but didn't reach out to touch him.

He stared out the kitchen window, barely acknowledging her. "What's there to talk about? You made a decision for the both of us."

With a shaky voice, she said, "Does it matter at all to you how I feel?"

He faced her. "Of course it does. I was thinking about you."

"Were you?"

He narrowed his eyes. "What does that mean?"

Despite her raging heartbeat, Lauren said, "Maybe you were more concerned about you than about me."

"That's not at all true. I was thinking of all of us." He pointed at her. "You're the one that's being selfish. You want a baby so bad you don't care what the consequences will be."

He acted as though he was completely detached from their baby, as if he had no connection to their son at all. He wanted to absolve himself, but she wasn't about to let him do that. "This is *our* baby. He's part of *us*. Doesn't that mean something?" She attempted to control the anger, disappointment, and sadness that threatened to spill down her cheeks.

"But he won't have a decent life. He'll never—"

"We've already gone through all of this."

He moved toward her. "And you still want to bring him into the world. Knowing that his life will be filled with suffering, that he'll never have a life of his own, never really do anything."

Her cheeks throbbed. He was trying to make this about the baby, as if he were being so magnanimous, but he wasn't. She wanted him to stop hiding behind some pretended noble gesture of doing what was best for their baby. "Why don't you just admit it?"

"What?"

"Come on, Paul, be honest." She placed her hand on her hip. "It's your life that you're worried about. How having a baby with Down syndrome will affect *your* life. Maybe the real issue is you wanted a perfect baby, and now that our son won't be perfect, you don't want him."

He raised his eyebrows, but kept his gaze directly on her. "That's a low blow."

Lauren cradled her head in her hands. Why did this have to be so complicated? She'd been thrilled to find out she was pregnant.

She'd never been happier. Then, boom, it had all turned into an emotional war zone—with her and Paul on different sides. This wasn't what she wanted at all. She'd lashed out and said things she didn't mean. "I'm sorry." Lauren wiped at her eyes. In a quiet voice she said, "I want us to be a family. I want you to love this baby."

He shook his head. "I just think it'd be better . . ."

She reached for his hand and placed it on her stomach. "This is our baby growing inside. He belongs to us. Can't we give him a wonderful and happy life?"

He withdrew his hand. "I don't know. I need to figure things out." He walked into the bedroom. After several minutes, he returned with a bag and some clothes in his hands. "I think we need some time to sort through all of this. I'm going to stay with my parents."

"You're leaving?" He might as well have slammed a truck into her chest.

"I need time to think."

He grabbed his car keys and left Lauren standing alone in the entryway.

She was stunned. All she'd wanted was a baby—a family—and now she had nothing. How could Paul leave like this?

Did she really have to choose between her husband and her child?

chapter 21

Monday morning, Lauren prepared to go to school. She hadn't heard from Paul since he'd left on Saturday night. Maybe if he had enough space, he'd realize that he wanted her and the baby. Maybe after he'd had time to think about it, he'd realize that his family is what mattered most. At least that's what she hoped.

She walked into her classroom and greeted the class. "After Mr. Campbell's presentation, I found an edited version of *Schindler's List* online. I know that we finished up our unit on memoir and the Holocaust, but I really wanted to show you this movie. It's based on a real man, Oskar Schindler, who made a difference. I've never shown this movie in class before, but it's a thought-provoking depiction of the Holocaust. Adolf Hitler caused so much devastation and was responsible for so many deaths, and yet ordinary citizens, like Mr. Schindler and like Milda, who never thought of themselves as heroes, took a stand and saved lives. Think about what you would've done. And think about what you can do now."

They spent the class period watching the film. Students gasped, and some of the girls even shed tears in parts. Lauren let her own tears fall, but they weren't just for what happened to the Jews, they were for what was happening in her own life.

At lunch she sat next to JoAnn.

After chewing a bite of salad, the older woman said, "I heard you showed *Schindler's List* in class today."

"Yes, It's a—"

"It's rated R."

Lauren shifted her weight in her seat. Was her judgment suddenly on trial? First, Paul questioned her decision to keep the baby and now JoAnn questioned her choice to show *Schindler's List*. Wasn't she capable of making good decisions? "I know, but—"

"We have a specific policy prohibiting R-rated movies." JoAnn crunched a carrot, her face showing her displeasure.

"I know the policy, so I found an edited copy that's appropriate for use in schools. The film is critically acclaimed and depicts some of the horrors of the Holocaust. It also shows how one man risked everything to help the Jews. The edited version isn't any worse than what's on TV."

"Doesn't matter if it's edited. It's an R-rated movie." JoAnn shook her head and grabbed another carrot. "You better hope Mr. Johnson doesn't get wind of this. We have to follow the policies, even if they don't make sense. And some parents may be upset, even though it was edited. You should have asked for permission first."

"I'm sure it will be fine." Why would parents object to a true story of a man who saved Jews from death? Besides, students read books with much more graphic details and mature themes every day in school. Why would a movie, especially an edited version, be so different?

"I'm sure glad I never have to worry about this stuff with my class. Not a lot of controversial movies about algebra." She laughed.

By the end of the day, the principal hadn't called for Lauren, so she left school feeling confident that JoAnn was overreacting.

When Lauren approached her condo, she saw Paul's car in the driveway. He was outside of it, leaning against the driver's side. Her heart dropped into her stomach, but she hoped he was back to tell her that he loved her and wanted to be a family, no matter what condition the baby had.

She got out of her car and smiled.

"We need to talk." He walked toward the front door, unlocked it, and went inside without saying anything. She followed him and shut the door behind her, the stale air hanging over them.

He turned and faced her. "I've been doing a lot of thinking."

"And?" She studied his face, trying to anticipate his answer.

After almost a minute of excruciating silence, he said, "I just don't think I can raise a child with special needs. That may make me a terrible person, but I can't do it. I want you to reconsider having an abortion." He glanced down at his hands.

She swallowed hard and folded her arms across her chest. "And if I don't?"

He clasped his hands together, but didn't look at her. "I don't know where that leaves us."

Hoping he didn't mean what she thought, she asked, "What are you saying?"

Paul shuffled his feet a few times. "I don't think we can stay together."

His words sucked all the air out of her lungs. "You want to end our marriage? Just like that?" A clammy feeling settled on the back of her neck—he wanted to divorce her because she didn't want to abort their baby. That didn't make any sense, but it didn't seem to matter, because Paul was willing to walk away because of it.

After several awkward moments, she moved toward the living room, trying to collect her thoughts amid the burning emotions that twisted like a tornado inside her. Finally, she said, "I can't believe you want to leave me because I want to have this baby. You're making me choose between our marriage and our son." *What kind of a person does that?*

"I'm sorry, but this is how I feel. I've spent a lot of time thinking about this and going over it in my head, but I keep coming up with the same answer." He paused. "I can't raise a baby with problems. It's not in me."

"How do you know that?" She wanted to reach him, to make him really think about what he was suggesting.

He shrugged. "I just do."

"Aren't you willing to even give this a shot?" If she could get him to think about this on his own, without the influence of his parents, maybe they'd have a chance. Maybe . . .

"I know you want me to and—" he paused "—I wish I could." He licked his lips. "I wish I were the man you think I am."

"But you are." She reached her hand out and placed it on his arm. "We can do this together. This is our family—"

"No." He stepped away from her. "I can't do it."

What he means is he won't. He won't even try. I guess he really isn't the man I thought he was. Through water-filled eyes she said, "If that's how you feel, then I guess we are at an impasse."

"If you'd reconsider . . ."

She shook her head hard. "No. This baby is a part of me. I'm not going to change my mind."

He drew his brows together. "You're not scared or worried about what life will be like with him?"

"Of course I am." Who wouldn't be scared to death at the prospect of raising a child with special needs? The very thought terrified her to her core.

"Then why go through with it?"

Lauren raked her fingers through her hair, trying to find the words to explain what she felt. "Because life isn't about having what you want, it's about learning to live with what you have."

He studied her.

"I wouldn't have chosen this to happen. But it did. And I choose to live with it." That's what it boiled down to—she was willing to live with it and Paul wasn't.

"I wish I was a better person, but I can't take this on." He shook his head. "Honestly, I don't want to."

Paul's confession ripped at her heart. "Then you've made your choice." She pressed her lips together.

"I'll come back later to get my things. I'll file the paperwork." He looked at her. "I wish things were different."

Paul left for his parents' house. Lauren sat in the living room and stared at the wall. Her marriage was over. And for what? Because she carried a child with an extra chromosome. Paul was not the man she thought he was. He wasn't the man that had promised to love her no matter what. How could he have no love for their child? How could he walk away from her and from their baby?

She rested her head against the couch. How would she cope? Could she raise this child on her own?

After thirty minutes of crying and soul-searching, she called her mom.

"Lauren?"

"Hi Mom." She tried to steady her voice, but failed.

"What's going on?"

"I think my marriage is over."

"Why?"

"Paul went back to his parents." She rubbed her forehead. "He can't deal with having this baby."

"So he left you?" The anger was apparent in her mom's voice.

"I don't know what to do or where to go from here." She sucked in a ragged breath.

"Come home." Her mom said it without hesitation.

"Back to Durango?"

"Yes. You can live with me. I'll help you."

Her mom's suggestion took her aback. If she went home to live with her mom wouldn't that be the same as admitting she'd failed? "But, Mom, you have your own life." She sniffed. "You have your job."

"I can retire. I've only kept working there for something to do."

"But—"

"We can make it work. If you want to keep teaching, you can apply here."

"I don't know. I love my job at the middle school, and my life is here." *At least my life* was *here*. The image of Paul as he walked out their door flashed across her mind.

"Why don't you think about it?" her mom said gently.

She swiped the back of her sleeve across her moist eyes. "Okay, I will."

Lauren ended the call and sat there, staring into the cold, empty darkness. She wrapped her arms around herself trying to comfort her demolished heart. No longer did she have her dream life with a great husband, a healthy baby on the way, and a fulfilling job. Now it was the worst kind of nightmare. Her baby had a debilitating lifelong condition, her husband had deserted her, and now she may have to relocate to live with her mom, which meant giving up her job. She felt like Humpty Dumpty. Would she ever be able to put the pieces of her life back together?

chapter 22

Lauren spent the rest of the week in a fog. She went through the motions of teaching her classes, but nothing seemed real. Life felt like it was suspended in that wakeful sleeping stage where she couldn't distinguish between the conscious and subconscious worlds. She spent the weekend mindlessly watching TV and texting her mom here and there, still holding out hope that Paul would come to his senses.

She came home after school on Monday and was in the condo for less than an hour when a knock sounded at the front door. She opened it and found Paul standing there. Immediately, her nerves caught fire. "Why did you knock?"

"I don't know."

The reason was obvious. He'd already moved out, both physically and mentally. The realization hit her with an explosive force, but she kept herself together.

He brushed past her. "I don't want this to be hard."

"Hard?" Was he kidding? He was leaving her because she wanted to have their baby. Hard couldn't even touch it.

"Yeah."

"You mean the fact that you don't want me or your son shouldn't be hard? What should it be?"

"I just . . ." He handed her some papers.

"What are these?" She held the stack out toward him.

"Preliminary." His eyes darted between her face and the papers in her hand.

"I see. You're in a hurry to dissolve our marriage." *How can he be so callous?*

"If I thought you'd change your mind."

"I guess we have irreconcilable differences." Lauren wanted to scream at him for not wanting to save their marriage and make a family for their son. She wanted to shake some sense into him and make him realize his mistake, but she knew better. He was firmly rooted in his decision, and once he made a decision, he didn't budge, especially if he had his parents behind him. "I don't want this to be ugly." She willed herself to be calm and detached so she wouldn't fall into a heap of quivering sobs on the floor.

"It doesn't have to be. We can split everything."

She wanted nothing tangible to remind her. The memories would be painful enough.

"I'll send you some extra money—"

"No." She wasn't sure how she'd pay her bills or take care of her son, but she didn't want to depend on Paul for anything. She'd do this on her own. "I'll take my share of our bank account and the Prius."

"You can keep living here." He said it as if this hadn't been a place where they shared their lives, as if it were only a building with no meaning.

"I'm going back home to live with my mom." It was her only decision now. "She's going to help with the baby."

He nodded.

She gazed at him, hoping to find a remnant of the man she thought she'd known and loved for the last seven years. "You're sure this is what you really want? It doesn't have to be this way." Lauren wanted him to gather her up in his arms, tell her that he'd been wrong, and promise that together they'd be a family. She waited breathlessly for his response.

After several moments, he said, "Yes, this is what I want. And I won't interfere with you raising the baby. You can make all the decisions. I don't want any ties . . ." His sentence trailed off.

"I see." She closed her eyes for a moment. "And this isn't your parents talking?" She had to ask.

"Lauren." He looked at her, his eyes cool and distant. "This is my decision. It's what's best."

She squeezed her fists. "It's best to erase us from your life?"

"You decided—"

"Don't you dare try to blame me just because I want to have our baby. *Our* baby." She pointed at him. "You want to divorce me because I'm having your son. Does that make any kind of sense?"

He stepped away from her. "I'm not going to argue—"

"Of course you aren't. How can you?"

"I've explained the way I feel." He waved the papers at her. "This is the only solution."

In a soft voice, Lauren said, "How did we get here, Paul?"

No response.

"Don't we want to fight for our marriage? Make it work? Won't you want to see your son?"

"Look, you made your decision. I've made mine." Ice clung to his words.

Lauren stood straight, drew in a breath of courage, and grabbed the papers from him. "What's the next step?"

Still balancing on the edge of an emotional cliff the next day, Lauren was grateful she still had her students and her job. She could find some solace there, even if it was only temporary. She'd need to tell Mr. Johnson about her plans to relocate. She hoped he'd be willing to give her a recommendation, so she could find another position in Durango. There was nothing left for her in Denver now.

While she was cleaning up after her last class, the principal walked into her classroom. "Lauren?"

"Yes?"

His face was solemn. "I got a phone call from a parent."

Lauren watched him. "Yes?"

"The parent complained that you showed *Schindler's List* in class last week."

She nodded.

"Perhaps I haven't been clear enough about our policy on showing movies."

She held her hand up. "Not your fault. I take full blame. I didn't even think about the rating. I simply thought it was a powerful way to end our study of the Holocaust."

"Even if I agree personally, we have a school policy prohibiting R-rated movies." He relaxed his shoulders a bit. "As long as you agree not to do it again, it shouldn't be an issue."

"It won't be an issue."

"Good. I know it's been a little bumpy lately but—"

"I'm going to be moving back to Durango after the school year is over."

He blinked. "You are?"

"To live with my mom." Needing to do something with her heavy, awkward hands, she pulled at the bottom of her blouse.

"Oh. Does she need help?"

"It will be mutually beneficial."

With a look of concern he asked, "Are you sure?"

"Yes."

"You've contributed so much to this school. Can I change your mind?" He held his hands out in front of him, encouraging her to stay.

Lauren smiled. "No. But thank you. I've loved working here." She meant it. Under any other circumstances, she wouldn't consider leaving.

"I'm sorry to hear this. I'll be happy to write you a recommendation if that will help."

"Thank you. I'll miss this school, but this is the right thing for me to do." She'd need her mom's strength and emotional support more than anything as she faced the rest of her pregnancy and the birth. Going to live with her mom was her only option at this point. She had nothing else.

The principal left. Lauren gazed around, sad at leaving the classroom that had been hers for four years. She had learned so much since beginning her career here, but she had a son to think about now.

chapter 23

The early morning June sun was just beginning to shower the neighborhood with light while Lauren packed the last of her clothing in the car. Paul would move back into the condo after she left and assume all responsibility for it. A pang of sadness punctured her heart as she took one last long look around. She'd had so many plans—so many hopes—but they were all gone now.

She'd finished all the paperwork at the middle school and said goodbye to her students. She'd even made a special trip over to see Calli, grateful to know that Calli and her family were working through things. Calli had realized how lucky she was to have such caring parents, even if they weren't related by blood, but it would take time for her wounds to heal.

The details were done, and all that was left was the drive back to Durango. She shut the front door and left the key in the mailbox according to her agreement with Paul. Despite everything, a small part of her wished Paul would come see her before she left, but she knew better. Besides, she reassured herself, it was better this way. A clean break would allow her to move forward and focus on what she needed to do.

After a long drive that alternated between gloriously high mountain peaks and flat, green valleys that stretched to the horizon, Lauren finally pulled into the driveway of her childhood home. She got out of the car and stretched then rolled her neck to relieve her tight muscles. Following her doctor's advice, she'd stopped every hour or so along the way to take a break from driving and get some water. Of course, she also needed to use the restroom every hour, so it had worked out well.

"Lauren!" Her mom waved and rushed from the house, grabbing Lauren into a tight hug. "I'm so glad you're here."

"Thanks, Mom."

"How was the drive?"

"Cathartic."

"Really?" Her mom studied her.

Lauren nodded. "I'm ready to start over here. And Durango is a familiar and gentle place—exactly what I need."

Her mom reached over and patted Lauren's belly. "Oh, look at that little bump you're sporting"

"He's growing. Everything with the pregnancy is fine so far."

"That's good to know. I called Dr. Paine and asked who he recommended for an OB. He said to call Dr. Hamilton."

"Thanks. I'll have to check into everything here."

"I'm just glad you're home where you belong. I'm so excited for my little grandson to be born." They walked arm in arm toward the front door.

"Don't get too anxious, we still have about five months to go."

After Lauren and her mom ate chicken salad for dinner and indulged in a few glasses of homemade limeade, Bethany came over. She gave Lauren a long hug. "I'm so excited you'll be here. We can hang out for the rest of the summer like we did way back when."

Lauren looked forward to spending time with her sister and the kids. "I think I'll have to pass on the tubing and river rafting this summer, though."

They sat on the couch. Bethany crossed her ankles and said, "How are things with the divorce?"

"Neither one of us wants it to drag on forever so we're trying to be amicable."

"Amicable about him deserting you and the baby?" Bethany frowned and shook her head. "I can't believe Paul."

"He has his reasons."

"And being a jerk is the biggest one. Who leaves his pregnant wife?" Bethany slapped at the arm of the couch.

Lauren didn't want to get into a big fight with Bethany, especially because she agreed with her sister, but what was done, was done. Paul had made his decision, and she'd made hers. Nothing was going to change that. "He doesn't want the responsibility of raising a baby with special needs. I understand his fear and anxiety. I'm scared to death."

"But you didn't abandon him or turn away from your own child." Bethany's eyes had the same anger Lauren had felt when Paul gave her the ultimatum.

"I know. But it is what it is, and it won't do me—or little Joseph—any good to focus on negative feelings."

"Wait. Joseph?" her mom said.

Lauren nodded with a smile. "Yes. I think he deserves a distinguished name from a man I loved with all my heart."

"Your dad would be very pleased to have a namesake." Her mom's eyes glistened.

"And his middle name will be Justin. I'm going to call him J.J. when he's older."

"Aww, you're going to make me cry," Bethany said, her expression soft.

"Let's not do that. I've done enough crying over the last while to last me a lifetime," Lauren said. "No more tears."

"Speaking of tears," her mom said. "Suzanne passed away on Monday."

"You didn't tell me," Lauren said, remembering the familiar heartache of losing someone she loved. "She was a sweet lady."

"Her funeral is tomorrow at her church on Third Avenue."

"Are you going?" Lauren asked.

"Yes. Will you come with me?"

Lauren smoothed her pants. Funerals weren't her favorite—all that grief was hard to take. "Oh, I don't know. I'm so tired, and I need to unpack."

"It'll only be for a couple of hours."

"What about Bethany?" Lauren pointed at her sister.

"I have to work at the hospital all day."

"Please?" Her mom gave her a pleading expression.

"Okay." Lauren couldn't deny her mom. Besides, Ethan had been kind enough to share his photos and talk to her classes, the least she could do was pay her respects.

That night she lay in the bed in her old room. Her mom had redecorated it, but the memories still swirled above her head. She'd had so many plans. She'd accomplished getting her degree and teaching certificate. She'd even found who she thought was her prince charming and married him, but he'd turned into a warty toad, and there would be no fairy godmother to help her now.

She was alone.

Alone and pregnant.

With a child that she had no idea how to care for.

Silently she promised little Joseph that no matter what, she'd do whatever she had to, so that he'd have a wonderful, happy life.

Even if that meant doing it alone.

chapter 24

Lauren awoke the next morning to a chorus of birds chirping right outside her window. Under other circumstances, she might have enjoyed their song, but her nausea was in full swing. She spent time in the bathroom until her stomach settled down. She splashed water on her face then went into the living room.

"You don't look so good."

"Thanks, Mom." She sat at the kitchen table and laid her head down.

"You know what I mean."

"Some days are rougher than others. I thought I'd be over the nausea by now."

"Probably has more to do with the emotional turmoil you've been through." Her mom set a glass of water on the table for Lauren.

"Could be." Lauren lifted her head and forced herself to take a sip.

"You don't have to come to the funeral with me if you're feeling sick."

Lauren brushed some stray hairs from her face. "Actually, I'd like to get out. Funerals aren't on my list of fun things to do, but I don't want you to go alone."

Her mom sat in the chair opposite Lauren. "I've gotten used to being alone. I don't like it, but I'm used to it."

"I know." Lauren laid her hand across her mom's. "But I'm here now, so we can go together."

Lauren took a dark brown skirt from her suitcase and pulled it up over her hips. It fit snugly across her stomach. "Guess I need to go shopping and buy some bigger skirts," she said to herself in the mirror. She grabbed a loose floral print blouse that covered her too-tight skirt and the growing baby bump.

On the way over to the church, Lauren felt like she'd been transported back in time. Most of the historic homes looked the same, trees still lined Third Avenue, and her mom complained that parking was the usual nightmare.

Inside the church, they sat toward the back. A large spray of pink carnations adorned the polished cherry wood casket, and arrangements of other flowers decorated the pulpit and surrounding areas. The overpowering, sickly-sweet floral scent was almost enough to make Lauren nauseated again.

Lauren recognized a few people sitting in the pews and hoped they thought she was simply home for a visit, not that she had to come home to live with her mom because she was a total failure.

After the service, she and her mom stayed in their seats while the crowd dispersed. Lauren didn't want anyone to ask her questions. When there was finally enough room, they both exited the building to the front.

"There's Ethan. I'd like to talk to him," her mom said.

Lauren trailed after her. Ethan was dressed in a charcoal gray suit with a periwinkle blue dress shirt, and a black tie.

"Oh, Ethan I am so sorry." She pulled him in for a long hug.

"Thank you for coming. I appreciate it, Mrs. Van Allen." He smiled, but Lauren recognized the sadness behind his eyes.

Ethan turned to Lauren. Not knowing what else to do, she gave him a hug, her heart unexpectedly racing when his arms encircled her. "I'm so sorry about your mom."

"Thanks." He stepped back. "Here for another visit?"

"Uh, not exactly."

He gave her a puzzled look.

"Are you in town long?" her mom asked him.

"I'm not sure. I need to take care of some things with the house so I can sell it."

"You're selling the house?" Lauren asked, noticing that the ease that she had felt before around him, had been replaced by . . . something.

"Yeah. I'm not much for being tied down. Besides, as much as I like Durango, my life is in Boulder."

Her mom clucked her tongue. "I can't imagine anyone else living there."

"I'll try to find you some good neighbors then." He winked at Lauren and her stomach flip-flopped. *Why am I having this reaction to Ethan?*

"Why don't you come over for dinner some night this week?" Lauren's mom said.

Lauren grabbed her mom by the arm and gently tugged her away. "Give the poor man a break. I'm sure he'll be busy trying to take care of things."

"I'd love to come to dinner, Mrs. Van Allen. Thank you."

"Thursday?" Her mom said with a smile.

"Works for me."

"Seven o'clock?"

"I'll be there."

As they walked back toward the car, Lauren adjusted her blouse because it had suddenly become tight and confining. "Mom, why in the world did you invite him for dinner?"

"He was one of Justin's good friends and he just lost his mother. I thought it was a kind thing to do. You two seemed to be getting along so well when we were at Suzanne's—"

"Mom."

"What?"

"Please don't be trying to—"

"I'm not trying to do anything. I wanted to invite the poor boy over for dinner. Is there something wrong with that?"

Lauren wasn't fooled by her mother's magnanimous gesture. "No, but don't think I'm not on to you." She pointed at her mom.

"Whatever do you mean?"

"You know what I mean."

"You're making entirely too much out of this. It's a simple dinner invitation. That's all."

Lauren gave her mom a look. How could she explain it? When she'd seen Ethan before, she was still married, and her heart was insulated from any effect he'd had on it back in high school. But now things were different. Very different. Her marriage was over. Her heart no longer had that insulation, and, worse, it was fragile. She'd need to protect it, and the way that she'd reacted to Ethan's hug made her feel . . . vulnerable. Confused. She didn't want to be attracted to anyone right now. Especially not Ethan Campbell.

chapter 25

Lauren spent the next few days looking for teaching jobs in Durango and surrounding areas. She readied her resume and clicked through the listings. A job popped up at Miller Middle School, which she'd attended years ago, so she read it and decided to apply.

Ironic that her new start would be in her hometown, but Lauren needed a clean break from Denver and all the memories there. A searing pain still held her heart. Some days, it was almost too much to even get out of bed, but she had no choice. She had to provide a decent life for herself and little J.J., no matter how daunting that seemed.

Late Thursday afternoon, after touring some small, musty apartments, she stepped inside her mom's house and quickly met the succulent garlic scent. "Are you making lasagna?" she asked.

"I sure am. And homemade French bread, a tossed salad, and some stuffed mushrooms. It's a new recipe, and since Bethany hates mushrooms I haven't been able to try it out. Cooking for one isn't much fun." She wiped her hands on the pink and white gingham apron she wore.

Though her mom didn't mean to, the comment stung. Lauren planned to find her own apartment, and once she did, she'd be on her own and essentially cooking for one. She didn't look forward to the loneliness.

"Lauren?"

"I'm fine."

"What did you do this afternoon while I was at work?" Her mom whisked some ingredients together in a small white bowl.

Lauren plopped onto a chair by the kitchen table. "I went to see a few apartments. I could probably afford one if I found a roommate."

"That's just silly." Her mom stopped what she was doing, and with hands on her hips, said, "Why would you need to get an apartment?"

"So I can start my new life." Such as it was.

"You can stay here indefinitely."

"Thanks, Mom, but I think I need to be on my own. You know, be an adult." Lauren played with the edges of a napkin. She didn't want to hurt her mom's feelings, but finding her own place was an important step in taking control of her chaotic life.

"I'm retiring and I can watch the baby while you teach. Sounds like the perfect arrangement to me."

Lauren shrugged. "I don't know." Maybe her mom was right, but she wasn't ready to give up yet. She had to at least try.

"Let's talk about it later. Can you help me with dinner?"

She gaped at her mom, her heartbeat quickening. *Oh no, tonight is the night.*

"Ethan will be here soon," her mom said.

chapter 26

A knock sounded. "Lauren, can you let him in?"

Lauren finger-styled her unruly hair and adjusted her shirt. She reluctantly walked toward the front door and opened it.

Ethan was dressed in khaki pants and a blue-striped dress shirt. He stepped into the house, his spicy cologne trailing closely behind. Lauren mentally yelled at herself for even noticing what he was wearing or how he smelled. The last thing she needed was to fuel this unwanted and impractical attraction. She assured herself it was simply the residual effects from being infatuated with him all through high school.

"Hey, Lauren."

She cleared her suddenly scratchy throat. "Hi, Ethan."

"It's nice of your mom to invite me over for dinner."

Lauren nodded. "Yeah, she's nice like that." She gestured toward the couch. "Would you like to sit down?"

Lauren sat on the chair across from the couch and laced her fidgety fingers in her lap, not sure what to say.

"Durango hasn't changed much, has it?" Ethan smiled. *It should be illegal to smile like that*, Lauren thought.

"No, it hasn't. It kinda feels like a time warp here. Like I could walk into the high school and go to all my classes," Lauren said.

Ethan laughed. "Yeah. Time is weird that way."

He looked at her and she tucked her hair behind her ear. He stood and walked over to Justin's senior portrait that hung on the wall. "Just like I remember him."

"When I come home to visit, I'm sure I'll hear his voice, and he'll come rushing up behind me and tickle me." The memories warmed her. Justin had been such a bright light in her life.

Ethan gave a slight nod. He faced Lauren and a somber expression crossed his face. He seemed to be trying to say something, but the words weren't coming out. Lauren studied him, waiting for him to speak.

After a few minutes he said softly, "You know, I still feel guilty."

"About what?" Lauren had no idea what he was talking about.

"I was supposed to go hiking with him that day. He was all excited to show me a new trail." Ethan half-smiled. "Said the view would knock my socks off."

"Oh. I didn't know." Lauren shook her head. "We assumed he'd planned to go alone."

Ethan moved to the couch and sat. "Yeah. I got called into work at the last minute. I told him I'd go with him the next day, but he didn't want to wait." Ethan leaned back. "If I'd gone with him, maybe . . ." He seemed to be lost in his thoughts.

"Time for dinner," her mom said from the kitchen.

Lauren stood and showed Ethan to the table.

"This smells delicious. I hardly ever have home-cooked meals." Ethan sat in the chair where her dad used to sit. Lauren sat next to her mom, trying to decide how she felt about Ethan being in her house, sitting at her table, and telling her he should've gone hiking the day Justin fell to his death.

"I hope you enjoy *this* home-cooked meal," her mom said, a smile splashing across her face.

"I travel a lot, and I get really tired of fast food. My mom was such a great cook." He piled some lasagna on his plate.

"And baker." Her mom handed Ethan the salad bowl. "She made the best apple pie I've ever eaten. Wish I could bake one like that."

"My dad loved her apple pie." He added salad to his plate then grabbed a piece of French bread.

"I miss cooking for more than one." She glanced at Lauren. "Now that Lauren will be living with me, I get to cook more."

Lauren gave her mom a sharp look. "Mom, you know this is only temporary."

Ethan turned to Lauren. "Are you and your husband moving back to town?" Ethan's gaze ignited her nerves.

"Not quite." She took a sip of water, hoping to wash down the bitter taste in her mouth.

"They're getting divorced," her mom blurted out. Lauren wished her mother had even a little restraint when it came to details of her life. It wasn't that she wanted to keep her impending divorce a secret from the world, but she didn't want Ethan to know. It was bad enough that she'd been the pathetic teenager who turned to Jell-O when he was around. She didn't want to be the loser who couldn't even stay married.

"I'm sorry," Ethan said with sincerity.

"Me too."

Ethan's fork clinked against his plate a few times, the only sound in the room. He took a bite of his lasagna.

"Suzanne was sure proud of your work," her mom said, seeming to finally sense Lauren's discomfort.

"She was my biggest fan."

Her mom's eyes lit up. "Maybe one of these nights you can show us some of your work."

"Ethan actually came to Denver and showed a few of my classes some photos he took of a Holocaust survivor and the woman who saved her. He talked to them about his experience."

"He did?"

"I thought I told you." Lauren glanced at Ethan. "It was a powerful presentation."

He smiled, and her stomach instantly reacted against her wishes. "I'd love to show you some of my other photos. There's one I took of the Aurora Borealis last year that even stuns me when I look at it."

"Come over any time," her mom said, a little too eagerly for Lauren's taste. The last thing Lauren needed was for her mom to play matchmaker.

After dinner and some light conversation, Ethan stood to leave. "Thank you so much for the dinner. It was great food and great company." He turned to Lauren. "Good to see you."

She nodded.

"Thanks again." He opened the door and left.

"Mom," Lauren said when she was sure he was gone.

"What?" Her mom walked into the kitchen and started rinsing dishes.

"You know exactly what."

Her mom shrugged. "Ethan sure is a nice young man."

Lauren handed her mom the plates. "Look, I know you didn't love Paul. But I did. I'm still trying to deal with all of this, and all I'm interested in right now is having my baby and making a life for him."

"Maybe—"

"No maybe. It's going to take a long time for my heart to heal and I can't worry about me. I need to focus on Joseph." She gazed at her mom with determination. "I mean it."

"Fine. I won't say another word."

chapter 27

A couple of days later, Lauren sat on her mom's couch checking her laptop for job postings in the school district. She sipped some lemon water as she scrolled through the listings for aides, cafeteria workers, and part-time janitors.

"What are you doing?" Bethany said as she walked into the house dressed in her blue scrubs.

"Trying to get a job, but there's not many out there for middle school English teachers."

"Have you checked other districts?"

"Yeah, but I'm really hoping to get a job close to town so I won't have to spend too much time away from the baby."

Kaylee and Jace came running from the back bedroom. "Mama," Jace shouted.

"Hi, babies." Bethany scooped both of them up in her arms. "Did you miss me?"

"Yes. Grammy made us chocolate milk and cupcakes. We read books and played chasing games," Kaylee said, her blond curls bouncing with each word.

"We had fun, didn't we?" Lauren's mom walked out of the hall.

"Thanks, Mom, for watching them. Sorry it was such short notice."

"Glad I could do it."

"I'm sure chasing kids on your day off wasn't what you planned." Bethany let Kaylee and Jace down.

"We had bonding time, didn't we, Jace?"

He nodded at his grandmother, giggled, then shot down the hall again after his sister.

"So I heard Ethan came over for dinner," Bethany said with a smirk. She sat on the couch next to Lauren.

Lauren gave her mom a look. "Yes, he did."

"And?"

Lauren bristled at Bethany's implication that she was still attracted to Ethan. "It was a nice dinner."

"Mom said—"

"I'm not talking about this." Lauren again focused on her laptop.

"Why?"

Was her sister trying to goad her into an argument or was she really that oblivious? "My marriage just broke up, for starters."

"It was only a matter of time." Bethany muttered it under her breath, but Lauren heard it.

She looked directly at Bethany. "What's that supposed to mean?"

Bethany straightened and said unapologetically, "We all knew it wouldn't last with Paul."

"What?" Since when did Bethany think her marriage was doomed to fail?

"We could feel the tension between you whenever you came to visit in the last year or so."

"There wasn't tension."

Bethany gazed at her, an eyebrow lifted.

"Maybe there was *some* tension. A little. Maybe." Lauren could concede things hadn't been perfect between her and Paul, but no one had a perfect marriage.

"Paul's a decent guy, I guess, but he was never your soul mate," Bethany said.

"He was my husband."

"And when things got too tough, he bailed." Bethany held her hand up. "Not exactly a prince charming."

Bethany was right. That's exactly what he'd done. He'd bailed. On her and their son.

"I'm sorry." Bethany reached over and hugged Lauren. "I didn't mean to upset you. I'm sure it can't be easy."

"Nope."

"I'm glad you're home." She caressed Lauren's arm. "I'm always here for you."

"I thought a baby would make things better, bring us closer together." She shrugged. "I didn't think things would be like this."

The next week, Lauren's nausea abated, but her nerves were on edge. She needed a job and she spent most of her time looking for one. If she didn't find something soon, she wasn't sure what she'd do.

While she was surfing the internet, a knock sounded. She rose and opened the door. Ethan stood on the porch and her stomach turned to mush. When would she finally be free of this awkward school-girl feeling? They were no longer teenagers. They were adults with much different lives—lives that had gone, and would continue to go, in very different directions.

"Hi," he said.

"Hi." She tried not to swallow her tongue. "Come in."

He stepped inside, a faint spicy scent following closely behind him. "I'm sorry to bother you."

"No bother. I was looking for a job." She gestured to her laptop on the couch.

"I'm sure you'll find something."

"I hope so. I really need one."

Ethan glanced around as if preparing to share an important secret. "I think I need some help."

"Oh yeah?" Sounded intriguing. The Ethan Campbell she knew never needed help with anything. Ever.

"I've been cleaning out my mom's house and trying to get it ready to sell, but I'd like another opinion, especially a woman's, on how it all looks. Do you think you could come over and tell me what you think?" He rocked back and forth a few times from his toes to his heels, almost as if he were . . . nervous. *No, that can't be it.*

"I don't know," she said dryly. "I'm pretty busy filling out *dozens* of job applications."

"Oh. I see." He pressed his lips together seeming uncomfortable, like he'd imposed on her.

Did he not get her sarcasm? "I'm kidding."

He gave her a dazzling smile and she knew he'd played her. She laughed and shut her laptop.

They walked down the street towards his house, the sunlight making jagged tree shadows on the asphalt. "No luck with a job?"

"Not a lot of teaching jobs here. Durango is so small," Lauren said.

"You're right, but nothing out there is quite like our unique city in the mountains."

"Yeah, I missed the small town life while I lived in Denver. I didn't even know most of my neighbors, let alone all their personal business." She laughed. "Nothing happens in a small town without everyone knowing about it."

Ethan stopped for a moment and gazed at her. "I'm sorry about your marriage."

She nodded.

He started walking again, but at a much slower pace. "Is it too nosy for me to ask what happened?"

Lauren chewed the inside of her lip. She wasn't sure how to explain what happened without revealing too much—Ethan didn't need all the gory details. "We couldn't make it work. After five years of marriage, we just got to a place where neither of us would compromise."

A couple of teenage boys rode past on their skateboards. Lauren's gaze followed them, nostalgic for the days when she was a teen and all she had to worry about was a bad hair day or whether or not her favorite song was in the top forty.

"That's tough," Ethan said, bringing her back to the present.

"Marriage *is* tough. Anyone who says different is either really lucky, or lying." A few birds streaked across the cloudless, deep blue sky. "I guess I had a different idea of what it would be like."

"You mean back when you were a kid?"

"Yeah." A nervous laugh fell out of her mouth. "You know, that awkward girl with the frizzy hair and a big gap between her front teeth."

"I don't remember."

Warmth ran across Lauren's cheeks—he probably didn't remember her at all. "Oh."

"Confession time." He kept looking straight ahead.

She watched him with trepidation.

His dimple showed as he smiled. "I always thought you had beautiful eyes."

Her heartbeat increased. "You did?"

"Still do."

Can someone get the license plate of that truck that just ran over me?

He laughed. "Your face matches your hair." He stuffed his hands into his pockets.

She touched her cheeks. "You're trying to embarrass me."

"If I remember right, that's pretty easy."

"Not as easy as it used to be," she lied.

She followed him into the house, hoping to focus on something else. Boxes were piled up in the corner and the walls were bare. "Looks like you've been busy."

"I found this." He handed her a snapshot of himself and Justin, with wet hair and bronzed skin, standing in front of the Animas River.

"Aww, look at my handsome brother. He loved kayaking. And rafting. And tubing down the river." Her eyes misted at the memories.

"He was crazy."

"You were both crazy. I'm pretty sure if my mom knew all the things you guys used to do, she'd still have a heart attack." She ran her finger across Justin's grinning face. "Sometimes, I try to imagine what he'd be like now."

"Probably still living life to the fullest."

"Yeah. So unfair that a guy with so much enthusiasm for life died so young." The empty place in Lauren's heart ached.

After a minute or so of silence, Ethan pointed to the room. "I'm thinking this pink was cool for my mom, but it probably won't appeal to most buyers. Makes me think of Pepto Bismol, which makes me think of puking."

"I think you're right." Lauren laughed then crossed the room and took inventory of it. "And you're lucky you asked for my help."

"I am?"

"Uh, huh." She pointed to herself with her thumb. "In another life, I was a decorator."

"Another life?"

"Well, I guess, besides teaching, I'd love to flip houses. I've been watching all those home shows for years. At first it was because I thought we'd be buying a house, but then I was hooked. Taking a house from dingy to fabulous is so exciting. At least it looks that way on TV."

"Then I'm glad I asked you." He stood and grabbed a real estate guide that was lying on the oak coffee table. "Too bad the housing market is terrible right now."

"Have you considered keeping it?" She didn't want to admit that she liked the idea of Ethan still having a connection to Durango.

"No. Home ownership isn't for me. Too big of a commitment. I like traveling the world and experiencing it. I'm not ready to settle down and have that kind of responsibility." He tossed the guide back on the table.

Squelching the disappointment that tried to surface, she nodded and smiled. "Your mom mentioned that to my mom." She sat on a wooden chair by a dark oak writing desk.

"Oh yeah? What'd she say?"

Lauren stretched her legs out in front of her and crossed her ankles. He'd had fun at her expense earlier. Now it was her turn. "She thought you were too much of a vagabond. She wanted you to get married and have a bunch of kids. You know, have a respectable job like a school teacher."

He gave her a knowing look. "Like a school teacher? She said that?"

Lauren twirled a strand of her hair "Too far?"

He closed his eyes for a moment and nodded. "Uh, yeah."

Turning serious, Lauren said, "I'm sorry about your mom."

"It's hard to lose someone you love." He tucked in a top flap of one of the boxes. "They say time heals all wounds, but I learned after my dad died, that the wounds never heal, you just figure out how to live with them without bleeding to death." He looked at her, his eyes forlorn. "I'm trying not to bleed to death right now."

Trying to lighten the mood, Lauren said. "Taupe."

He wrinkled his forehead. "Huh?"

"For this room." She stood and fanned her arms out.

"I can see that."

"And we could repaint the cabinets in the kitchen. White would brighten up the whole room."

"Okay." He rubbed his chin.

"Do you want to invest much money in the house?"

"It depends. What are you thinking?"

"Maybe some travertine tiles in the kitchen. If you laid them yourself—"

"I don't think I want a huge project. I'll be leaving tomorrow for an assignment."

"Where?" She looked at him in his faded blue jeans and v-necked white t-shirt that hugged his toned chest, reminding herself that although they seemed to have passed the awkward stage, that was as far as it was going to go.

"Alaska."

"Wow, that sounds amazing." She wished she could travel, but her life's circumstances prohibited anything like that.

"Alaska is gorgeous. Reminds me of Colorado, with less people and more wildlife. Fantastic photo ops."

"I'd love to see some more of your photos."

"Yeah?"

She nodded.

Ethan grabbed his laptop, placed it on the coffee table, and sat on the couch. He tapped some of the keys then gestured for Lauren to sit next to him.

The screen erupted in an eclectic mix of photos that looked more like works of art. "Wow, these are beautiful."

"I'll show you one of my favorites." He clicked through a few screens until he stopped on a shot of tall pine trees silhouetted against a darkening sky with flecks of red raining down. "The Aurora Borealis."

Lauren was speechless at the sense of wonder captured in the photograph.

"Still stuns me that I took that." He clicked on another one, and an image of the sky with green swirls across it popped up.

"Wow."

"It's amazing how every night it's a different display of lights. I never get tired of watching it."

"I've always wanted to see the Northern Lights. I've heard it's breathtaking."

He looked at her intensely, causing a tingle to slip down her spine. "It's more than that."

"What do you mean?"

He paused for a moment, his eyes pensive, yet soft. "It's life-changing. Makes you realize how immense and beautiful this world is and how there has to be some greater power to it all."

Lauren blinked. Ethan had so many layers to him—many more than she'd thought he had.

"Being up there, away from it all, and just absorbing a natural wonder like this makes me think there's more. There has to be." He cleared his throat, seeming embarrassed by his emotions. "Here are a few photos I took in Hawaii last year."

He clicked through a folder, and several shots of breaking waves appeared. One picture caught Lauren's eye. She leaned in to see it more clearly. "Is that a palm tree I can see through the curve of the wave?"

"Yeah." He scooted the laptop closer to her.

"How did you do that?"

"A very expensive telephoto lens." He clicked on another photo with a surfer inside the cresting wave.

"These are fantastic."

As she leaned in to see the photo more closely, he moved his arm around her, encircling her while he kept his hands on the keyboard and clicked through photos. "I'll show you some that I took in the Middle East."

She tried to focus on the photos instead of how close his face was to hers and how his breath was warm on her neck, making her skin erupt in goose bumps.

An image displayed of a young boy with a tear cresting on his lower lid. He had dark hair and hollow eyes. He was sitting in a corner, covered with filth. Lauren blinked back her emotion.

"I snapped this one a couple of years ago right after a bomb went off not too far away. I think it best illustrates the grief and terror over there."

Lauren couldn't speak. The haunting gaze of this unknown boy held her captive.

"It's hard to look at him, isn't it?"

She nodded, still aware of his close proximity and the spearmint scent that tickled her nose when he spoke.

As if also realizing how close they were, Ethan removed his arm and stood abruptly. "That's some of my work."

"You are very talented. Gifted," she said without making eye contact.

"Thanks." He shut the laptop.

She stood and surveyed the room, trying to ignore the connection she'd felt to him. "So back to the house."

"Uh, yeah. I'll be gone for the next couple of weeks, but"—he tapped the side of his thigh a couple of times—"I wondered if you'd be willing to help me when I get back?"

Considering the alternative of sitting in her mom's house alone and dwelling on her less-than-stellar life, she said, "It might be fun to do this project. It'll help get my mind off . . . things."

His dimple showed again. "I'll let you know when I'm back in town, and we can get together."

"Sounds good."

"Great. It's a date," he said.

She looked at him.

He held a hand up. "I didn't mean that the way it sounded."

His little-kid look of embarrassment amused her. "You'll need to move these boxes out of the way so we can get to the walls," she said.

"Will do, boss." He saluted her. "I'll text you when I get back."

She left his house and walked slowly back to her mom's, trying to stop the smile that broke through. Having this project would help keep her mind occupied. And, she had to admit, working with Ethan Campbell was both unexpected and intriguing. But only in the most platonic way, of course.

chapter 28

Lauren awoke to the mid-July morning sun streaming in through her window. She'd hated that light coming in when she was a teen. Now she loved to rise early and try to get as much done during the day as she could. Today she had plenty to do, beginning with a doctor's appointment.

"How are you feeling?" Her mom asked as Lauren walked into the kitchen.

She filled a glass with water. "I think I might be over the nausea part, hopefully."

"You have your doctor's appointment today?"

"Yes. Dr. Hamilton. He has an office over by the hospital."

"Do you want to meet me for lunch?' her mom asked while she poured herself a glass of orange juice.

"Actually, Ethan texted me. He's back and wants me to come over."

Her mom tried to hide a slight smile.

"Listen, Yente, it's not like that. Stop trying to be a matchmaker."

"Me? I'd never." Her mom feigned an expression of shock.

Lauren set her glass in the sink. "I'm helping him get his house ready to sell. He needed some advice. That's all."

Her mom laughed. "And he came to you?"

"Hey, I studied design before I decided to go into teaching. Besides, I love redecorating." A pang of sadness shot through her.

"I was waiting to decorate my own home, but that's obviously not going to happen now."

Her mom gave her a side hug. "Well, this will be good for you."

"That's what I think." She swallowed back the sorrow forming in her throat. "It'll help me keep my mind off the mess that is now my life."

"Have you told him you're pregnant?"

"No, why would I?" It was none of his business.

"Well, it's starting to be more obvious." Her mom smiled. "Maybe he'll just think you ate too much lunch."

"Very funny. I'm sure it doesn't matter one way or the other."

Her mom grabbed her purse and headed toward the front door. "Let me know what the doctor says."

"I will."

The office was decorated in muted tones of green and several beige padded chairs lined the highly-textured wall. Lauren checked in with the receptionist, then found a copy of *People* magazine to flip through while she waited. She stopped on a story about one of the Kardashians then read about Amanda Bynes. Even though it was wrong, she found some comfort in reading about celebrities' troubles because it momentarily took her mind off her own.

About fifteen minutes later, a short nurse with silver hoop earrings called her back, weighed her, and took her urine sample. She led Lauren into a small room with an exam table.

Lauren hadn't met the doctor, but Bethany said he had a good reputation at the hospital.

The door opened and a tall, thin man with mostly black hair and some graying at the temples walked in. He extended his hand. "I'm Dr. Hamilton. Nice to meet you." His caramel brown eyes seemed sincere.

"You too." She gave a courteous smile.

"I've gone over your file. You're having a boy with Trisomy 21."

"Yes." Somehow, the medical term seemed even scarier than the more common one of Down syndrome.

"Your blood pressure looks fine and your weight is good. Let's listen to the heartbeat."

Lauren laid back and the doctor measured her stomach. He smoothed the cool jelly then put the monitor on her belly. She heard Joseph's heartbeat—a strong, definite heartbeat.

He gave her a tissue to remove the jelly. "You can sit up now."

She wiped her abdomen. "Thanks."

He leaned against the wall. "Everything seems normal, but babies born with Trisomy 21 can have some problems. We'll try to eliminate as many concerns before the birth as possible. Of course, we can't prevent everything, so you need to be prepared."

His words echoed in her ears. *You need to be prepared.* A rough reminder that everything was not normal. "Okay."

"Will your husband be in the delivery room?"

"Actually." She cleared her throat. "We're in the process of a divorce."

"Oh."

She stared at the ground. "He didn't want me to go through with the pregnancy." Saying it aloud made her feel so ashamed of Paul. How could a father not want his own child?

"I see." His voice was calm, even kind. "You plan to keep the baby?"

"Yes."

"We can't change the fact that your son has an extra chromosome, but what we can do is make the environment as positive as possible, so he can have the best chance to grow and learn. A diagnosis like this can be frightening, especially because of the unknown, but I know several children with Down syndrome, and your life with your son can be full of wonder and love. It may not be what you planned, but it can still be good."

Lauren wanted to believe her life could be wonderful, but as a soon-to-be single mom of a baby with special needs, her fear of the unknown was almost crippling.

"Would you like to meet other moms of children with Down syndrome?"

"I think so. Maybe" The idea both terrified her and soothed her at the same time. Meeting moms would make her own situation all too real, but at the same time, it might allay some of her fears—at least that's what she hoped.

"I can put you in touch with a friend of mine who has a young son."
Lauren smoothed her hair. "I feel overwhelmed by all of it."

"That's completely normal, even expected. It might help to talk to her and get the perspective of someone who's been where you are right now."

"I'd like that. I think." She nodded and wiped at her eyes—she'd become a bundle of nerves and tears since the diagnosis.

"Will you have any other support?" He gazed at her with concern.

"My mom and my sister both live here. I grew up in Durango, but I've been in Denver for the past several years." That part of her life was now over.

"We'll get through this." He smiled, warmth emanating from his face. "If you have any questions, please don't hesitate to ask." He paused. "Life isn't always what we expect it to be, but we can make the best of it."

"Thank you."

Lauren left the appointment feeling like she'd found a doctor who would not only be competent, but would also offer her some emotional support. She'd need all the support she could get.

Lauren went back to her mom's and changed into sweats because her middle had grown enough to make her pants uncomfortable and she didn't want to wear her skirt over to Ethan's.

She texted Ethan then walked to his house and rang the doorbell. He opened it, wearing some faded blue jean shorts and a Denver Broncos t-shirt. She averted her eyes from the form-fitting shirt and refused to notice his toned calves. She chastised herself, because she wasn't at all interested in anything with anyone, especially Ethan. She had more than enough to deal with.

"Did you get some paint?" she asked while gazing around the room.
He shook his head. "Nope."
"Why not?"
"I haven't been to the store yet. Besides, I need your help to choose the right color."
"Then let's go."

An hour later, they returned from the store with several cans of water-based paint and other painting supplies. Lauren had made sure it was okay to paint with latex paint even though she was pregnant. They'd decided that the whole house needed a paint job, but they'd start with the living room first.

"I can't remember the last time Mom painted this house." He set the cans on the living room floor. "It was probably back when I was in high school—fifteen years ago. Or more. You know, when vomitous pink was popular." He laughed.

"A fresh coat of paint makes a huge difference." Lauren had watched enough home makeover shows to know that a drab room could become stunning simply by adding new paint. It was an inexpensive way to make a dramatic change.

"Let's get started. I'm at your disposal."

Ignoring his mischievous grin, Lauren said, "We need to tape off the windows, protect the outlet covers and baseboards, and spread those plastic sheets over the floors and furniture. The prep work is the most important step." She smiled. "Unless you want to replace carpet and scrape paint off the windows."

"Well, maybe if you weren't going to be such a sloppy painter ."

She put her hands on her hips and tilted her head. .

He laughed. "To your expertise."

"I'm just repeating what they say on those home shows. It can't be that difficult to repaint a room. Right?"

"I have no idea." He shrugged. "You were the decorator in another life, remember?" Ethan teased. He opened a package and pulled out a plastic drop cloth. "I've never done this before."

"That makes two of us." She stepped over to him and grabbed an end of the twisting drop cloth. "I guess we'll learn as we go."

Lauren climbed up onto a chair and reached to remove one side of the drapes.

"Be careful," Ethan said. "I don't want you to get hurt." He moved over next to her.

"I'll be fine." She stuck her hand out, inching her fingers over to the far side of the rod.

"I think you should let me do that."

Lauren stretched a bit too much and started to lose her balance. She took a step back to steady herself, but it was too late.

She fell backwards—right into Ethan's waiting arms.

"Oh," she said, as she looked into his mesmerizing eyes. Their gazes interlocked, and his strong embrace sent electricity coursing through her body, causing a sensory overload. She'd dreamed of a moment like this so many times back in the day, never imagining it would ever happen. Her heart felt as though it might leap from her chest.

"Are you hurt?" Lauren watched his full, deep red lips move and wondered what it would be like to feel them on hers. Would his kiss be gentle and tentative or strong and . . . *Wait. What am I thinking? This is wrong. So wrong.*

"Lauren?" he said, breaking into her irrational thoughts.

She clumsily moved out of his hold. "Sorry about that. I . . . uh . . . thanks for catching me."

"Happy to help." His smile grabbed at her stomach, and she mentally yelled at herself for thinking such ridiculous things. *Get back to the job at hand and forget about anything else.*

After an hour or so of taping plastic over the windows, putting masking tape around the outlet covers, and placing tarps on the floor, Lauren surveyed the room. "We've done a fine job, if I do say so myself."

"Agreed," Ethan said, a playful twinkle in his eyes.

"I think we're ready."

Ethan sat on the plastic-covered couch, making a crinkling sound. "It's almost dinner time. Are you hungry?"

"Not really." She set the masking tape down by the paint cans.

"You don't eat much." He eyed her. "Are you on a diet?"

"Excuse me?" Maybe he'd noticed her growing belly? She pulled at her shirt, making sure it covered her stomach.

He stood, a sheepish expression on his face. "That came out wrong. Because you don't need to be on a diet. Of course. I just meant . . . Never mind." He stumbled over his words, and it made Lauren chuckle to herself.

"You go ahead and eat. I need to run back to my mom's anyway. She'll be home from work and I want to check on her." Lauren did want to check on her mom, but she also wanted to tell her about the doctor's appointment.

chapter 29

Lauren found her mom in the laundry room pulling clothes out of the dryer, the lavender scent of the fabric sheets filling the small room and reminding her of when she was a kid, back when life wasn't so complicated. "Hi, Mom."

"Hey, honey. How was the appointment?" She piled the clothes into a basket.

"Good. The doctor said everything seems to be fine." Lauren bent down and grabbed a sock that had fallen to the floor. She stuck it in the basket. *If only everything were fine. If only . . .*

"Was he nice?"

"Yeah." She took the basket from her mom and carried it into the living room, which was the official folding room. "He's going to get me in touch with a friend of his who has a child with Down syndrome." She set the basket on the floor in front of the couch and her mom sat.

"What do you think of that?" Her mom grabbed a blue towel.

"It all seems surreal. I know what the test results have said, but there's still a part of me that hopes they're wrong." She sat by her mom and picked up a dishtowel from the basket. "If I had the power to change Joseph's chromosome count, I'd do it in a heartbeat. Does that make me a bad person?" As much as she loved the little person growing inside her, this pregnancy had changed things in ways she'd never imagined, and the fear of what was ahead weighed heavy on her heart.

Her mom stopped folding the towel in her lap. "No, it doesn't make you a bad person. It makes you a real person."

"The whole thing scares me." Her shoulders slumped. "I know absolutely nothing about raising a baby, and I know even less about taking care of one with special needs."

Her mom took Lauren's hand in hers. "You'll know what to do. Listen to your instincts. This is your son and you need to trust that you'll know how to take care of him."

"I've never known anyone with Down syndrome and reading about it on the internet scares me. Actually, it completely terrifies me." So much could go wrong. Would she ever have a normal life with her son?

"Then stop reading about it on the internet." She patted Lauren's hand. "Really. Maybe meeting this friend of the doctor's will help."

"Maybe." What if it didn't help? What if Lauren had a bad reaction to meeting this woman and her child? What if it scared her so much she didn't recover? What if . . .

"How about we watch *When in Rome* while we fold clothes?" her mom said, jolting Lauren out of her thoughts.

"Oh." Lauren shook her head, reminding herself that she'd only come back to check on her mom and tell her about the appointment. "I'm going to go back to Ethan's to help him paint the living room."

Her mom shook her head. "You can't do that."

"Why not?"

"Because you're pregnant. The fumes are dangerous." She folded a yellow towel and set it on the couch.

"I researched it, and as long as it's latex paint it shouldn't be a problem."

"I don't think it's a good idea."

"But I told him I'd help." Was it that she really wanted to paint that aging room and give it a face lift, or was it something more? She refused to answer such a preposterous question.

"You don't want to take a risk with the baby do you?"

"I think you're overreacting." Lauren stood. "I'll be back later."

As Lauren walked to Ethan's in the evening air thick with an earthy, pine scent, she couldn't help but replay what her mom had said. What if paint fumes *could* harm her baby? Did she want to take that chance? By the time she reached Ethan's house, she'd decided she didn't want to take any risk with her son. He deserved the very best chance she could give him, and if there was even the most remote possibility something might harm him, it was her duty to avoid it.

"Hey," she said as she entered the house. Paint supplies lined the wall on one side of the room.

Ethan stood there with a paint roller in his hand. "Ready? I think with the two of us we can get this done pretty fast." He struck a pose. "Besides, I'm Super Paint Man."

She laughed at him standing there with the roller raised above his head and a goofy grin on his face, reminding her of Justin.

"Let's get going on this project."

"Well, Super Paint Man, I'd like to, but I can't. I need to get back to my mom's. She needs me to . . . reorganize the pantry and some cupboards. I promised her I'd help." It sounded totally lame, but she didn't want to do anything to hurt J.J., and she didn't want to tell Ethan the real reason.

"Oh," His hand dropped to his side and disappointment flashed across his face.

"I'm sorry. I totally forgot." Lauren felt stupid offering such a silly excuse. Why didn't she just call him with it instead of coming over to tell him? She refused to answer that question.

"No worries." He cracked a smile. "I can get this sucker all painted tonight. You did most of the real work with all that taping."

"Can I come by and see it after you're done?"

"Sure." He seemed distant. "I'll let you know."

Lauren walked back to her mom's. She needed to stay in control. Feeling upset that she couldn't stay and help Ethan was unacceptable. Nothing could ever be between them, even if it were at all possible that he was interested, which she had no reason to believe he was. But even if he were, her first priority was her son, and if his own father didn't want him, why would any other man? She needed to stay focused on Joseph and stop thinking about Ethan or allowing herself to feel anything about him.

That night she lay in bed, her mind in a tangle. She'd thought her marriage to Paul would last a lifetime. That's what she'd planned— to have a family with him, to build a life, to grow old together. But she was here. In her old bedroom. Alone and pregnant. As if on cue, the baby fluttered in her stomach like a tiny, delicate butterfly.

She didn't know how things would turn out exactly, but one thing was certain, she had to protect her son and give him a decent life.

chapter 30

Lauren spent the weekend helping her mom in the backyard. She loved working in the rose garden in the corner. Her dad had started it years ago as a Mother's Day surprise. She remembered how excited her mom was when he brought her out blindfolded into the yard. He'd removed the blindfold and showed her a single, red rose bush. Her mom had thrown her arms around his neck and kissed him. Over the years, he'd added more roses. Lauren's favorite was the one with yellow petals and red tips, but the original bush still held a special place in her heart, because it symbolized the love between her parents. Digging her hands into the soft, cool ground, she inhaled the sweet scent of her daddy's rose garden.

She hadn't heard anything from Ethan and figured he was busy working on his house. She was wise to stay away. With her heart so vulnerable, she needed to be extra careful to protect it. No need in forming any kind of attachment to Ethan anyway. As soon as he finished prepping the house for the market, he'd be on his way back to Boulder. He wasn't going to be in Durango long term like her.

Right after her mom left for work Monday morning, someone rapped on the door. Lauren pulled her robe around her and looked through the peephole.

Ethan. *Oh no. What is he doing here? And I'm in my old robe.* The tips of her ears warmed. Maybe if she didn't open the door he'd go away.

He knocked again.

She ran her fingers through her hair. *I can't see him like this.* She stood there silently hoping he'd give up.

The doorbell rang. *Why is he so persistent? Maybe there's some sort of emergency.*

Worried something might be wrong, she opened the door slightly. "Hi, Ethan."

"Oh. Did I wake you? I'm sorry—"

"No. I'm having a slow morning." Very slow.

"I just thought, maybe, you might go with me to pick out that tile."

"Now?" She pawed at her hair and tried to keep her dragon breath to herself.

"Yeah. I thought we could get started today." He paused. "Unless you have plans."

Of course she didn't have plans. Her life was pathetic. "Uh."

"I should've called. Or texted. I'm sorry." He stepped back from the door.

"No, it's fine."

"I can come back."

"Give me half an hour?" She hoped that'd be enough time to shower and get dressed.

"Sure."

Exactly thirty minutes later, he was in her driveway, and her hair was still wet. Punctuality wasn't her favorite quality in a person at the moment, but at least she was dressed and managed to put on some mascara and lip gloss.

They arrived at the home improvement store with a list she'd written on the way over.

"We'll need to pick out the tile first," she said as they found a basket and headed inside the store.

At the large display, Lauren found travertine tile.

"What about this?" Ethan pointed at some ceramic tile.

Lauren picked up a piece. "Look closely at the edges of this tile." "Yeah?"

"Notice how there's a faint line between the design and the edge?"

He nodded.

"That means the design has been stamped on." She sounded like an expert, but the truth was, she was an expert home-improvement-show-watcher, especially over the last few months.

"A stamped design is bad?"

"Look at these." She showed him a travertine tile.

"Much nicer."

She smiled.

"Lauren Van Allen?" said a high-pitched voice from behind her.

Lauren spun around to see Kathy Jacobsen—a much rounder Kathy Jacobsen than she'd known in high school. "Kathy?"

"Yes." Kathy eyed Ethan up and down. "And Ethan Campbell?"

He smiled and tipped his head.

"I definitely remember you from high school." She glanced at Lauren with a smug look. "I had no idea the two of you got together. Who would've thought that? Right, Lauren?" Kathy's tone insinuated that Ethan was too good for Lauren in high school and in Kathy's opinion, apparently still was.

"Oh." Lauren's tongue swelled. "We, uh . . ."

"We're shopping for tile for the kitchen. Lauren is set on those ceramic ones, but I like these. What do you think?" Ethan picked up a travertine tile.

"Definitely the travertine. They are much, much better. You have such a good eye for this, Ethan. You're a natural." Kathy arched an eyebrow and smiled. She flipped her blond highlighted hair back with her fingers. *I can't believe she's actually trying to flirt with Ethan.* Lauren wanted to remind Kathy that they'd graduated from high school years ago.

"You still live here in town?" Ethan asked.

"Yes. I married John Kartchner. You remember him?"

"Yeah," Ethan said with enthusiasm.

"He teaches at Fort Lewis College. We have two kids," Kathy said, giving Lauren a condescending sideways glance that made Lauren want to punch her.

"That's great." Ethan was a saint to keep being so nice to Kathy with her snooty attitude.

"Do you two have any?"

Lauren's face burned. The truth would come out that she and Ethan weren't together and Kathy would feel so validated.

Before Lauren could say anything, Ethan put his arm around
Lauren and pulled her close. "Not yet. But we're working really hard
on it. Aren't we, honey?" Ethan winked, and Kathy's face reddened.

Lauren swallowed the laugh aching to leave her mouth.

"Well, it was nice seeing you both. Maybe we could get together
for dinner some time." *Kathy barely acknowledged me in high school and is
being so rude right now. Why would I want to spend any more time with her?*

"Sounds awesome, Carol," Ethan said.

"It's Kathy."

Ethan shrugged. "Sorry."

Kathy walked away, miffed.

Lauren turned to Ethan and swatted him playfully on the arm.
"You're bad."

"I didn't like the way she was treating you."

"She was like that in high school. No big deal."

"You deserve to be treated much better than that." A serious
expression crossed his face. "You deserve to be treated like a
princess."

Suddenly feeling shy, she said, "Thanks."

He picked up a piece of the travertine. "How many do we need?"

Ethan purchased the tiles, mortar, grout, and various tools.

On the way back to the house, he said, "Thanks for the help
on this project. It's hard being at the house without my mom." He
glanced at her. "Having you there helps."

When they got to the house, Ethan brought all the supplies inside.

"Uh, oh. We forgot a tile cutter," Lauren said. "I thought I put
everything on my list."

"A what?"

"We need to be able to cut the tiles."

"I think there's a saw in the garage."

"This is a very specialized tool."

"Do I need to buy one?"

Lauren recalled when her dad had remodeled the bathroom
some years ago. "You know, my dad might have bought one. He

tiled around the bathtub. It might be in the garage or the shed in the backyard. I can go home and check."

"Sounds good."

Lauren walked back to her house and looked up a tile cutter on the internet so she'd be sure what it looked like. She rummaged through the garage then checked the shed. No luck.

She dialed the number for a local rental shop and drove over to pick one up. On her drive back to Ethan's, she found confidence in her ability to solve a problem, and she looked forward to seeing Ethan's face when she brought the tile cutter.

Bustling with pride in getting the tool they needed, Lauren knocked on the door, a smile playing on her lips. Ethan opened it, and over his shoulder she could see a tall woman with sleek, dark hair pulled back into a ponytail and with legs that went up to her neck.

Lauren's face flushed. "I'm sorry, I didn't realize someone would . . . be . . . here." The exotic woman didn't even glance in her direction.

"No worries. Come in." He opened the door wider.

When Lauren stepped inside, the woman gave her a contemptuous glare.

"I can come back later," Lauren said, pulling at the collar of her shirt.

"Sounds like a good idea," the woman said in an accent Lauren didn't recognize.

"Lauren, this is Shawntae." Ethan said it casually, like he didn't notice—or chose to ignore—the bulging cloud of awkward that hung over the room.

Shawntae? What kind of a name is that? Lauren forced a smile and said, "Nice to meet you."

"We were in the middle of something." Shawntae's over-sized brown eyes bore into Lauren.

"I'm sorry—" Lauren started.

"Actually, we're done," Ethan said.

Lauren wasn't sure what to do. She felt like the proverbial third wheel.

"Ethan, I came all this way to speak with you." Shawntae reached out her hand for Ethan. "Please?"

Lauren wished she could evaporate. These two had history, and she was the unwelcome intruder. She wanted to be anywhere but there.

"Let's go somewhere," Shawntae said.

Ethan shook his head then opened the door and inclined his head toward it.

Shawntae pushed out an angry breath. She brushed past Lauren and rushed over to an expensive-looking silver car. Throwing the car door open, she slid inside. The tires squealed as she left.

Lauren cleared her throat. "Um, I didn't mean—"

"Shawntae has a hard time with no." Ethan shut the front door.

"You don't need to explain anything." But she wouldn't complain if he did.

"I met her a few years ago on a shoot in Egypt. She was a model."

"Obviously," she said under her breath.

"I traveled a lot and so did she. Things didn't work too well so we broke it off a few months back. She called me from London last week. I told her not to come out here, but she didn't listen." Ethan gestured to the north wall of the living room. "What do you think of the paint job?"

Apparently, Ethan was done talking about Shawntae, so Lauren took his cue and inspected his work. "Looks good. I mean, the flamingo pink was, um, *beautiful*, but this is a nice change." She smiled.

"I even started on the bedrooms. I guess once you get the knack of painting it's pretty easy." His confident stance showed his pride.

"You've done a lot of work."

He nodded.

"I have the tile cutter in the back of my car."

Ethan hefted the tool onto the driveway, his biceps flexing. "How do we run it?"

Luckily, Lauren had also researched that, so she showed him how. He seemed more than impressed.

Back in the house, Ethan said, "Doing this remodeling is kind of fun. Great for a change of pace." He picked up a yellow bucket and a few tools. "Ready to get started?"

"Whenever you are."

They walked to the kitchen where a pile of travertine tile sat.

"Have you done *this* before?" he asked.

"No, but I've watched lots of people do it on TV."

"Isn't that kinda like watching *Grey's Anatomy* and then expecting to go into an operating room and remove a kidney?" He laughed.

"Ha ha. Very funny. " She picked up a tile. "I'm impressed you already prepped the floor with backer board." Lauren knelt and set the tile down.

"Wasn't that hard." He crouched down next to her. "Not like laying tile."

"It should be pretty simple." She sounded more sure than she actually was, but Ethan didn't need to know that.

"I don't want to wreck the floor."

"Trust me."

He gave her a questioning look.

"Really. We can do this." She needed to prove she could do something right and tiling a floor was as good a project as any. "What design would you like?" She gathered a few more tiles and laid them down.

"I don't care." He picked up some tiles and put them down next to her, inadvertently brushing his arm past her leg, making goose bumps erupt on the nape of her neck. "Any design that will make someone want to buy this house works for me."

Ignoring her rapping heart, she turned the tiles then eyed the outcome. "Diagonal would be nice."

"Whatever you say."

"It's not my house."

"Pretend it is."

His comment made her stomach fall and, for a moment, she imagined this house being hers and Ethan's. Together. She shook the thought from her mind and attributed it to wanting to make a home for her son. Ethan just happened to be part of the scenery she used.

They marked off the area and started laying the tiles from the middle of the room. Lauren set out a diagonal pattern. "We need the spacers." She picked up a package of white plastic Xs. "We need to put them between all the tiles so the grout lines will be even."

Ethan mixed the mortar and they began setting tiles.

She felt his eyes on her, so she looked up.

"You're amazing. I'm impressed you can do all of this."

She sat back, not used to such a compliment. Paul hadn't been very free with praise.

"I'm glad you're here," he added.

"Thanks." She was sure the warmth colored her cheeks.

After a couple of hours of measuring, sticking the little spacers down, and placing tiles, Lauren's muscles were on fire. She was sweaty and tired and wanted a break. She wiped her face with the back of her hand and Ethan grinned. "What?" she said.

He reached over and swiped at her cheek, his finger leaving a hot spot. "You had a smudge." She wiped again and he started laughing. "Now it's all over your face."

She dipped her finger into the mortar then flicked some onto Ethan's face. "Now it's on yours."

He scooped out some into his hand, and she jumped to her feet. "Whoa." She held up her hand. "Wait a minute."

His grin grew wider and he started after her, grabbing her from behind. She struggled against his sturdy hold. "I wonder what I should do with this handful of mud?" He opened his hand, his palm filled with the gray goop.

"Come on. I only flicked a little bit at you."

"All's fair." He drew his hand closer to her face, the dusty smell of the mortar circling her nose.

"No way." She struggled even more and started squealing. "Please, don't."

The doorbell rang. "Saved by the bell." Ethan let go of her, dropped the mud into the bucket, and opened the door. A young man with a big nose and a shaved head stood there with a pizza box in his hands. Ethan handed the kid some money.

He turned to Lauren, holding the box. "In the mood for pizza?"

The scent of garlic wafted over to her and made her hungry instead of nauseated. "I think I am."

They washed up then sat on the couch. Lauren sank deep into the cushions, letting herself relax.

Over the pizza, they talked about the latest weather, some current events, and how the Broncos should've won the last Super Bowl.

Ethan's phone rang. He looked at it and stood. "Excuse me for a minute." He walked down the hall and answered in a quiet voice.

A pang of irritation shot through Lauren, even though logically she knew she had no right to be bugged that someone had interrupted their casual, unplanned dinner. It was probably that Shawntae woman.

When Ethan came back into the room, Lauren stood. "Thanks for the pizza. I'd better go. My mom will be worried."

"Don't you feel like a teenager again living with your mom?" She was sure he meant to tease her, but the ease of the night had shifted and it came across as annoying.

"I don't have any other options right now," she said curtly.

"I didn't mean—" he started, an expression of regret on his face.

"No big deal. Really."

She left his house telling herself she was being ridiculous. Ethan had every right to be involved with another woman, or several, if he so desired. It was none of her business.

And she didn't care.

At all.

chapter 31

The next day, while her mom was at work, Lauren checked her email at least a dozen times hoping for a request for a job interview. Nothing. She checked the district website a couple of times just in case a job posted that she hadn't seen. She didn't want to succumb to desperation so she told herself that something would turn up soon.

After taking a shower, applying some make up, and fixing her hair, she found a cute outfit and put it on. She felt a little better about things and decided to indulge in some comfort food. Piling chocolate chip ice cream into a bowl, she sat on the couch and watched a trashy daytime talk show.

During the midst of a screaming tirade by an over-sized woman with spiky black hair and a bright red face, the doorbell rang. With bowl still in hand, Lauren answered the door.

"Ethan." She tried to discreetly hide the bowl because she didn't want him to think she sat around the house eating ice cream all day.

He stepped inside. "I called you, but—"

"Oh. My phone must still be on vibrate back in the bedroom."

Ethan glanced at the TV. "Wow, that woman looks like she's about to explode."

"Her best friend just . . . uh, never mind." Sitting home, eating ice cream, and watching a low-class talk show definitely equaled loser. She flicked the TV off.

"I need your expertise with grouting those tiles. Are you free today?" His gaze went to her hand still holding the bowl with her leftover ice cream.

"I'm pretty busy."

He nodded slowly. "I see."

"I've been doing lots of . . . And trying to get some . . . You know, I have stuff that . . . I'm doing." If she tripped over her words any more, she'd be on the floor.

"Uh, huh."

They both laughed.

Lauren put her bowl in the sink then walked with Ethan to his house.

Lauren's phone vibrated as she walked inside. She pulled it from the pocket in her capris. "Hello?"

"Hi. Is this Lauren Wilson?" a female voice asked.

"Yes."

"This is Lillian Thomas. I'm the administrative assistant at Durango School District 9-R."

Lauren's chest constricted. "Hi."

"I was calling to see if you'd be available for an interview on Monday morning at ten o'clock at Miller Middle School."

"Absolutely." Lauren sounded too eager. Maybe that'd work against her. Should she say something else?

"Great. I'll put you down then. Thank you."

"Thank you so much. I really appreciate it. Thank you." There she was being all eager again. Lauren said goodbye before she could sound any more desperate.

"Good news?" Ethan asked, his eyes inviting her to share.

"Yeah. An interview at Miller on Monday."

"Awesome." He grabbed an empty box. "They'd be crazy not to hire you. You're a great teacher."

"You think so?"

"Oh, yeah. You were amazing the day I was in your class." He reached out and touched her arm, sending shivers up to her shoulder.

She stepped back, retreating from his touch. "Thanks."

"I need to get some stuff packed in the back bedroom before I start on the kitchen floor again."

She nodded, but her mind was focused on her upcoming interview. She had to nail this interview so she could secure a job. If she had a job, then—

Ethan cleared his throat, bringing her back to the moment. "Guess I'll go back to my old bedroom." He started toward the hall, and she followed him.

"Looks like your mom didn't ever change your room." She handled a soccer trophy. "I feel like I've stepped back into the nineties."

"Mom kept asking me to come home and pack it up. But I never got around to it."

"Too busy traveling all over the world and taking photos of gorgeous models?" She arched an eyebrow.

"Something like that." His eyes saddened. "I thought I'd have plenty of time to come home and take care of it. I guess I thought she'd live forever." He sounded melancholy.

Lauren sat on the bed.

"I was in Portugal when she told me about her cancer. I was stunned." He set a box on a wooden desk. "I sure miss her." He pulled some books off a shelf and placed them in the box. "And my dad. It's only me now." He paused. "I'd like to think they're together somewhere. Maybe Mom is making Dad an apple pie and they're laughing. They both loved to laugh."

"I remember your parents together. They seemed so happy."

Ethan looked at her. "They were. I don't even remember them fighting. They just liked to be together. My dad always said what a good woman my mom was, and Mom always said Dad was the love of her life. And that's how they acted." He shrugged. "That's the kind of marriage I'd like. Someday. Down the road."

"Yeah." That was the kind of marriage she'd wanted too.

"I'm sorry. I didn't mean to—"

"No need to apologize." She gave a slight smile. "Maybe you should keep the house and this connection to your parents." Lauren couldn't imagine losing her childhood home with all of its memories.

"I don't want to live in it."

"Maybe you could rent it out." She leaned back on the bed. "I might know someone who would be interested in renting it."

He faced her. "Who?"

"As much as I love my mom, I'm not sure I can live with her indefinitely." Lauren's life may be in shambles at the moment, but now that she had a job interview, she had faith she'd be able to put the pieces back together. And she'd need her own place before the baby came.

"I'll think about it." His face showed no expression, and Lauren tried to discern what that meant. Was he opposed to her, or anyone, renting the house? Maybe he really did want to cut all ties for good. Or maybe he didn't. Lauren wished she could read him.

She rose and took a framed photo of Ethan and Justin off the wall. They were dressed in their high school soccer uniforms making ridiculous faces. The corners of her mouth lifted as she remembered her brother's countless goofy expressions. "You guys were so crazy together. I'm sure your soccer coach wanted to strangle you more than once."

"Yeah. I'm pretty sure he said that a few times. Justin's love of life was contagious."

Lauren stared at the photo, her thoughts on her brother. "I don't really know what happens after we die, but I hope he and my dad are together, maybe even chasing after adventures somewhere out there."

Ethan nodded.

She placed the photo in the box, a pang of grief coursing through her. It wasn't fair that Justin had been ripped from her.

"You can have that if you'd like."

"Really?" She picked up the photo and lightly brushed her fingers across Justin's face. "I'd like that." She wasn't sure if her heart swelled because she could have this photo of her brother or because of Ethan's kind gesture. Either way, she was touched.

They both worked to pack up the rest of the room, Lauren enjoying the easy conversation between them.

Ethan picked up one of the boxes and she tried to ignore how his biceps engaged and stretched the fabric of his shirt. He stacked it on another box against the wall. She picked up a couple trophies, trying to balance them in her hands. She took a few steps and dropped all the trophies on the floor. "I'm so clumsy."

Ethan said, "I'll get those."

"No, I can get them." She bent down at the same time as Ethan and they knocked heads, which threw her off balance and she fell back.

"I am so sorry," Ethan said. He offered her his hand.

As soon as she placed her hand in his, a sizzling sensation shot up her arm. He pulled her to her feet then brushed her hair back from her forehead. He gently rubbed the sore spot with his fingers while she reminded herself to breathe.

"Does that feel better?" he asked, his gaze holding hers.

Lauren wanted to lose herself in his magnetic eyes, feel his strong, steady arms slowly wrap around her, pulling her so close to him they'd almost be as one. She wanted to feel his mouth on hers and taste his kiss and . . . and . . . She shook her head. *Stop thinking about kissing him. It can't happen. It can't.* She took a few unsteady steps back, wiping at her searing face.

Ethan looked at her with a perplexed expression.

"Uh, I need to go." Lauren's head and heart were in a violent argument. If she stayed much longer, she was afraid her heart might win, and that would be disastrous. Kissing Ethan would only lead to another broken heart. And she couldn't risk that.

chapter 32

Early Monday morning Lauren sat up in bed. The room was still cloaked in darkness. She hadn't heard from Ethan since she'd run out of his house, flustered and confused. He probably thought she was crazy for acting the way she did, but she had to protect her heart. It had been through the wringer with Paul, and she wasn't about to serve it up to Ethan so he could take a piece of it. They needed to remain friends and that was all. No more impulsive thoughts about kissing him.

The baby kicked. *I know, J.J., I'm not going to let anyone hurt you. I'll protect both of us, I promise.* With that, she tucked thoughts of Ethan into the back of her mind.

Lauren rose from bed and went into the bathroom. When she returned, she parted the blinds in her bedroom window. The sun was beginning to rise, sending its rays over the mountains. *Good. I'll have plenty of time to get ready for my interview so I won't be stressed.* Going into it, she knew her pregnancy would count against her, but there wasn't anything she could do about that.

Taming her curls with some gel, Lauren pulled her hair back into a loose ponytail. She swiped some mascara across her lashes and added some tinted lip gloss then tried on several outfits to see which one hid her growing belly. It almost seemed like her stomach had protruded over night.

Though the round belly sent a thrilling sensation through her, it also reminded her that Paul wasn't here to share it—that he'd purposely *chosen* not to share it. And why? Because their baby was imperfect. She pulled her shirt tight around her middle and gazed at her reflection in the mirror. No matter what, she couldn't wait to meet her son. Whatever that brought with it, she'd deal with. Or at least learn to deal with.

On the drive over to the middle school, she sang to the radio hoping to dilute her nerves. She'd only had one previous interview for her last job, so she wasn't an expert interviewee by any means. She had to trust that whatever happened would be the best thing.

Lauren pulled into the same parking lot that had been there since she'd attended Miller. She parked then closed her eyes for a moment. Breathing in and out a few times, she opened the car door and made her way into the familiar school.

Those on the committee seemed nice. They asked several questions, and Lauren did her best to answer them.

Before the interview concluded she said, "I need to tell you that I am expecting a baby. He should be born in mid-November. I realize that may be a problem, but I promise to work my hardest."

"Congratulations," a middle-aged woman said.

"Thank you." She argued with herself if she should tell them about Joseph's diagnosis. It may mean she'd need extra time away from work to deal with medical issues, but her mom had agreed to help, so maybe it wouldn't interfere with work. She decided to only discuss it if she was offered a position.

"We'll be in touch," the principal said.

Lauren left the school unsure as to how it went or what the outcome would be, but she'd done her best and that was all she could do.

That night at dinner her mom asked her about the interview. After Lauren gave her the play-by-play, she said, "I'm thinking, if I get the job, I'll go ahead and find a place to rent."

"Not this again." Her mom sat back against the chair. "Why don't you like living here? With me?"

"Mom, it has nothing to do with you. This is about me." Lauren needed to feel in control of her life—be the victor, not the victim. "I *need* to take care of myself and my baby."

"But I can help you."

"Letting me stay here now has been a huge help."

"Then stay indefinitely." Her mom's eyes pleaded with her.

"I don't want to make you feel bad. I know you want me to live here, and I really appreciate the offer, but I need to prove to myself that this divorce won't destroy me—that I can, and will, provide for my family without Paul. I might be down, but I'm not out, and I am going to make a wonderful life for Joseph. Can you understand that?"

Her mom gave a slight nod.

Lauren rose and took her plate to the sink. It clinked softly as she set it down. "Let's not talk about it anymore tonight. I don't even have a job yet." She faced her mom. "Why don't we watch *Sabrina* and have some popcorn? You love Harrison Ford *and* popcorn."

chapter 33

A week passed without any word from the school district. Or Ethan. She assured herself she was glad she hadn't heard from him. Talking to him, and seeing him, would only confuse things, and she needed to keep her head clear so it could be in charge and make the right decisions.

Lauren busied herself with reading everything she could about birthing, taking care of a newborn, and raising a child with special needs. She even found a few groups on Facebook. The fear of having a baby with Down syndrome was still constant, but she figured that if she educated herself, she could alleviate some of that fear. At least she hoped so.

She thought back to her unit on the Holocaust. Prejudice seemed to come from fear, which was a result of ignorance. Maybe if people were more educated about Down syndrome they'd be less likely to let fear make them jump to conclusions and become prejudiced. She'd never thought much about Down syndrome before this diagnosis, but now she'd become a member of a club she'd never wanted to join.

"What are you doing?" her mom asked as she came into the living room after work.

"Reading about Down syndrome." Lauren set her laptop aside. "Knowledge is power, right?"

Her mom put her brown bag on the couch. "They're such sweet, wonderful people. A young man who works at the grocery store always has a smile and works hard to pack my groceries. He's good at his job."

Lauren stretched out her legs, noticing that her toenails needed polish. "I never thought much about Down syndrome, or any other disability—I figured it wouldn't affect me so why worry about it." She caressed her belly. "When Joseph is born, it will change everything."

"Guess what?" He mom peered at her. "Having a baby changes everything. Period."

The doorbell rang. Lauren rose to answer it while her mom disappeared down the hall.

"Hi," Ethan said. "Bad time?"

She drew in a quick breath. "No. Come in."

He stepped inside. "I can come back."

Lauren shook her head slightly. "No. It's fine." She absently pulled her shirt over her middle.

He studied her and she had to look away from his intense gaze. "Is everything okay?"

"Yeah."

"You took off so suddenly—"

"Oh. That." Her mind worked quickly to come up with an excuse, but nothing came.

"Did I do something—"

"No." She held her hand up. "I just . . . I needed to . . ." She couldn't tell him that she'd had an almost uncontrollable urge to kiss him. How would that sound?

Ethan's brows knit together while he watched her.

Changing the subject, she asked, "Is there something you needed?"

"I wanted to see if you'd be interested in renting my house."

She brought her finger to her lips."Shh. My mom doesn't like the idea of me moving out at all. She was really upset when I mentioned it."

"Oh." He plunged his hands into his pockets.

"But *I* still think it's a good idea," she whispered. "I need my own space." *And space for my baby boy.*

"I just got back from an assignment and need to leave again. In fact, I'm on my way to the airport." He inclined his head toward the driveway.

"Okay." She didn't like the disappointment triggered by Ethan leaving.

"If you're interested—" He rocked back on his feet—"I'd like to give you a great deal on it."

"Yeah?"

He grinned and that obnoxious dimple appeared again. "I'll swap you rent for taking care of things."

"I can totally pay rent." She waved her hand. "Actually, that's a lie. I don't have a job yet, but I'm hoping that'll change soon."

"I need someone to look after the place, and you need somewhere to live. It'd benefit both of us."

She hated how his eyes sparkled when he spoke, and even more, she hated that she noticed it. "I'll have to ease my mom into the idea."

"I'm going to Japan. I'll be back in a couple of weeks or so and you can let me know then." He glanced at his watch. "I'd better get going."

"Have a good trip. We'll keep an eye on the house while you're gone."

"Thanks. I'll see you when I get back."

"Sounds good." Actually it sounded great. But it shouldn't. *Remember, no complications.*

Lauren watched him jog back to his car and get in. He was even better looking now than he was in high school. More than that, though, he was kind and thoughtful and considerate. He made her laugh and being around him made her feel good. He'd been a bright spot in her dismal life. But he'd be going back to his apartment, and his life, in Boulder eventually. He was only in Durango temporarily. She knew that, and was grateful she was protecting her heart, but somehow she wished . . .

"I always thought he was a nice, handsome young man," her mom said, startling her. "It'd be—"

"Mom, don't start." Lauren turned around, sure her cheeks betrayed her. "I'm not going to date Ethan. I'm not going to date anyone." Lauren collapsed on the couch. "My divorce isn't even final yet."

"But your marriage is over."

Lauren grabbed a throw pillow and played with the fringe. "That it is. Actually, it's been over for a long time. I'd hoped things would change when I found out I was pregnant. I really thought . . ." she didn't finish her sentence.

"Having a baby would make your marriage better?"

She nodded. "When we first got married, things were awesome, but the more he worked, the more distant he became. The pregnancy overwhelmed him. And with the diagnosis, it was too much for him to handle."

"Nominating him for sainthood?"

"Hardly. Just trying hard not to wallow." Some days that was easier than others.

Her mom walked to the kitchen. Over her shoulder she asked, "Why did Ethan come by?"

"He's leaving for a photography assignment and asked if we'd keep an eye on his house." Not a complete lie, but nothing that would tip her mom off that she might really move out and catapult them into another uncomfortable discussion.

chapter 34

Lauren spent the next two weeks watching her belly grow and trying not to stress out about her job situation. If she didn't get a job, she wasn't sure what she'd do. She checked other district websites and filled out applications hoping something, anything, would turn up. Since she'd wanted her divorce over quickly and without a lot of drama, she'd agreed to no alimony from Paul. Severing all ties with him would be for the best.

Thoughts of Ethan had tried to creep in, but she'd successfully barred most of them from taking up residence in her head. She was confident that Ethan had no romantic interest in her anyway, so as long as she kept her thoughts in check, there was no problem. And that's what she needed, a simple, uncluttered life.

Lauren was in the kitchen, making tacos when her mom came home from work. "Hi, Mom. Dinner is almost ready."

They sat at the table eating and chit-chatting when her mom asked, "Have you heard anything about a job?"

Lauren shook her head. Without warning, tears filled her eyes. "If I don't get a job . . ."

Her mom patted her hand. "You will."

"I feel completely overwhelmed by all of this. Nothing is turning out like I planned. My marriage is over, my baby has Down syndrome, I have no job and no prospect of one. I don't know what

I'm going to do." Through sobs she said, "It wasn't supposed to be this way."

Her mom reached over and caressed her shoulder. "I know. I'm sorry."

"I'm trying so hard to keep things together, and the harder I try, the more they fall apart."

In a quiet voice, her mom said, "Maybe . . ." She didn't finish her sentence.

Lauren wiped at her tears then brushed her hands on her shirt. "What?"

"I don't want to upset you."

"Too late."

Her mom tapped her fingers on the table. "I don't want to add to it."

"Mom, say what's on your mind."

"Have you thought about giving the baby up for adoption?"

"What? Are you serious?" Lauren couldn't believe her mom would suggest that she give her baby away.

"Even though I'm perfectly happy to take care of Joseph, it will be very hard to be a single mom. Especially to a baby with special needs. Who knows what you'll be facing."

"But he's a part of me. My son. I can't give him away." The mere thought made her miserable.

"Maybe that would be best for him though."

"I think adoption can be a wonderful opportunity, but that's not what I want to do. It's not the right choice for me." The memory of Calli talking to her about being adopted rammed into her mind. "I want to keep him." She sniffed.

"There are lots of good families anxious to adopt—even a baby with Down syndrome."

"But he's my baby, and no matter how hard it is, no matter what I have to face, I will. I don't know how, but I will." Her resolve began to build again. "I'm not going to give up."

"You're sure?" Her mom studied her.

"Yes. Absolutely." Lauren had never been so sure of anything.

"Good."

"Good?"

That was not what she expected her mom to say.

"I wanted to make sure you've thought about all the options and that you are certain you want to raise this baby. Taking care of a child is exhausting and seldom easy. I imagine having a baby with special needs will be even more demanding."

Lauren sat back against the kitchen chair. "I don't know what will happen, but I do know that I've loved this baby ever since I knew I was pregnant, and I'm willing to do whatever it takes to be the best mom I can to him."

"You don't have to do it alone."

"Please don't suggest I start seeing Ethan."

Her mom blinked. "I wasn't going to. I meant *I'll* be here." She paused. "But it's interesting you jumped to that. Is there something you need to tell me?"

"Of course not." There was nothing to tell her.

"Okay." Her mom used that I-don't-really-believe-you-tone.

"Really. He's a world-traveling photographer. Neither of us is interested in a relationship. Besides, even if I were, which I'm not, he wouldn't want a ready-made family."

"He still doesn't know you're expecting?"

"No. It's none of his business and it has nothing to do with anything." She crossed her arms over her chest.

"I can see that."

Frustrated by her mom's implication, Lauren stood and took her dishes to the sink, rinsed them off, and placed them roughly in the dishwasher.

chapter 35

The next week, Lauren met Bethany at their favorite restaurant downtown. They sat outside in the courtyard, the late August sun casting shadows through the canopy of leaves above them.

Within ten minutes, Jace had thrown the silverware on the ground and Kaylee had spilled Lauren's water all over the table.

"Mommy, I'm hungry. Can I have a pizza?" Kaylee said.

"Sure." Bethany wiped at the table with a napkin.

"And a corndog?" Kaylee pointed at her menu.

"No. One or the other."

"But I want both." She stuck her lower lip out.

"This is why I don't bring these kids with me. I thought Matt would have a day off today and could watch the kids, but then he got called in." Bethany tucked her hair behind her ears.

"Never a dull moment with the forestry service, right?" Lauren tried to ignore the envy that poked her. Bethany seemed to have the perfect life.

"Or with my kids." Bethany reached over and unwound Jace's fingers from the salt shaker.

Jace screamed, "No."

Bethany frowned at him and told him to stop.

"But they're both so cute." Lauren gave her sister a cheesy smile.

"Did you ever hear from the school district?"

Lauren shook her head. "Nope. Since school has already started, I guess I didn't get that job." She flicked a piece of ice off the table.

"What are you going to do?" Bethany handed a crayon to Jace, encouraging him to color on his children's menu.

"I'm going to substitute teach until I can find something else. I don't really have many options."

"Maybe that'll work out better. You can take time off when you have the baby."

"Except no benefits and no stability. I wish . . ." Lauren didn't finish her sentence. Wishing things were different wouldn't make them so. She knew that well enough by now.

Bethany grabbed a sweetener packet from Jace and wagged her finger at him. He gave her a wide grin. She blew out a breath then looked at Lauren. "Have you heard from Ethan since he's been gone?"

The mention of his name sent an unwanted flutter through her stomach. "Yes."

Bethany's eyes lit up. "And?"

Trying to douse the flame of excitement that flashed across her sister's face, she said, "He's staying in Japan for an extra week or so."

Bethany didn't attempt to hide her disappointment. "Oh. Nothing else?"

The wooden chair creaked as Lauren adjusted her weight. "My divorce isn't even final yet. Why are you trying to make me date Ethan?"

"Mommy, my tummy is making noises," Kaylee said.

"I know. We're all hungry, baby." Bethany rubbed her daughter's arm then handed her a red crayon. "We'll order any minute."

Jace threw a crumpled napkin on the floor, so Lauren reached down to fetch it.

Bethany shook her head and rubbed her temples. "Some days."

"You're lucky." Lauren played with a fork in front of her. Not only was Lauren almost divorced, but her child may never do normal things like dump salt on the table or throw silverware on the floor.

Bethany looked at her, empathy in her eyes. "I hate seeing you alone."

"And I hate being alone, but it is what it is." Paul had made his choice, and she'd made hers. No matter how hard it was, she had to think of her baby.

"You don't have to be alone."

"Beth, I appreciate what you're trying to do, but divorce and a baby with special needs is a lot of baggage for me to deal with, let alone anyone else."

"Maybe Ethan wouldn't mind."

"The last thing I want is to worry about a relationship with anyone. I can barely handle my own life."

"So you just want to be alone and raise this baby on your own?"

"Let's be real here. If his own father doesn't want him, what makes you think any other man, anywhere, is going to want my son? That's the reality." Saying it out loud left her edges raw. No one chose to have an imperfect baby—Paul had proven that. Why would Ethan be any different?

Bethany tightened the strap on Jace's highchair. "I think you're making Ethan guilty of Paul's crime."

chapter 36

The following Monday, Lauren was called in to substitute at Animas Elementary School. After a long day of answering questions and teaching a class full of six-year-old bundles of energy, her patience was shot and her ankles were swollen. She wanted nothing more than to go home, even if it wasn't *her* home, put her feet up, and lose herself in a bowl of ice cream. Middle school kids were tiring, but young children were absolutely exhausting. She had much more appreciation for elementary school teachers now.

Shortly after she arrived, there was a knock on the door. She opened it and Ethan stood there. "Uh, hi."

"Hey. Sorry I didn't text or call. I need to replace the battery in my phone."

"Come in." She opened the door and gestured for him to come inside and sit down. "How was Japan?"

"Awesome. Lots of photos I can use."

The air weighed heavy with awkwardness as she sat on the other end of the couch.

He shifted his weight. "I was thinking we could go get a bite and discuss the details of you moving into the house." Was he asking her on a date? That wouldn't be a good idea. *Definitely not a good idea.*

"When?"

He shrugged. "Now? I'm hungry, but if you aren't, we can discuss the details here, and I'll eat later. No big deal." He said it casually, but his body language seemed to indicate otherwise. Or maybe she was reading too much into it. It was a simple get-together, not a date. The last thing she needed was a date anyway. Her feelings were still too raw, and she was far too vulnerable. Obviously.

"Yeah, that'd work."

"I need to run back to the house, but I'll be back in fifteen minutes. We can go to Lady Falconburgh's."

"I love that place." She found her smile. "It's *so* Durango."

He left, and a few minutes later her mom opened the door with a grocery bag in hand. "I thought we'd like some salmon tonight. I have a special recipe I want to try." She set the bag on the table. "A woman at work gave it to me."

"Sounds good."

"Why are you looking at me so funny?"

"I'm not." Lauren tried to have a blank expression. She didn't want to tell her mom she was going to dinner with Ethan, because her mom would make it into something it wasn't.

"What's going on?" He mom stepped over to her.

"Nothing."

"Lauren?"

"I can't eat dinner with you." She paused. "I'm going to eat with Ethan."

"I see." Her mom tried to conceal a smile, but Lauren caught a glimpse of it.

"It's not like that. It's not a date."

"So what is it?"

Lauren hesitated. Which was worse? Her mom thinking it was a date or knowing it was to discuss her moving into Ethan's house? "Dinner with a friend."

In her closet, Lauren found a flowing skirt and a blouse that seemed to hide her growing waist. Even though it wasn't a date, which it *definitely* wasn't, Lauren wanted to look nice—just in case she saw someone she knew at the restaurant. She dampened her hair to liven up the curls then touched up her makeup. Grabbing her perfume, she misted her neck. After all, she didn't want to smell bad, even on a non-date.

Lauren walked into the living room.

"Wow," her mom said with wide eyes.

"What?"

"You sure look nice for a—"

"Mom," Lauren interrupted, "I always dress like this when I go out in public. Don't make something out of nothing."

"And perfume, too." Her mom wore an expression dripping with implications.

Lauren rolled her eyes. Why was her mom being so ridiculous? So what if she wore perfume? Was there a law against smelling good? It wasn't because of Ethan, and her mom needed to stop acting like Lauren had some hidden agenda.

A knock sounded.

"Sounds like he's here." Her mom opened the door. "Hello, Ethan."

"Hi." He looked at Lauren. "You look beautiful."

"Thanks." Lauren shifted her weight, unsure how to react to his compliment.

"Are you ready to go?" His voice was like Dove dark chocolate, rich and smooth.

She nodded, trying to ignore how his hair curled at the edges and how his eyes danced as he spoke and especially how his smile drew her gaze to the perfect lips that framed it. *This is not a date. This is not a date. This is not a date.*

They chatted in the car, and by the time they arrived at Lady Falconburgh's, Lauren's nerves had settled enough that she could act like a normal person. They sat at a booth toward the back of the restaurant.

"I always come here when I'm in town. I usually see a few classmates," Ethan said.

"One of the things I missed in Denver was the quaint, small town feel of Durango."

"After dinner, we should walk along Main. I haven't done that in years," he said.

They ordered their meals from a young college-aged girl with a colorful tattoo on her upper arm.

"Are you still interested in housesitting?"

"Definitely."

"I still want to sell it, but I need to be free to do some assignments right now."

"I can take care of it for you. No problem."

"How's the job search going?"

"Not great." She sipped her water. "I've been subbing, but that isn't very dependable. Hopefully, that'll change so I can pay rent."

"I'm not worried about that. You'd be doing me a favor by taking care of it. Besides, my mom wouldn't like it to sit there empty." Ethan took a bite of his Reuben sandwich.

Lauren suddenly caught sight of an old friend sitting at the bar across the room. *Oh no. I don't want to talk to Chase. I hope he doesn't see me.* She twisted around, turning her back to him.

"What are you doing?" Ethan asked.

"There's a guy over there that Paul and I used to hang out with back in college. I'd feel really awkward if he came over here and started asking me about Paul."

"We can go if you'd like."

"No, it's okay. He probably won't notice."

Ethan's gaze locked on Lauren's, and her heart froze. "Tell me more about what happened with Paul."

Lauren pushed her salad around with her fork. "I guess we started drifting apart a few years ago, but I didn't want to admit it. This last year Paul spent so much time working, I hardly ever saw him. " She poked a tomato. "I tried to pull us together, but his first priority was work. Not me." She didn't dare share what a selfish jerk Paul had been, because she'd only sound like a bitter ex. "We finally hit something we couldn't agree on, and there was no going back."

She wanted to tell Ethan exactly what it was, but something held her back. Fear? Was it so bad that she enjoyed talking to him and didn't want to ruin that? Once he knew she was pregnant, he wouldn't want anything to do with her. A divorced, single mom, especially one with a child with special needs wasn't attractive to anyone. The child she carried was damaged, and by extension, so was she. Maybe she was misjudging him based on Paul's actions, but her heart was too fragile to take that chance.

"What was it?" he asked.

"We wanted very different things, and neither of us was willing to compromise." She wanted their baby, Paul didn't.

After a few minutes, Lauren said, "What about you? Why haven't you gotten married? Settled down like your mom wanted?"

He shrugged. "Haven't found the right woman, I guess." He sipped his soda. "Maybe someday, when the time is right."

They finished their meals, and Lauren was relieved when Chase left without seeing her.

After dinner, Ethan and Lauren walked along Main, peering into windows. "Some of these stores have been here forever," Ethan said.

"Do you ever think about coming back here for good?"

"Not really. I love the outdoors, the river, mountain biking, skiing."

"I remember that." A sudden breeze prompted Lauren to fold her arms as they walked.

"But I love being able to travel and see things like the pyramids, Chichen Itza, the Alps, the Vatican. This world is amazing." Ethan's face lit up. "I want to experience all of it."

"Makes it difficult to have a relationship that way."

"Are you offering?" He glanced at her with a glint in his eyes.

Her face turned to fire. If he knew she was pregnant, especially with a child with Down syndrome, he wouldn't even joke about it.

He walked ahead of her. "Let's get some candy here. I love gummy bears."

"You do?"

"You sound shocked."

He opened the door for her, and she walked past him into the store. "I thought you'd be a licorice kind of guy."

"Nope. Gummy bears all the way. Especially the red ones."

They sat on a bench outside the store. Lauren ate a dark chocolate truffle. Ethan grabbed a red gummy bear. "Oh, no, you aren't going to eat me are you?" he said in a high-pitched voice.

"Why, yes I am, little gummy bear," he answered in a deep voice.

"No, no. I want to be free to run in the meadows and chase butterflies."

"But you are much too delicious for that."

"Oh, nooooo." With that he popped the bear into his mouth.

Lauren looked at him, trying to conceal a giggle. "That was, um, weird."

"Are you telling me that your gummy bears never begged for freedom?"

She slowly shook her head. "No. Can't say that they did."

"I guess you missed out then."

They laughed and spent the next few minutes talking. They walked back along Main then crossed over to a side street where they ran into Kathy Jacobsen and her husband, a short guy with a receding hairline. *Of all people. Sometimes, living in a small town has definite drawbacks.*

"Oh, hi," Kathy said. "You remember my husband, John?"

Ethan shook his hand. "Good to see you."

"Kathy said she saw you."

Ethan and Lauren both nodded. Lauren didn't know what to say.

"John and I just finished dinner, but we'd love to get some dessert and coffee with you."

"Oh," Ethan said. "That'd be great, but we're headed in here for some dancing." He tipped his head toward the Wild Mustang Saloon.

Kathy made a face. "We don't dance."

"That's too bad. We'd love to have you join us," Ethan said.

Lauren elbowed him.

"Maybe another time," Kathy said.

Ethan smiled then guided Lauren into the building. Once they got inside, Lauren said, "I think she's stalking you." They laughed.

A crowd of people stood near the walls, while several couples were line dancing to an Alan Jackson song.

"Come on, let's dance," Ethan said.

"I'm not much of a dancer. I'm really bad at it, actually."

Ethan cocked his head. "It's either dance or go back outside and hang out with Kathy."

"You win." Lauren followed him out to the dance floor. "But you're going to be sorry."

Ethan stood next to her and started doing the dance steps. He made it look so smooth and easy, like he was made to move like that.

Lauren clumsily tried to follow along. She turned the wrong way and stepped on Ethan's foot, bumping into him and practically knocking him down. "I'm so sorry."

"It's okay." He lifted his foot and shook it.

"I broke your foot." Lauren brought her hand to her face. "I told you. I'm terrible."

"My foot is fine."

The cowboy-hat-wearing DJ announced, "We're gonna slow it down. Gents, find your favorite lady for *I Melt* by Rascal Flatts."

Without warning, Ethan pulled Lauren close to him and they started swaying on the dance floor.

"I'm so sorry about your foot."

"No worries."

"I haven't done much dancing." Paul didn't like to go dancing. Paul liked to work, and when he wasn't at work, he wanted to watch sports. They hadn't gone out together very often over the last couple of years.

"Boulder has some great places to country dance."

"Do you go a lot?"

He nodded and Lauren gave a laugh.

"What?" He looked at her.

"I didn't picture you as a country dancing kind of guy."

"Oh yeah?" He gently pushed her out into a twirl then tugged her back to him. Without warning, he dipped her slightly.

"Guess I was wrong," she said. "You're full of surprises."

They circled around the floor a few times. Lauren let down her defenses and simply enjoyed herself, until Ethan rested his smooth-shaven face against Lauren's cheek, making her nerves go wild. "Maybe we just need to stick to slow dancing," he whispered, his breath tickling her ear and sending an electric current down her neck. *This is a very bad idea.*

Lauren stepped back then turned and hurried outside. The cool night air was a welcome relief to her burning face.

"What's wrong?" Ethan said.

Lauren started walking. "I can't do this."

He grabbed her shoulder. "Do what?"

She faced him. "This." She held her hands out in front of her.

"What is *this?*"

"I don't know, but I can't do it." She started walking again.

"What are you talking about?"

She spun around. "You. Me. Dancing."

"Did I do something wrong?"

"No. I just need to go home."

On the silent ride back to her mom's, her head and heart had an all out war. By the time they arrived at the house, her head was back in charge.

Ethan turned the engine off. "Lauren, can you talk to me?"

"I'm sorry. I didn't mean to run out like that." She knew she was acting erratic.

"What's going on?"

"Nothing. I'm fine. Really." How could she explain to him that he made her feel things she didn't want to feel? That he made her think things she didn't want to think. That she needed to protect herself and her baby.

"Do you want to talk about it?" The tenderness in his voice appealed to her heart to share what she was thinking, but her head warned against it.

"I need to figure some things out. That's all." Being around him muddled her mind and made it too hard to logically make decisions.

"Do you still want to housesit?"

She nodded. "Yeah. Having a place to myself will help."

"I have an early flight in the morning, but I can come over before and help you move your things over."

Though it was a kind offer, Lauren didn't need to spend any more time with him. "I don't have much. It's no big deal."

They got out of the car and walked up to her door.

Ethan reached into his pocket. "Here's the key." He handed it to her, leaving his fingers in her palm for several seconds.

She drew in a breath. "Thanks. I'll take care of it for you."

"I'll be back in a few weeks," he said.

They stood there without moving. Her head screamed to go inside the house, but her feet were cemented to the ground. He inched closer to her, his lips so near she could almost feel them on hers.

Suddenly the porch light flipped on and the door opened.

Lauren stumbled back. "Mom."

"I thought I heard something out here."

Ethan coughed. "Hi, Mrs. Van Allen."

"Would you like to come in?"

He glanced at Lauren. "No. I better get home. I have to be at the airport early tomorrow."

"All right." Her mom left the doorway.

"Thanks for dinner," Lauren said, grateful that her mom had inadvertently stopped her from doing something she'd regret. "I'll take care of the house."

When she walked in, her mom was sitting on the couch knitting. "How was dinner?"

"Good." She sat on the couch and decided to dive into the subject of moving. "I'm going to housesit for Ethan until he sells the house."

Her mom looked straight ahead, her face solemn. "So you're moving out?"

"Mom, I'll be down the street."

Her mom sat silently, the knitting needles rhythmically clinking together.

"Please don't be upset. I'll still need your help with the baby."

Her mom kept knitting. "How long will you be housesitting?"

"I don't know, but if I get a job, I'll find my own place eventually."

Her mom nodded. "Did you finally tell Ethan about the baby?"

"No."

"Why not?"

"It hasn't come up. Besides, it has nothing to do with my ability to housesit." That was the truth. At least most of the truth. "I'll move my stuff in this weekend."

"Fine."

"Mom, you knew I wasn't going to live with you permanently."

She stopped knitting and looked directly at Lauren. "Am I that hard to live with?" She went back to working the needles quickly.

"No. That's not it." She paused. "I've lived away from home for years and I want to be independent again. I want to prove I can live without Paul. That my life didn't end because he left me." *That was it.*

After a few moments of silence her mom put the needles down and peered at Lauren. "I'm proud of you. I don't want you to move out, but I'm proud of you for not giving up."

"Thanks."

"I know you worked hard to make your marriage successful. I can't say I'm sorry that it's over, except that it's made you sad. And that makes me sad. But you are a survivor, and I'm proud of you for trying to put your life back together."

Empowered by her mom's confidence in her, Lauren said, "I can't let anything get in my way of making a new life. I have no idea what that means because I've never had a baby, and I have no idea what his having Down syndrome will involve, but he's my son and I owe him the best life I can make for him."

"You aren't bitter about all of this?"

"Oh, I've had my moments, believe me." She raised her hand. "But if I drown myself in bitterness, how will that help me or Joseph?"

Her mom studied her then smiled. "When did you become so wise?"

chapter 37

Lauren moved her things to Ethan's over the weekend and tried to get settled.

Monday evening, she received a call to substitute at Fort Lewis Mesa Elementary School, a small, rural school about twenty miles or so out of town. Young kids weren't her favorite age group, but she needed the money, so she accepted the job.

The nip of the early morning, mid-September air met her as she left Ethan's house and made her way to her car. She headed through town and down the state highway toward Fort Lewis Mesa and arrived at the school fifteen minutes before it started. She was directed to a classroom down the hall. About ten minutes later, twenty-four second graders filed into the room, including a little girl with blond hair and glasses. Lauren recognized the facial features immediately. A plump woman with small eyes and a long nose followed the girl and sat beside her.

Lauren introduced herself to the class, but her gaze kept darting back to the little girl. When the kids began a math worksheet, Lauren made her way over to the girl.

"Hi," Lauren said with trepidation.

The girl said nothing.

"This is Amber Rose," the woman said. "I'm her aide. My name is Janet Lewis."

"Hi," Lauren said.

"Amber isn't verbal yet." She patted Amber's arm. "Do you know anything about Down syndrome?"

Lauren's hand reflexively touched her stomach. "Not much."

"Amber knows sign language." Janet made a fist then stuck her thumb up between her forefinger and her second finger. "This means toilet. That's an important sign. Amber isn't potty-trained yet, so we're working on that."

"Oh, I see." The idea that this child wasn't yet using the bathroom struck Lauren hard. Would her son not be potty-trained at this age?

"I'll be with her one-on-one, so you won't need to worry much about her. She'll be going to her special ed. class in a bit."

Amber looked at Lauren with large brown eyes, magnified by her glasses. She gave Lauren a smile then went back to coloring boxes on her paper.

After school, on her way back to Ethan's house, Lauren pulled into a park that overlooked the river. She sat on a bench and watched the water crest over rocks, spilling white bubbles down its path. The leaves overhead waved in the breeze and birds chattered somewhere near. She kicked off her shoes and wiggled her toes into the soft, cool dirt beneath.

She never thought she'd come back to Durango to live. Be divorced. Pregnant. Alone.

How was she ever going to raise a child on her own, especially a child that would need so much? What if Joseph never spoke? What if she had to learn sign language just to communicate with him? What if he never learned to use the bathroom? What if he simply watched life pass him by? What if? What if? What if?

Joseph started kicking her, so she rested her hand on her belly. After an hour of sitting on the bench, she wiped the tears away and made her way home.

Not long after Lauren arrived at the house, she opened the door to her mom and invited her in.

"I thought you'd want this." She handed Lauren some mail.

Lauren thumbed through it until she stopped at an envelope. She knew exactly what it was and her heartbeat thundered in her ears. With trembling hands she held it out in front of her then slowly opened the envelope. Sure enough there it was in black and white. Her marriage was dissolved, and a pit of sadness settled in her stomach.

"Can I do anything?"

Lauren shook her head. "No. Just makes me feel like a failure all over again." A part of her wished she'd made it more difficult for Paul, wished she'd made him hurt the way she did. She had every right to be angry and to have made this process as hard as possible. But what would that have accomplished, except to make her miserable? It wouldn't have made Paul love her enough to work it out or made him love their son. And Joseph deserved love, not hate and anger. No matter how much Paul had hurt her, she needed to move on with her life and focus on the baby. She vowed that Joseph would never feel anything but love.

The next week, after a long, exhausting day of substituting, she opened the door and there stood Ethan. "Hey, what are you doing here?" She stepped behind the door, wishing she'd worn a looser shirt.

"Sorry." He came inside the house. "My assignment fell through and my place in Boulder flooded from the apartment upstairs, so they're doing some work on it. I figured this would be a good time to come out here and finish tiling by the sink in the bathroom."

Lauren nodded.

"I would've called, but right after I replaced the battery on my phone, I lost it and had to get a new one." He glanced at her, his gaze settling on her stomach. "I lost all my contacts." He kept looking at her stomach.

She bit her lip. "It *is* your house."

He set his suitcase on the floor.

No need to hide the obvious. "Yes," she said.

"What?" He shifted his weight.

"Yes, I am pregnant." She paused. "And, yes, Paul divorced me knowing that I'm carrying his child."

Ethan nodded, as if he'd just solved a puzzle. He sat on the arm of the couch. "Wow."

Not wanting to go into any details, she said, "I can move back in with my mom."

"I'm sorry I didn't give you any notice."

"Let me put some stuff together, and I'll be out of your way." She hadn't planned to go back to her mom's, but she was sure there wouldn't be any objections.

He followed her into the bedroom. "When are you due?"

"November." She tried to say it as matter-of-factly as possible. He didn't need to know that she feared her world would turn upside down in six weeks.

"I can't believe—"

"I don't want to talk about it." The last thing she needed was to break down in front of Ethan. Better to keep her emotions under control. "It's fine."

He put his hand on her shoulder, and her knees nearly buckled. "It isn't fine."

She blinked. *Do not lose control.*

He caressed her arm. "You don't deserve this."

Against her wishes, her eyes filled with tears, and her bottom lip trembled.

Ethan pulled her into an embrace, and despite knowing better, she melted into his strong arms and inhaled his spicy scent. They stood there, intertwined, for a few minutes.

Finally, she stepped back. "I'm sorry."

"Don't be. That's what friends are for. Right?"

She nodded while wiping the moisture from her cheeks. He'd turned an embarrassing moment into something tender, and she was grateful he was there. She needed a friend.

He brushed a tear from under her eye then traced his finger down her cheek. Without warning, he laid his lips across hers. She lost herself in the warmth of the moment and in the connection between them. His mouth explored hers, and his hands gently held her face.

The passion began to build as she yearned for more. Suddenly realizing what was happening, Lauren pulled away then rushed out the door, her heart beating rapidly. She jumped into her car and raced back to her mother's, the kiss still smoldering on her lips.

chapter 38

When Lauren opened the door and hurried inside, her mom asked, "What's going on?"

"Ethan came back unexpectedly," she said breathlessly. "Can I move back in with you?"

"Of course." Her mom stared at her from her seat on the couch. "What happened?"

Lauren tucked her hair behind her ears. "His assignment fell through and—"

"That's not what I meant."

Lauren shrugged. "I don't know what you're talking about."

Her mom gave her a you-know-exactly-what-I'm-talking-about look.

"He came home, and I decided to come back here. Obviously, I can't live in his house *with him*. Is there a problem?" She wanted to deflect her mom's suspicions. After all, she wasn't even sure what had happened.

"No problem at all."

"Thanks." She walked back to her room and realized she'd left her clothes and toiletries at Ethan's. *Now what am I going to do?* She fell onto the bed.

"Do you want something to eat?" Her mom asked as she poked her head in the room.

"No. I'm not hungry."

Her mom sat on the bed next to her. "I promise things will get better."

"It feels like everything that could possibly go wrong, has." Including the kiss that still weighed heavy on her lips. Why did he have to kiss her? Just when she thought she was in control of her feelings, he had to go do something that jumbled them all up. Besides, he may know about her pregnancy, but he didn't know everything, and if he did, he'd regret that kiss. A kiss that made her lips ache for more every time she thought about it. A kiss that was better than she'd ever imagined back in high school. A kiss she'd gladly repeat again and again and again if her situation were different—if she weren't pregnant with a defective baby.

"I know, but things will work out."

"I hope so." *What* did she hope would work out? She had no idea.

"For now, you have a place to live and food to eat." Her mom patted her leg. "And you'll have a sweet baby—"

"I'm scared to death to have this baby."

Her mom squeezed her hand. "I'll be here for you."

"I don't have any idea what to expect."

"Did you ever talk to the doctor's friend?"

"No." Lauren had meant to call, but hadn't found the time, somehow.

"Why not?"

She played with her fingers. "I guess talking to her would make it all too real."

"But it is real."

"I know." Lauren pursed her lips. "I'm trying to embrace all of it, but in the back of my mind . . . I keep hoping . . . he'll be born and be totally fine." She rubbed her forehead. "I know that's totally unrealistic. And it makes me feel like a terrible person."

"You aren't a terrible person. It's only natural you'd be scared of the unknown. But you have me and Bethany. We're not going anywhere."

"It feels like I have no control over anything. Staying in Ethan's house and being on my own gave me a little sense of control. Now he's back, and that means I'm here living with you." She paused.

"That's not a bad thing, but it makes me feel like a failure all over again. Like I'm swimming upstream against a current ten times stronger than me."

Lauren rested her head on her mom's shoulder. It wasn't enough that she was divorced and pregnant, now her feelings about Ethan were all twisted into a pretzel. Did she dare think he was interested in a relationship with her? A divorced, pregnant woman with a boatload of baggage? Why would he want anything to do with her? And once he found out she carried a baby with Down syndrome he'd bolt, just like Paul. Right?

Yet a tiny flicker of hope—a flicker so small it was barely there—sparked inside her. What if she'd been wrong all along, and there was a chance?

chapter 39

Lauren checked her phone the next day and found a voicemail from Ethan. *Hey, I, uh, wanted to see how you were doing. Maybe get together sometime. Give me a call.*

She listened to it at least five times. Each time she wanted to respond, but something held her back. The kiss had changed things. She had to admit she wanted a relationship with Ethan, but it wasn't fair to saddle him with a child with special needs. Even if he wanted to explore a relationship with her, adding a baby with Down syndrome complicated everything. She could tell him, but what if he reacted like Paul? She couldn't take another rejection like that. Her heart would never recover a second time. She didn't know what to do, so she did nothing.

Several days later, Lauren found a posting for a teaching position on the district website. She filled out the application and sent it off, keeping her fingers crossed that she'd get the job, but knowing it was out of her hands. She simply had to trust that everything would work out.

That afternoon, she drove over to her doctor's office. The crisp air and changing leaves proclaimed the full-blown entrance of autumn. She pulled her over-sized sweater tighter around her as she made her way into the building.

"Looks like everything is going well." Dr. Hamilton measured her stomach. "Babies with Down syndrome tend to be small. Usually about six pounds." He listened to the heartbeat. "Sounds good. Did you ever get in touch with my friend?"

"No," she said, a warm flush crawling up her neck.

Dr. Hamilton peered at her through his glasses. "You don't want to talk to her?"

She sat up and pulled her shirt down. "I don't know." Truthfully, she had mixed feelings. She wanted to know more about Down syndrome so she could help Joseph, but a small part of her still wanted to deny it, wanted to pretend everything was fine. In fact, some nights she went to bed hoping she'd wake up in the morning to discover that this had all been a bad dream—a vivid one—but a dream nonetheless, and her life hadn't been thrown into complete chaos.

"It may help you to speak with someone who's been where you are." He placed his hand on her shoulder. "I know it's difficult. Are you having second thoughts?"

"No."

"Talk to my friend. I think she can put your mind at ease a bit." He smiled.

After Lauren left the office, she sat in her car and found the note with the woman's phone number tucked in a pocket of her purse. She stared at it, her fingers shaking. What if visiting this woman made things worse? What if it was a terrible experience? What if it made her even more anxious to give birth?

She put the note back in her purse and drove home. Of course, Dr. Hamilton would probably ask her again at her next appointment, and she'd have to explain that she was too frightened to talk to his friend, because that would make it too real.

Who was she kidding? No matter how she might wish otherwise, she was going to have a baby with Down syndrome. Avoiding this woman wouldn't change the truth. Talking to her might even help.

When she got to her mom's house, she pulled out the number again and punched it into her phone.

"Hello?"

"Is this Patricia Olsen?"

"Yes, it is."

"Hi, my name is Lauren Wilson. Doctor Hamilton gave me your number because I'm about to have a baby with Down syndrome." She still wasn't comfortable saying the words out loud.

She laughed. "He does that. You're the first one to actually call me."

"Oh. Well, I don't want to impose."

"No, no. I'd love to speak with you in person, if you'd like. You can meet my son, Preston."

"I . . . I . . ."

"It's up to you, but I'd be happy to answer any questions. I know how scary it is to know your baby is going to have a disability. But if I could tell you anything, I'd tell you to take a breath and enjoy your baby. It might be different than you expected, but that doesn't mean it will be bad."

Feeling more at ease, Lauren said, "Maybe we could meet tomorrow afternoon. If that works for you?"

"Let me check my calendar. Ah, yes that'd work. You're welcome to come to my home."

"Okay."

Patricia gave Lauren her address, and they hung up. Joseph would soon be here, and Lauren needed to be as prepared as possible. She hoped the visit would go well and she wouldn't unintentionally say or do anything offensive since she was still so new to the Down Syndrome Club.

The next day, Ethan sent her a text asking to see her, but she didn't respond, because she still didn't know how to respond. She felt disoriented and unable to make sense of her thoughts and feelings about Ethan, so she refused to think about him. Or the kiss.

She drove over to Patricia's home. It was a nice house that looked like a wood cabin with a green Pro-Panel roof and a few pine trees in the yard. She stepped up to the front door and rang the bell.

Patricia, a thin, thirty-something woman with shoulder-length brown hair, opened the door. Behind her stood a boy that looked to be about four-years-old with light hair and bright blue eyes. He peeked around his mother's legs.

"Preston, can you say hi?"

He smiled but said nothing.

"Come on in."

The home was warm and welcoming with the scent of just baked cookies wafting through it. Toys were strewn about the great room. Preston stayed close to his mom.

"He's a little shy with strangers." Patricia tousled his hair.

"How old is he?"

"Six."

"Oh. I thought—"

"He was younger?" She smiled then offered Lauren a cookie. "Our kids tend to be smaller, so they look younger." Patricia gestured for Lauren to sit on the brown leather couch.

"I'm having a little boy."

"Preston was born with a heart defect and he was only a few months old when he had open heart surgery to repair it. But he's doing great now. You'd never know." She reached her arms out and Preston snuggled onto her lap.

"He's adorable."

"When he warms up, he's quite the flirt. His teachers at school tell me that all the time."

"So he goes to school?"

"Oh, yes. In a regular classroom most of the day with an aide."

Preston watched Lauren intently.

"Hi," she said.

He smiled, and the skin around his eyes bunched up, making his eyes look like crescent moons.

"I'm sure you're scared to death. I know I was." She handed Lauren a cookie. "If I'd known then what I know now, I wouldn't have spent time worrying about stuff. Besides his heart surgery, he's been pretty healthy. Colds here and there. He did have problems with his thyroid last year."

Preston reached over to the plate and took a cookie. His eyes brightened as he sunk his teeth into it. "Mmm," he said with a grin.

"He likes that." Lauren laughed.

"Oh, yeah. He loves chocolate chip cookies. And ice cream. And chocolate pudding. Hates peanut butter and broccoli."

"Sounds pretty normal."

"Yes. That's something I've learned." Patricia said. "Preston is my third child, and he's more like my other children than not like them."

"But there are differences."

"Sure. He had some feeding issues when he was a baby. He isn't fully potty-trained yet, and he doesn't speak much, so he's in speech therapy."

"He doesn't communicate very well?"

"No, no." Patricia waved her hand. "Preston communicates fine. Just not with a lot of words. He pantomimes what he wants or uses signs, but he's starting to use more words."

"Are all kids with Down syndrome not very verbal?"

"Depends. The ability of skills can vary widely. It's true that they share some characteristics, but it's also true that they are unique. They all have their own strengths and weaknesses, like the rest of us."

"But he's always happy?"

Patricia shook her head. "That's pretty stereotypical. In my experience, he's like my other kids. He's happy, but he can get mad or start crying when he doesn't get his way. He has moods like the rest of us. And he can be so stubborn."

"Do you ever wish . . . I mean, do you ever think about . . ."

"What life would be like if he didn't have Down syndrome?"

Lauren nodded, feeling like the question was rude, but wanting to know the answer nonetheless.

"No. He is exactly as he should be. I believe things happen for a reason. Preston is the way he's meant to be. I've learned so much from him." Preston climbed down from Patricia's lap and ran over to play with one of his toy cars. "I won't lie and say everything has been a day in the park. We've had our share of problems, but I wouldn't trade any of it. Preston is such a light in our family. He reminds me to be grateful, to appreciate life, and to take time to enjoy the journey instead of rushing to the destination. You know, take time to smell the roses." She laughed.

"I like that."

"Oh, it's a way of life for him. He literally stops and smells roses whenever we pass by them. He loves them." Patricia smiled, easing Lauren's anxiety.

Preston started spinning around, holding a toy car in each hand. He sang out unintelligible words as he spun.

"And he loves to sing." Patricia clapped her hands. "Sing, Preston."

"He seems to be very loved."

"He is. We all adore him. I remember when I delivered him and one of the doctors said that we couldn't change the fact that he has an extra chromosome, but we could change the environment he grew up in. We had the power to make it whatever we wanted."

"What did you do to help him when he was a baby?" Lauren took a bite of her cookie, feeling even more at ease. She suddenly wished there were a way she could transfer all of this woman's knowledge and experiences into her own mind, so she'd know how to be a good mother to Joseph.

"I played lots of classical music, sang to him, read him books, talked to him, and spent as much time cuddling with him as possible. The time went by way too quickly."

Preston came over and made some sort of sign.

"He wants another cookie." Patricia gazed into her son's eyes. "Preston, what do you say?"

"I . . . want . . ." He finished with a garbled word.

"We're still working on the word *cookie*." She handed him a cookie, and he ran off and found a Star Wars action figure.

Lauren stood. "I've taken up enough of your time."

Patricia rose from the couch. "You know, having children changes your life. Jeremy, my oldest, has dyslexia. My daughter, Sophie, contracted RSV when she was a baby and almost died. I've learned that part of being a parent means we take what comes, good and bad, and we love our children, no matter what." Patricia waved at Preston. "Even though your baby will have some challenges, he's still your child and you will find such joy in raising him."

"Thank you."

"I hope this visit has helped."

Lauren nodded. "It has." It was true. Patricia seemed genuinely happy to have Preston, and he was a pretty regular kid.

"Please feel free to call or come over any time. I'm happy to answer any questions."

Lauren walked out the door and got into her car. She rested her hand across her bulging belly. As if in response, the baby kicked. Would Joseph be like a typical kid? Would he sing and play and love chocolate chip cookies? Would his eyes crinkle when he smiled? Was it too much to hope that her life would be more normal than not?

Meeting Patricia and her adorable son made Lauren grab onto the hope that maybe her dream wasn't so far out of reach after all.

chapter 40

The following Wednesday, after Lauren had come home from substituting at Escalante Middle School, she opened the front door to Ethan.

"Hey," he said. She didn't let herself notice his captivating eyes or the stubble on his chin that made him look like he'd just come home from a weekend in the mountains.

"Hi, Ethan."

"I think you've been avoiding me."

"No, I . . . really . . . I've been . . ." She stumbled over her words.

"Let's go for a drive. The leaves are starting to turn up in the mountains, and we have an hour or so left of daylight."

"I'm not sure I can leave right now." Lauren feared that her heart might overpower her head if she spent time with Ethan.

"Come on." His eyes insisted. "We need to talk."

Reluctantly, she agreed and followed him out to the car, reminding herself to stay firm in her decision and not let her heart get carried away with silly notions.

The bright yellows and brilliant oranges made the La Plata Mountains look like they were on fire. An early storm had dusted the tops of the peaks with snow, making the scene picture-perfect.

Ethan found a place to pull off the dirt road. He tapped the steering wheel with his hand. "Here's the thing. I don't want to be tied down."

"Okay." What did this have to do with her?

"I travel all over the world. I like it. And I like my life."

"I'm glad." Lauren watched him while he fidgeted in his seat.

"I've been in several different places—exotic places—taking photos over the last few weeks, and all I could think about was . . ."

She waited for his answer, unsure of what he'd say.

He turned and faced her, his expression serious but vulnerable. "What it would be like to come home to you every day."

Lauren's heart dropped to her stomach as warmth exploded through her body. *To come home to* me *every day? Did I hear him right?*

Ethan drew in a breath. "From the time I came over to your mom's for dinner and found out you were getting divorced, I haven't been able to get you out of my head. That's why I asked you to help me with the house. Why I kept showing up at your mom's. Why I asked you to housesit. But you didn't seem interested." He paused. "So I took extra assignments figuring I could get you out of my system." He laughed. "I thought it worked, until I kissed you."

"All these years. No strings. No real attachments." He laid his head back. "Now it's different." He looked at her, the intensity of his gaze making Lauren's nerves sizzle.

"I don't know what to say," she said.

"I don't expect you to say anything. I just needed to tell you. I came back because I wanted to see you again." He looked out the windshield. "Instead, I made you upset."

"Not upset."

"You didn't return my phone call or reply to my text."

Lauren rubbed her temples. She wanted to tell him that she'd thought about him, that she'd been afraid to hope he felt something for her, that she'd longed for another kiss, but her fear that he'd abandon her like Paul, once he found out about Joseph's condition, made her keep that to herself. No matter how she felt or how he *thought* he felt, she couldn't risk it. "I can't . . ."

"I know you feel something too."

He was right. She ached to have his arms embrace her and feel his warm lips smothering her with long, deep kisses, but he didn't know what it really meant to be with her. She didn't even know what it would mean to have a baby with special needs, and she certainly wasn't going to thrust that on Ethan.

"Even if I do, it would never work between us."

"Why not?"

"Trust me on this. I know." She'd learned that from Paul.

"What does that mean?"

"It means that you don't want to be stuck with a ready-made family."

"What if I do?"

She shook her head. "You don't understand."

"I want to."

Tell him about Joseph, her heart said. *He cares about you.*

Don't tell him. Remember how Paul reacted. He'll do the same thing, her head countered. *Even if he says so, no man really wants to be stuck with all this divorce baggage and a baby with all sorts of problems on top of that.*

But maybe it wouldn't matter to him. Maybe he'd be able to love Joseph. He isn't Paul.

No. This is a bad idea. You'll regret it. He'll break your heart and you'll feel even worse.

"The truth is, I'm not ready to have a relationship."

"We could take it slow."

"I'm sorry. I don't know when, or if, I'll be ready for something more and that's not fair to you."

"I'm willing to wait."

Lauren needed to cut him free. He might think he wanted to be with her, but when he found out about Joseph it would be different. She didn't want to endure a messy break-up after Joseph's birth. If she sent him away now, she could get over him before she got in any deeper. "I don't want you to wait."

He studied her. "This is how you want it? Really?"

"Really." She twisted her watch around her wrist. "And it's probably best if we don't see each other anymore. At all. I'm going to live with my mom indefinitely, so I won't be able to housesit." Cutting all ties was the best idea. He'd thank her later.

After several minutes, he started up the car. "I'll take you back to your mom's."

They drove back in silence, her mind reeling in a thousand directions. *This is best for everyone. Ethan wouldn't want to be stuck with Joseph and me. If things were different . . .*

Ethan stopped the car in front of her mom's house. "I'm going back to Boulder on Sunday. If you change your mind, you know where to find me."

She wanted to tell him not to, but she couldn't. Lauren opened her door. "Good luck with selling the house and have a safe trip back to Boulder." She got out of the car and went into the house without looking back.

chapter 41

Lauren kept thoughts of Ethan out of her head, or at least tried to, for the next few days. At times, she wanted to run to his house, throw her arms around his neck, and tell him she never wanted to leave, but that happened in books and movies, not in real life. In real life, there was no such thing as happily-ever-after. Time would heal her wounds, and she'd move on. Without Paul. And without Ethan.

The following week, Bethany invited her to go shopping at the mall—the people in Durango called it a mall, but it was much more accurate to call it a mall-in-training.

"This would look cute on you after you have the baby," Bethany said, holding a print blouse in her hands.

"Right now I feel like a hippo so I'm not thinking about any clothes."

Bethany rolled her eyes. "But we're shopping."

"You're shopping. I'm along for the ride." She let out a sigh.

"Let's get some lunch then."

They sat inside the large-paned window of the restaurant on Main Street. Lauren watched people as they walked past. Her heart stopped for a moment when she spotted a guy with dark hair across the street. *Not Ethan. Stop looking for him. He's gone and he's not coming back. Get over it and stop thinking about him.*

"You can always tell the tourists from the locals, huh?" Bethany smirked. "One of these days, we should do the tourist thing and ride the train to Silverton."

"Maybe." Lauren's thoughts were miles away—somewhere north of Denver.

"Funny that we've lived here all our lives and have never gone on the train, especially since it's so famous," Bethany said.

"Yeah." Lauren swirled the water in her glass with her straw.

"It's expensive, but maybe we should take the kids and splurge on the Polar Express this year. It's starting up again next month, around Thanksgiving."

Lauren didn't say anything.

"Hey, where are you?" Bethany poked her.

"What?" Lauren focused back on Bethany.

"I said we should take our kids on the Polar Express."

"Sounds fun, but I don't know if Joseph will be able to do that." Lauren wasn't sure what her baby would be able to do, if anything. She didn't want to dwell on the negative, but she had to be realistic—Joseph's possible health issues could prevent him from doing even the simplest things.

Bethany waved her hand. "I'm sure he will."

"You have no idea what he will or will not be able to do. He's not going to be like your kids." It sounded bitter even though she didn't mean it to. She wanted to be positive and upbeat, but the truth was, she was scared to death and feeling totally incapable of having her baby, which led to almost unbearable guilt. She should be excited to meet her son, but some days, she dreaded it.

A waiter came to their table and brought them the meals they'd ordered.

Bethany pushed her salad around her plate. "Lauren, I know I have no idea what it will be like to raise a child—"

"I'm sorry. I didn't mean to be so snappy." None of this was Bethany's fault.

Bethany peered at her. "Something's bothering you besides the baby."

Lauren shook her head. "Nothing." The last thing she wanted was Bethany delving into, then analyzing, her non-relationship with Ethan. It was a waste of time.

"Come on." Bethany pointed at her. "You are the worst liar I know."

"I am not." Lauren fidgeted in her chair. She absolutely did not want to discuss Ethan. Not now. Not ever. She'd made the right choice and that was the end of it. No need for a discussion.

"Tell me what's going on." Bethany leaned in, waiting for Lauren to spill her guts.

"There's nothing to tell."

"I've known you all my life, and I know when you're trying to hide something." Bethany's eyes grew wide. "It's Ethan, isn't it?"

Lauren gritted her teeth, wishing her sister would stop badgering her.

"It is." Bethany sat back, a smug grin on her face. "What happened?"

"Nothing. And no, it's not Ethan. It's . . ." She couldn't even come up with something to finish her sentence.

Bethany gave her the I-don't-believe-you-for-one-minute expression.

Knowing she was beat, she tried to play it off as nonchalantly as possible to prevent any more discussion than necessary. "It's no big deal. Ethan came home last week. That's all." It sounded simple enough, and she hoped Bethany would leave it at that.

Bethany studied her then a look flashed in her eyes. "Did Ethan ask you out?"

Her sister was getting on Lauren's nerves. "Why would you say that?"

"Come on, why won't you tell me what happened?"

Why wouldn't she tell Bethany? Was she afraid Bethany would talk her into changing her mind? Make her believe it *was* possible that she and Ethan could be together despite everything? Maybe telling Bethany would help her make sense of it.

"Lauren?"

"Ethan didn't ask me out." Lauren paused. "He said he came back to see me. That he'd been thinking about me." She tapped the table with her fingers. "He said he wants to be with me. Have a relationship."

Bethany clapped her hands together. "Awesome. That's the best news I've heard. You've always had a thing for him."

"You mean my high school crush?"

Bethany nodded.

"That was years ago and totally unrealistic and juvenile. We're both completely different people now."

"You should date him."

Lauren shook her head. "No. Not gonna happen."

"Why not?"

"Seriously?" Was her sister that dense?

"He knows you're divorced, right?"

"Yeah." She felt like she had a tattoo stamped on her forehead alerting everyone to that fact.

"And pregnant?"

Lauren rested her hand across her large belly, remembering Ethan's reaction. "Now he knows."

"And he still wants a relationship with you?"

"He only thinks he wants to be with me. If he knew . . ."

"The baby has Down syndrome?"

"Yes." She rubbed her stomach. "If Joseph's own father doesn't want him, why would Ethan?" The truth still sliced through her like cut glass. Paul didn't want his own child.

"So you didn't tell him about the diagnosis?"

"No." Lauren rolled the napkin between her fingers. "Much better to not get involved."

"But—"

"I'm serious. I need to take care of my son and forget about a man. This is about J.J. now, not me."

"It doesn't have to be that way."

"Yes, it does. If Ethan knew—"

"He'd what? Bolt?"

Lauren nodded.

"And you know that because?"

Lauren shook her head and rolled her eyes. "I knew it was a mistake to talk to you about this."

"Only because you are being completely unreasonable."

"Not unreasonable." Lauren caressed her stomach, imagining she was stroking Joseph's back and wanting to think about him and not Ethan. "I want to protect my son."

"More like your heart."

"Is that a crime? After all I've been through, do you blame me?"

Bethany reached across the table and placed her hand on Lauren's. "Paul is a loser. He deserted you and his son, but that doesn't mean Ethan would do the same. Don't you get that?"

Lauren shrugged. "Not willing to take that chance."

Bethany wagged her finger at Lauren. "For a smart woman, you can be really stupid."

chapter 42

Lauren spent the next few weeks living at her mom's, substituting at different schools in the district, and trying to prepare for the birth of the baby.

She hadn't seen or heard from Ethan. She didn't expect to, but it still left her feeling sad. Lauren touched her lips, remembering the kiss that still sent a shiver down her spine when she thought of it—a kiss that would have to remain simply a memory.

A week passed when she received a phone call.

"This is Susan Knolls from district 9-R, and I was calling to schedule an interview for a position at Escalante Middle School."

"Oh, yes." Lauren sat up straight and drank in a deep breath. She thought they'd hired someone else.

"Can you come in next Wednesday at four o'clock for an interview?"

"Yes." Of course she could. This is what she'd been waiting for. Maybe things were going to turn around.

"We'll see you then."

She ended the call, relief washing over her. If she could land a job at Escalante, doing what she loved, then she'd be able to find a place of her own and begin building a life for herself and for little Joseph. A real life, not the silly notion of some fairy tale.

The following Wednesday she had her interview. They asked her several questions, including what she planned to do with her baby, and she told them her mom would be watching him.

"Your resume looks great, and the kids have responded well to you when you've substituted here," Mrs. Vail, the principal, said.

Lauren smiled. "Being able to substitute at different schools has shown me how much I love teaching in middle school."

"The job begins in January," the principal said.

"Perfect timing."

"Thank you for coming in. We'll let you know." Mrs. Vail stood, as did the others on the panel.

Lauren left the building feeling hopeful. She desperately needed a stable, dependable job, and this one seemed to be exactly right for her.

A few days later, Lauren opened the front door to a princess and a Dalmatian dog. "Wow, you two are the cutest kids ever."

Kaylee and Jace walked into the house with Bethany behind them. "Remind me to never try to sew Halloween costumes on the day of the carnival."

"They're adorable."

Lauren's mom came into the living room. "Aww, look at you two." The kids ran to her and hugged her.

"I like your costume," Lauren said to Bethany, who was dressed in all black with a pointed black hat on her head.

"Kaylee insisted I dress up. A witch was all I could think of. Besides, I could never compete with your costume."

"You like it?" Lauren spun around, showing off her pink sweatshirt with baby bottle nipples sewn in two rows down the front that covered her distended belly.

"I love it."

"I had some spare time on my hands so I thought I'd make it."

"It's genius."

"I pretty much look, and feel, like a big pig." Lauren shrugged. "So I might as well dress like one, right?" She adjusted her pink pig nose.

Bethany laughed. "You'll have the best costume for sure."

"What's on the agenda?" Lauren's mom asked.

"We'll trick-or-treat at the houses on Third Avenue then go to the carnival at the school," Bethany said. "This is all my kids have talked about."

As Lauren walked beside her mom along the tree-lined street, she watched Bethany with her kids. Bethany obviously loved being a mom. She hoped that Joseph would be able to do normal things like going trick-or-treating so she could sew him costumes and enjoy being a mom like Bethany.

Lauren leaned down to help Jace adjust his costume. When she stood, she was practically face-to-face with Ethan. Her heart somersaulted. *What is he doing here?*

"Hi," he said. He wasn't dressed in a costume, but he didn't need to be—he took her breath away simply by standing there.

"Hi." She glanced down at her bulging, pig belly, heat rising to her cheeks.

He laughed. "Did you make this costume yourself?"

"Yes."

"Hi, Ethan," her mom said. "What brings you out here?"

"This is the place to be on Halloween. I used to come here when I was a kid, but I haven't been in town for Halloween in years. There's an offer on the house so I came back to do some paperwork and thought I'd check it out."

He glanced at Lauren, and even in the dim street lighting, his intense gaze captured hers.

"Would you like to join us?" her mom asked.

Lauren shot her a look, but her mom ignored it.

"Thanks, but I'm—"

"We're going to a carnival afterward. It'll be fun," Bethany added.

Lauren wanted to strangle her mom and her sister. She didn't want to spend time with Ethan. She *couldn't* spend time with him. "Leave the poor guy alone. I'm sure he has plans," she said.

"Actually, it sounds great." He smiled then spoke to the kids. "This next house has the best candy ever. At least it did back when I was a little trick-or-treater. Let's go knock on the door."

Lauren swallowed hard and commanded her silly heart to stop trying to jump out of her chest.

While they trick-or-treated, Lauren made sure to keep some distance between her and Ethan.

At the school carnival, she did the same, spending her time taking the kids to booths and watching them play games.

After an hour at the carnival, both Kaylee and Jace were crying. "Too much fun for these two," Bethany said. "We'd better go home. Mom wants to come back to my house and help me put them to bed."

"I'll come too," Lauren said.

"No, that'd be too many." She turned to Ethan. "Could you take Lauren home?" Bethany was so obvious. Ripples of irritation coursed through Lauren.

"Sure," he said. "If that's okay with her."

Lauren seethed at being set-up, especially when she explicitly told Bethany she didn't want to be involved with Ethan. But she didn't want to be rude, so she smiled and said, "Thanks."

They walked back to Ethan's car, the cool air settling in for the night. At the car, Ethan leaned against it, looking up at the clear black sky. "I love how you can see so many stars here. It's like an explosion of shimmering diamonds."

Standing so close to Ethan under this blanket of stars was much too dangerous. It made her want to abandon her common sense, but she knew better. It had to be this way. "When are you headed back?"

"After I sign papers."

"Oh." The words cut her. As much as she didn't want to get involved with him, she didn't want him to disappear either.

"I accepted the offer a few days ago and came back here to sign and clean out the house."

"That's great news." She tried to smile, but her face disobeyed her.

"It's a young family. I think my mom would be happy to have children living in the house."

"Yes, she would." Images of kids running through a house, filling it with laughter, brought a heaviness to Lauren's chest. That's what she'd wanted a lifetime long ago.

"I'll miss Durango, but it's time to move on." He turned and faced her, making her heartbeat thunder in her ears.

"Moving on is good," she whispered.

He drove her back to the house, and she tried to ignore how his cologne called out for her to embrace him.

"Thanks for the ride." She opened the door and got out. "Good luck with the house sale."

"Thanks."

"And good luck with your photography." It sounded lame.

"Good luck with . . . everything."

She shut the door and watched him drive down the street. Why did life have to be so hard? So unfair?

chapter 43

A week later, Lauren was mopping the floor in her mom's kitchen when a pain crossed her abdomen. She was sure it wasn't anything to worry about since her due date was still two weeks away.

The doorbell rang so she walked over and opened the door.

"I found some of your things when I was cleaning up and wanted to bring them over," Ethan said. He had a box in his hands.

"Oh, thanks.".

He set the box on the sofa. "Everything is a go on the house."

"That's good." Was it? Once he left, would she ever see him again?

"I have a few more things to do then I'm leaving for an assignment in Paris."

"Paris? I'd love to go there someday." Another pain, this time crampy and hot, enveloped her stomach. She dropped the mop.

"Are you okay?"

"Yeah. Probably too much mopping." She tried to laugh, but wanted to cry instead.

"Or the baby."

Again, a pain yanked her insides. "No. Not this soon."

"I've heard babies don't always respect time." He took her by the arm, gently prodding her toward the sofa.

"That may be true, but I'm sure—" she stopped mid-sentence and grabbed at her side.

"Let's get you on the couch."

With Ethan's help, Lauren made her way across the living room. "I'm sure I'll be fine. I don't want to keep you."

"Lauren, I'm not leaving you."

"My mom drove to Telluride for the day with one of her friends. But I can call Bethany if I need to." She clenched her teeth.

Ethan studied her, concern flickering in his eyes. "Maybe we should go to the hospital."

"No. We don't need—" Another cramp. Her skin was clammy, and sweat collected at her hairline.

"I think we do."

"You don't understand."

"I think it's pretty clear. You're having a baby."

"But I can't. My mom's not here and—"

"I think you can with, or without, your mom."

Ethan reached out and helped her stand. "I'm taking you to the hospital."

"I need to call Bethany."

Ethan grabbed her phone. "I'll call her."

"Do you know how to use my—" She bent over and stifled a scream. The pain was growing more intense. How could she be having the baby? Didn't childbirth come with more warning than this?

"Bethany didn't answer."

"Did you leave a message?"

"No." He tossed her phone on the couch. "I think we need to go right now."

Houses and buildings blurred together as they raced across town to the hospital. Lauren clenched her fists together and concentrated on not yelling the words that flowed into her mind. "I'm so scared."

He rested his hand on hers. "You don't need to be. I'll be right here with you."

"I can't ask you to do that."

"You're not asking."

They pulled in front of the hospital, and Ethan ran around to help her out. "I need some help," he shouted.

A woman with a wheelchair approached them. "How close are the contractions?"

"Close," Ethan said.

"I'm not ready for this baby," Lauren cried.

"A little too late for that." The nurse laughed. "I'll have your husband sign you in while I take you directly to the OB floor."

Lauren closed her eyes. She thought she might die from the pain before they even reached the labor area.

The nurse asked her some questions, but all she could do was moan. In a faraway place she heard Ethan's voice. She reached her hand out for him.

"I'm here. I'm not going to leave you."

"My mom. My sister," Lauren said then moaned through another contraction.

"I'll try to get a hold of them."

The next little while was a haze as people moved around her. The pain seemed to ease up for a minute here and there, but it was so intense she wasn't sure she'd live through it. She wasn't sure she *wanted* to live through it.

"Please, get this baby out," she cried.

"The doctor is on his way," a female voice said.

Ethan placed a cold washcloth on her head. "I hope this helps."

"I can't do this." Waves of pain cascaded over her. How did any woman ever give birth? This was like having a semi truck drive over the top of her.

"Yes, you can. I know you can. You can do anything." He stroked her head.

Finally, the doctor showed up. "Looks like you're ready to push."

"Shave my head, cut off an arm, I don't care. Just get the baby out," Lauren said, tears slipping down her cheeks.

"I need you to bear down to the count of ten. Can you do that?"

"I don't know."

"You can," Ethan said. "I'll count for you."

Lauren could hear Ethan counting. She squeezed her eyes shut and pushed.

"Again," the doctor said. "Can you do that again?"

"It hurts." A forest fire raged inside her.

"Come on, Lauren. Push," Ethan said.

She pushed again.

"I need you to push until we get to ten," the doctor said.

With every ounce of strength she had, she pushed until she felt like her guts would spew out. A burning sensation was followed by pure ecstasy as the pain subsided.

"The baby is out," the doctor said. "A baby boy."

Lauren's head fell back. She'd never been so relieved. Almost immediately, she raised it back up to see her son. His face was swollen, and he had a little clump of hair.

The nurses gathered around the baby, so she rested her head against the bed.

"You were amazing," Ethan said.

"Hardly."

"I am in awe of what you just did. You brought a life into the world."

"I don't think I had any choice."

He brushed some damp hair from her forehead. "I've never seen anything like this."

"I'm sorry you were pulled into it. Not my plan." Now that she was through the intense pain, it was replaced by an overwhelming sense of mortification. Ethan had just watched her give birth. She wanted to dig herself a hole and hide in it for . . . forever.

A nurse walked over with the baby in a tightly wrapped blanket. "Would mommy or daddy like to hold him first?"

Ethan stepped back. "His mom."

The moment the nurse set Joseph in her arms, Lauren's heart swelled inside her with a love she'd never experienced. *Her son.* She couldn't stop staring at him. He seemed perfect in every way. And even if he wasn't, it didn't matter. He was a part of her.

The best part.

"Do you want me to try your mom and sister again?" Ethan asked.

"They'll both be so mad they missed it. Who knew it'd be so fast?"

Ethan leaned in and gazed at the baby.

Not wanting him to see, Lauren pulled Joseph closer to her and used the blanket to shield his face from Ethan.

Ethan tucked the blanket back down. "He's beautiful."

She stared at Ethan. "You can see it, right?"

"What?" Ethan kept his gaze on the baby as he tenderly touched Joseph's cheek, the gesture bringing moisture to Lauren's eye.

"He has Down syndrome."

Ethan smiled at Joseph. "Does that matter?"

Shortly after the birth, Ethan said he needed to meet with his real estate agent so he left. Lauren didn't want to think about how his absence made her feel empty. Not long after, Bethany showed up.

"I can't believe you had the baby so fast. And so soon."

"I'd been having contractions, I guess, all day, but I didn't realize it. I thought it was my stomach freaking out. All of a sudden, they got super painful."

"And Ethan brought you in?" Bethany sat next to the bed.

"Yes." Still feeling embarrassed, she added, "He was here through the whole thing."

"In the room?"

Lauren nodded. "Yep. In all my glory."

"Wow."

"I know. At the time, the entire Denver Broncos could've been there, and I wouldn't have cared. Now that it's over, I'm not sure I can ever face him again. He saw me give birth."

A nurse wheeled in a bassinet with Joseph swaddled inside. "He's had his bath and everything seems to be fine."

"Can I hold him?" Bethany stood.

"Sure," Lauren said.

Bethany took Joseph in her arms then sat on the bed next to Lauren. "He has Dad's nose, don't you think?"

"I think he's the most beautiful thing I've ever seen." Though the characteristics of Down syndrome were present—the flat nose bridge and skins flaps on the inside of his eyes—Lauren's heart melted each time she looked at him.

Bethany sniffed him. "He smells like a newborn."

Joseph yawned then let out a cry.

"Are you going to nurse him?" Bethany asked.

"I don't know. From what I researched, he has weak mouth muscles and probably won't be able to."

"You should try anyway. I loved breastfeeding my babies. If he can, you'll feel such a bond with him." Bethany handed him to Lauren.

"I can't believe he's finally here. I was so scared, but now that I have him in my arms, everything seems right with the world."

Lauren traced around Joseph's eyes and nose, the wonder of this little life igniting a deep sense of awe.

After a minute or so, Bethany asked. "What happened to Ethan?"

"He had to meet about the house. He's leaving for Paris soon."

"And you're going to let him?"

"Of course." What other choice did she have? She rocked Joseph, and he fell asleep.

Bethany stood. "You are so frustrating."

"Look—"

"No, you look. He came with you to the hospital and stayed through the delivery—"

"That doesn't mean anything, except that he's a nice guy."

Bethany pointed at Lauren. "Who cares about you. A lot."

"He'd do the same for anyone." Lauren had to admit that Ethan was a rare breed. He was kind, compassionate, and caring.

Bethany let out a loud sigh. "Why are you so stubborn? He told you he has feelings for you."

"That was before he saw Joseph."

"So how did Ethan react when he saw the baby?"

"He said it didn't matter."

Bethany raised her arms toward the ceiling. "See? You've been wrong about him all along. He wants to be with you and he doesn't care about Joseph having Down syndrome. He is *not* Paul."

"He was being nice, that's all. I went into labor right in front of him. His only choice was to bring me to the hospital. Then he stayed out of a sense of obligation." It was so obvious, why couldn't Bethany see that?

Bethany gave herself a face palm.

"I keep telling you that nothing is going to happen."

"Because you won't let it."

"Because he has his own life, and I have mine. Very different lives." Lauren caressed Joseph's cheek. "Besides, even if it makes no difference to him that Joseph has Down syndrome, I have no idea what the future holds, and I'm not going to thrust that on him or anyone else. It wouldn't be fair to burden him with the unknown."

A stout nurse with dirty blond hair walked into the room. "The doctor is here to examine your baby. May I take him to the nursery?" She showed Lauren her identification.

Lauren tucked him in the bassinet and watched as the nurse wheeled him away. "I never knew I could love anyone so instantly. And so completely."

"Welcome to motherhood." Bethany picked up her things. "I need to go. Matt is home with the kids."

"Thanks for coming to see me."

"Mom will have a coronary when she finds out she missed the whole thing."

"I didn't think it'd be a problem for her to drive up to Telluride. She must've forgotten her phone." Lauren twisted her hair into a loose bun.

"See you later." Bethany left.

Lauren laid her head back. She had a son. A perfectly imperfect son. Her heart was swollen with love for him. Now that she'd held him in her arms, the idea that Paul wanted to abort him was even more heinous. Though it still hurt that he abandoned them, Lauren was glad he wouldn't be in the picture. He wasn't the man for her nor the father for Joseph.

She hadn't planned to be a single mom, but Joseph deserved a life and he deserved love. That's all she needed to worry about.

Thirty minutes later, the nurse brought Joseph back to her. Dr. Rico, the pediatrician she'd found, followed the nurse.

"Your baby is doing well," he said. "No problems."

"Other than the Down syndrome," Lauren said.

"Down syndrome itself is not a problem, but it can cause some problems. He's doing great. You'll need to bring him into my office for a follow-up exam, and we'll monitor him closely. You can enroll him in a program here in town for children with disabilities, so he'll have access to therapy and other services."

Lauren didn't want to be rude, but she didn't want to discuss any of this. She simply wanted to hold her baby and snuggle with him. "Thanks, Dr. Rico. I'll make an appointment."

The doctor left, and she picked up Joseph. He had the beginnings of red fuzz on most of his head. His face was still swollen from the delivery. She pulled out his hand and touched each of his chubby fingers.

She stared at him in wonder then pulled him close. In a whisper she said, "I'll always be here for you. No matter what."

The door flew open, and her mom rushed to her bedside. "I cannot believe you had the baby while I was gone. I leave for one day, *one day*, and you have the baby. I'm so mad, I could spit."

"Hi, Mom. Would you like to hold your grandson?"

"Can I?" She dropped her purse on the bed.

Lauren placed Joseph in her mom's arms. "Oh, look at him. What a sweet boy."

"Isn't he wonderful?"

"Tell me everything that happened."

Lauren proceeded to tell her mom the whole story.

"Where's Ethan now?" Her mom peered at her.

"I don't know." Why did everyone think she knew where Ethan was or what he was doing? It wasn't her place to know. Or to wonder. Or to care. Or to think about him and wish . . . No, it wasn't her place, and her heart needed to obey her. "He went home. He's leaving for Paris."

"I see." Joseph started to fuss, so her mom put him on her shoulder and patted his back.

"Please, don't say anything. He was awesome to be here during the birth, even if it embarrassed me for the rest of my life, but that's it. Don't try to make it anything more. Please."

"Whatever you say." She gave Joseph a kiss and handed the squirmy baby back to Lauren.

As soon as Lauren took him, he settled down.

"I'm going back to the house and get everything ready for you to come home."

"I think it'll be tomorrow afternoon."

That night, Lauren lay in the uncomfortable hospital bed. The euphoria of the birth had worn off, and she stared into the empty darkness. Somehow, some way, she had to make it all work. Despite her defiance to her sister and her mom, a small part of her wished that included Ethan. But that was too much to hope for. Wasn't it?

chapter 44

The next day, Lauren and Joseph were released from the hospital, and her mom took them home.

For the next several days, Lauren recuperated and took care of Joseph. He slept almost all the time, but started to stay awake more here and there. She marveled when he yawned, when he cooed, and even when he cried. Despite the extra chromosome, he seemed to be like a normal newborn baby. He struggled to nurse, so she bottle-fed him most of the time.

About a week after the birth, Lauren was in her room, changing Joseph's diaper when her mom appeared at the door.

"Someone is here to see you." Her mom wore a sour expression.

"Who?"

Her mom didn't answer. She turned sharply and walked away.

"Mom?"

Lauren dressed Joseph and swaddled him with a fuzzy blue blanket. She walked out into the living room and froze.

"Hi," Paul said.

Lauren blinked. Finally finding her voice she said, "What are you doing here?" She hugged the baby tighter as if protecting him.

Paul glanced at the floor. "I wanted to see you. And the baby."

He wanted to see the baby? The one he'd cut all ties to? The one he'd so easily discarded? Trying to be civil, she said, "How did you know?" She hadn't contacted him and she was sure her mom hadn't, either.

"I still have a few friends here from college. I asked one of them to check on you. He told me."

"Chase?"

Paul nodded.

"You've had him watching me?" Lauren wasn't sure if she should be angry or creeped out.

"Not like that." He shrugged. "I just . . . I wanted to know."

"Why?" She scowled at him. "You wanted no ties to us. Remember?" She patted Joseph on the back.

"Can we go somewhere and talk?"

Lauren wasn't about to go anywhere with him. He was lucky she didn't toss him out of the house. "Here is fine."

"But—"

"I'm not listening in," her mom said from the kitchen.

"Mom, would you mind giving us some privacy?"

"Fine. I need to run to the grocery store anyway. But I'll be back *soon*." She gave Paul a stern look as she passed him and went out the front door.

"She still doesn't like me," he said.

"Can you blame her?"

"No. In fact, I take all the blame. For all of this."

"You do?" Lauren couldn't believe *that* came out of his mouth.

He looked at her. "I've missed you."

Was he serious? He missed her? "I see."

"My dad pushed for the divorce. He and my mom said it was for the best. That I didn't want a baby with problems."

"And?"

"I figured they knew better." He shrugged. "With all the stress of opening up the other office and the pressure my dad was putting on me, it seemed like it was the best decision." He paused. "But I miss you."

Lauren watched him, but said nothing. She'd wanted to hear him say this months ago. But now? What did he expect her to do?

He kicked at the floor. "I told my dad I want to open my own practice."

"You *what?*" Lauren sat on the couch with the baby. Paul was going to leave his dad's firm? She didn't see that coming.

"It wasn't worth it." He sat in the chair across from the couch. "I didn't like who I'd become. I want to focus on family law. You know, help families that are struggling."

"Wow. I never thought I'd hear you say this. You were so committed to the firm."

"I know, but I realized my dad was pulling all my strings. I wanted to think he was right, that he knew what was best, but he was wrong." He raked his fingers through his hair. "I . . . was wrong."

The last person she'd expected to see in her mom's living room was Paul. And to hear him say these things was messing with her mind and her heart. She couldn't allow him to do this to her.

He gestured toward the baby. "May I?"

Lauren considered his request. He'd abandoned them both, said he didn't want any connection to them, and now he wanted to hold Joseph? "I don't know." She was reeling from his admission and wasn't sure what to do.

"Please?" His eyes pleaded with hers.

Against her better judgment, she handed Joseph to his father.

"He has your red hair."

"Not much of it."

"I can't believe he's my son." Paul's eyes misted.

"He's healthy too. No heart defect. No problems with his lungs or intestines. The doctor checked him over thoroughly."

Paul touched the baby's hand and held it in his. Paul smiled, but Lauren refused to let it affect her.

She cleared her throat. "And he doesn't have the single crease in his hand."

"What does that mean?"

"He'll probably use his fingers normally and may not need extra therapy for that. But, he does have hypotonia, which means his muscles are weaker so he'll need physical therapy. And he failed his hearing test so I'll need to follow up on that."

"Because of the . . ." he didn't finish.

"Yes, because of the Down syndrome. There may be other things as well, but for now, Joseph's okay. We're going to take it one day at a time."

"You named him after your dad?"

"Yes."

A tear slipped down his cheek. "I'm so sorry I wasn't there. I'm sorry I wasn't at the delivery. I'm sorry that I was such a coward."

"I'm sorry too."

He gazed at her. "What if . . ."

She held her hand up. "Let's not go there."

"You're right. I'm sorry." Paul brushed his finger against the baby's cheek.

After a few minutes of silence, a knock sounded.

Lauren rose and went to the door. Her heart squeezed tight when she saw Ethan standing there. "Uh, hi." She didn't open the door fully.

"Is this a bad time?"

Couldn't be worse. "Well . . ."

"I can come back later."

"That might be best."

"Don't let me stop you from having someone come in," Paul said.

Lauren opened the door wider, and Ethan walked into the house. His gaze fell on Paul, and Lauren wished she could disappear. How in the world did Paul and Ethan come to be in the same room? And worse, in her mom's house? How did this happen?

"I'm Paul. I'd stand, but I don't want to disturb my son."

"I'm Ethan. A friend of the family. I live down the street. Or used to."

"He was good friends with Justin in high school. His mom recently passed away and . . ." Lauren didn't need to explain anything to Paul. He didn't deserve any explanations.

The baby started to fuss, so Lauren reached down and took him from Paul. "He's hungry."

"I'll wait while you feed him," Paul said.

"It might be a while. He's still learning to suck." Lauren needed some space. Paul's visit was totally unexpected, and she needed time to process everything he'd said. "It'd probably be better if you didn't wait."

"Oh. I'm crashing at Chase's place." He turned to Ethan. "Lauren and I knew him back when we were in college at the Fort."

Feeling the awkward tension in the air, Lauren said, "Tell him I said hi." The baby started crying louder. "I really need to feed him."

"Can I come back later?" Paul asked.

Lauren's shoulders tensed. "I don't know." He'd laid a bombshell at her feet and she wasn't sure what to think or how to feel, except that she wanted him to leave, so she could try to clear her head..

"Can I call you?"

Lauren gave a slight nod and Paul left. He *was* Joseph's father and if he wanted to have a relationship with his son she shouldn't stand in his way—at least that was what the logical part of her brain said. If only he'd come to this same decision several months ago, before their life together disintegrated.

Joseph had settled down and was nearly asleep, so Lauren laid him in the bassinet by the hallway then collapsed on the couch. The emotional angst was almost too much. She wanted to hate Paul for what he'd done—punish him for hurting her so deeply by keeping the baby from him—but Joseph wasn't some kind of pawn. She couldn't in good conscience deny Paul from being a father, if he were *serious*. But was he? Could she trust him after all that had happened? Honestly, she didn't know. She wished he'd never shown up.

"I should probably go," Ethan said, jerking Lauren out of her thoughts and reminding her he was still there.

Feeling like she needed to explain things to Ethan, she said, "I didn't know he was going to be here. I didn't tell him about Joseph's birth because . . ."

"Looks like he wants—"

"He deserted me. And our son." She looked at Ethan, hoping to convey how Paul had shattered her heart and left her broken.

Ethan sat on the couch next to her. "Are you still angry with him?"

"I don't want to be. I want to focus on Joseph and do what's best for him." She stood and crossed the room to check on the baby. He slept peacefully in the bassinet.

Lauren wanted to say more to Ethan. She wanted to tell him how he'd become part of her life and how it wouldn't be the same if he walked out of it. A sense of panic settled in. She didn't want to let him go again, but how could she ask him to stay? It was too complicated. Wasn't it?

"You'll know what to do." He stood.

If only that were true. She had no idea what to do, especially about her feelings for Ethan. "I feel so confused."

Ethan's gaze captured hers. With a few steps he closed the gap between them, and her heart went into spasms.

"I'm not confused," he said with conviction.

"What do you mean?"

"I know what I want."

She stared into his eyes, wanting to drown herself in them.

"You. That's what I want."

"No. You don't."

Ethan studied her. "Why do you say that?"

"Because."

He brushed a wisp of hair from her face. "Because?"

She stepped back. "Why would you? I'm a single mom with an imperfect baby."

"Is that what this is about?"

Her throat became thick. "Why would you want us? Paul didn't." She searched his face, hoping against hope she might be wrong.

Ethan blinked. "He left you *because* of the baby?"

She nodded.

"Because he has Down syndrome?"

"Why would *you* want Joseph when his own father didn't?"

Ethan glanced at the ceiling, the corners of his mouth lifting. "This all makes sense now."

"It does?"

He gazed at her and her heart fluttered. "You were pushing me away because you thought—" he reached out and cradled her head—"I'm not Paul."

"I know." A tear teetered on the edge of her lower eyelid. "But you said you didn't want to be tied down. That you liked the freedom to travel and see the world."

"I thought that's what I wanted."

"And you have gorgeous, exciting models all over the world. Women without all this baggage."

His hands traveled to her shoulders, his forehead against hers. "I don't want them. I want a woman with depth. A woman who's loved and lost. A woman who's been kicked, but gotten back up. A woman who's sacrificed." She watched his lips as he spoke. "And brave. You're the most courageous woman I know."

"Me? I'm afraid—"

He put his finger to her lips then traced them with his thumb. "Courage isn't the absence of fear, it's being afraid, but going forward anyway."

"You really think I'm courageous?" She'd never thought of herself that way.

"Yes. You sacrificed your life with Paul to give life to Joseph. *You* are his rescuer."

"Like Milda?"

Ethan's eyes moistened. "Like Milda."

"I love that comparison." She smiled. "I'm Joseph's rescuer." She paused. "I guess, in a way, he's a modern-day holocaust survivor."

Ethan nodded then caressed her shoulder. "And you are beautiful. Inside and out."

His lips were only inches from hers. Slowly, he brushed his warm lips across hers then laid them gently on her mouth, tenderly exploring hers. She melted into the kiss, pressing her body against his and eliminating all distance between them. The kiss deepened as she let go of all her anxiety and inhibitions. She never wanted this moment to end.

He pulled away and peered at her. "I love you. I love Joseph, and I want to be part of your life if you'll let me."

She stepped back unsteadily, still reeling from his kiss.

"I don't want to pressure you or stress you out. You have enough of that." He let go of her. "I'll be at my mom's house."

"Your mom's? What about the sale?"

"Change of plans."

Ethan had laid his cards on the table. So had Paul. They both wanted a life with her and Joseph, and it was up to her to make the right decision. Could she trust Paul and make a life with him again without any regrets? If she chose Ethan, would Paul still want to be part of Joseph's life?

chapter 45

Lauren sat in her bed that night, snuggling Joseph close to her. Her heart was so full of love for him, she was sure it would explode any minute. She never thought she could love someone so completely. The future was filled with all sorts of uncertainty, but one thing she knew for sure was that she loved her son fiercely, and she needed to do the right thing for him.

Maybe Paul deserved another chance. He was Joseph's father and maybe she was being selfish by not wanting to forgive Paul and give him another chance.

She caressed Joseph's fingers, marveling at how even though he had an extra chromosome his fingers were in the right place. So were his toes, his eyelashes, his nose. She tenderly kissed his flat nose bridge, the most apparent physical marker of Down syndrome. "I love you. I wish I knew what to do."

She rubbed the soft fuzz that covered his head. "Your daddy wants another chance. He wants to love you and be a family again, but I don't know if I can trust him. If things get too hard will he run away again? Will he let your grandparets influence him?"

Joseph whimpered, so Lauren rocked him back and forth, the warmth of his little body against hers making her heart swell even bigger.

"But Ethan was there when you were born. He loves us. He's a good man who's never done anything to hurt us. He'd be a good dad to you, but you might lose a relationship with your father."

Joseph yawned and the skin around his eyes crinkled. Lauren smiled. "I just want to do right by you my sweet boy. I want to make the choice that's best."

The next morning, she awoke to the scent of bacon wafting through the hall. "Hi, Mom," she said as she walked into the kitchen.

"I thought we could have a nice breakfast. You need plenty of nourishment. No more eating like a bird."

Lauren munched a piece of chewy bacon. Life was so much better with bacon. "I'm starving."

"So what are you going to do?"

"About what?" She tried to play innocent, but she knew exactly what her mom wanted to know.

"Paul."

Lauren shrugged. "I don't know. He wants another chance."

Her mom's face scrunched up. "And?"

"Joseph deserves a family. He deserves to have his father in his life."

"But—"

"I know, Mom. I'm completely aware of what Paul did, but he said it was his parents pushing him. Now that he's realized that, maybe things really would be different."

Her mom shook her head.

"I know how you feel about him, but I need to do what's best for Joseph."

"What about you?"

"It isn't about me."

Her mom pointed at her. "Don't be a martyr."

"I'm not. I'm simply trying to do what's best for my family."

They finished breakfast without saying anything else. Joseph started to cry, so Lauren went back to the bedroom to get him. After she changed his diaper and fed him a bottle, she checked her phone. Paul had left a voicemail asking to see her again. She called him back and invited him to come to her mom's house so they could talk.

She walked back into the kitchen to tell her mom. "I don't know why you're even considering this." Her mom leaned against the kitchen counter, a look of disdain on her face.

"He *is* Joseph's father—"

"Really, Lauren. I have to say my piece."

Lauren held her hand up. "I already know what you're going to say. It's the same exact things I've said to myself."

"Then why? Why would you go back to him? Do you still love him?"

"I don't want to discuss this anymore with you."

"But—"

"I know you love me. I know you want what's best for me, but can you please trust me to do the right thing?"

Her mom let out a breath then reluctantly nodded. "I'm going to Bethany's. I'll see you later." She tossed a dishtowel on the counter and left.

Lauren sat on the couch, waves of nerves crashing in her stomach. She wanted to do the right thing. She wanted to do what was best for Joseph. But what was that? Was it best to put their family back together, knowing that Paul had deserted them? Knowing that Paul didn't want Joseph?

Maybe his parents had pressured him, but Paul was an adult, a man capable of making his own decisions, and he'd still turned his back on them. He'd left her when she needed him most. Yet he was here, asking for another chance. Didn't he deserve that?

She got up and checked on Joseph. He was sleeping soundly in his crib. Lauren sat on a chair in the kitchen, drumming her fingers on the table, thoughts of Ethan seeping into her mind. Ethan had been there for her. He didn't desert her, or Joseph, and now he wanted to be a part of their lives. She couldn't deny the strong connection she felt to Ethan, but he wasn't Joseph's father. Did that matter? The more she thought, the more muddied her mind became. She needed to focus on her son, not on her feelings for Ethan.

After a few minutes, she stood and filled a glass with water. The doorbell rang, and it startled her, making her spill the water on the counter. She hurried to clean it up then walked to the front door, each step making her heart beat more furiously. *What is the right thing to do?*

"Hi," she said as she opened the door.

Paul came in, dressed in khaki pants and a blue dress shirt. "Where's Joey?"

"Joseph," she corrected, "is taking a nap."

"He seems to sleep a lot. Is that normal? I mean, do normal kids sleep a lot?" He patted the side of his leg. "I didn't mean—"

"It's okay. Why don't you sit?" She gestured to the couch in the living room.

Paul sat and rubbed his hands on his pants. She hadn't seen him this nervous since their first date years ago at Leo's downtown. He'd asked her out after he'd knocked her food tray out of her hands in the cafeteria at Fort Lewis College. His face had turned almost purple as he apologized. He'd promised to take her out to eat to make up for it. From their first date, they'd been inseparable. Paul had won her heart easily, and their life together was a dream. But that was then. Before they'd moved to Denver. Before he'd started working with his dad. Before they'd known about Joseph's condition.

Paul peered at her and asked, "Can you forgive me for being so selfish and so stupid?"

Lauren smoothed her hair. She wasn't the same woman she'd been a year ago, a few months ago, or even a few weeks ago. Joseph had changed her. What Paul had done was terrible, possibly unforgivable, but as his eyes pleaded with hers, she couldn't withhold her forgiveness. "Yes. I can forgive you."

Paul let out a breath. "I was afraid you'd never forgive me for what I've done. Pressuring you to have an abortion then leaving when you didn't. I left you when you needed me the most."

She nodded, and moisture built behind her eyes. They'd lost so much—time together, Joseph's birth, bonding as a family. No matter what the future held, it wouldn't change the past or the way it could've been.

"I wish I could take it all back. Rewind time." The pain was clearly etched on his face.

"Except you can't."

"I know. I've missed so much."

"You have." She didn't harbor anger toward Paul, but she felt sorry for him. She pitied him for listening to his parents, for sacrificing their family, for missing out on Joseph's birth.

He edged closer to her, his gaze reaching out to her. "But we can go forward from here. We can put the past behind us and focus on our family. I want you and Joseph. I want our family." He took her hand in his. "We can start over. Just the three of us."

Months ago, she'd ached to hear this. All she'd wanted was for Paul to want their family, all of them, no matter what. She wanted him to love their son unconditionally. "What about your parents?"

"I told them I was coming down here to see you. My mom says there's been some breakthroughs in research and people are talking about reversing the effects of Down syndrome. We can look into that. We'd want to do everything we can to help him be normal. My parents said they're willing to finance whatever he needs. My dad even consulted with a plastic surgeon he knows about facial reconstruction to minimize the effects. We don't have to do that, of course, but it might be an option."

A cry sounded from the back bedroom. "I need to take care of the baby."

"I'll wait."

"I think it'd be better if you go. I need some time."

Paul jumped to his feet. "Whatever you say." He made his way to the door. "Talk to you soon?"

She gave a slight nod.

By the time she made it back to the bedroom, Joseph had fallen asleep again. Lauren watched him, his chest rising and falling rhythmically. He looked so peaceful, so unaware of the turmoil between his parents. She rested her hand on his arm. He didn't deserve turmoil. He deserved unconditional love. He didn't ask to be born with an extra chromosome, he only asked to be loved. And that's what she would do.

Love him exactly the way he was.

When Lauren came back into the living room thirty minutes later, both her mom and Bethany stared at her.

"What happened?" her mom asked.

"What did Paul want?" Bethany said as she stepped toward Lauren.

Lauren held up her hands. "Before you both get all worked up and start spewing fire, he wanted to see Joseph." She didn't want to tell them the rest—they'd flip out for sure.

"That's it?" Bethany said, eying her sister.

Lauren nodded, but didn't look at her.

"I don't believe you. What else did that snake say?"

"He wanted to see his son," Lauren met Bethany's gaze.

"Oh, so now he admits he has a child?"

"Yes." Lauren tried to keep her voice even.

"Oh, please." Bethany studied Lauren. "And there's more, isn't there?"

Lauren said nothing.

"He wants you back."

Lauren hated that Bethany could read her so well. She chewed on her lip, but still said nothing.

Bethany narrowed her eyes. "You aren't going to fall for any of this are you?"

"What's that supposed to mean?" Lauren held her ground. Did Bethany think she'd developed amnesia? No one was more acutely aware of what Paul had done than Lauren, but he was still the father of her son and that meant something.

"He deserts you and then waltzes back into your life, expecting to pick up where he left off? After what he did—"

"Look, Beth, I know you mean well, but you need to back off." This was Lauren's choice, Lauren's life, not Bethany's. Lauren was growing tired of Bethany treating her like a child who was incapable of making the right decision.

Bethany threw her hands in the air. "Unbelievable."

"Let's not get upset." Her mom walked over to Lauren and caressed her arm. "What did he say, exactly?"

Lauren glanced at her sister, whose face glowed red. "Pretty much what Bethany said."

"What do you think about it?" Her mom was a much better diplomat than her sister.

"Mom, you can't encourage this. Paul is a complete jerk. Lauren deserves so much better." Bethany shook her head.

"I agree. But, this is her call to make. Not ours."

Lauren's insides were twisted into a giant knot. She didn't know how she felt or what she wanted. "I need some time to process all of this. I didn't expect Paul to show up." Or Ethan to profess his love. A few months ago, no one wanted her, or her baby. Now she had two men wanting to be part of her life.

"What can we do?" Her mom asked.

"Can you keep an eye on Joseph for a little while? I need some fresh air."

"Sure. Bethany and I will watch the baby. Take as much time as you need, but take it easy."

Lauren followed the still well-worn path behind her house that led down to the river. It had been her escape ever since she was young. Whenever she was stressed or anxious, she'd sit on a boulder next to the river and watch the water flow downstream. The bubbling river that traveled past her in its rhythmic motion always settled her raging emotions.

Today was no different. The water flowed past rocks, large and small, while the crisp November air licked her cheeks.

She'd thought her life with Paul was over. She'd thought he was firmly in her past, and she was prepared to move forward and provide a good life for Joseph and herself. Without Paul.

Now, he was back and it stirred feelings in her. He wanted to make their family work. Maybe he deserved another chance.

She picked up a rock and threw it into the churning water, making it splash across a boulder.

She could forgive him, but could she forget? Could she erase the fact that he'd insisted she terminate the pregnancy, that he didn't want Joseph? He'd let fear rule his reason. Would that happen again? What if Joseph had medical issues down the road? Would Paul walk away from them? What if raising Joseph was too hard for him after all?

And Ethan? He'd been there when she needed him. He hadn't left her. He said he loved her and her son, but he wasn't Joseph's biological father. Did that matter? He'd been a self-proclaimed wanderer, was he really ready to settle down with a pre-made family? Take on the responsibility of a child with special needs? It was a lot to ask of anyone. Maybe the connection she felt to Ethan was fleeting.

Too many questions bombarded her mind and sent her stomach into nervous convulsions. *I have to make the right choice.*

Glancing up at the blue, cloudless sky, she looked for an answer, but it wasn't there. The answer wasn't in the sky or in a book or even in her family's opinions. It was in her heart.

She had her answer.

Now she needed to act on it despite what anyone else thought.

chapter 46

The next afternoon, she met Paul at a bench that overlooked the river. Storm clouds collected, casting a gray shadow on the day.

He sat next to her, and for several minutes neither of them said anything. Finally, Lauren broke the silence. "You know, this river is the same today as it was when I was a kid."

"Yeah. It's a nice river." He folded his arms across his chest.

"It is, but it's also constant."

Paul gazed at her.

"This river has stayed its course and will continue to do so. It's dependable, steady."

Paul nodded. "That's how rivers are."

She turned to him, filled with a sense of calm conviction. "I need a river."

"Huh?"

"I need steady, immovable."

Paul's face registered her point. "I thought you forgave me."

"I do forgive you." She kicked at the ground beneath the bench. "But I can't trust you."

"I've changed." He pulled his hands to his chest. "I won't desert you again. Or Joseph. I promise."

He seemed sincere, but he didn't get it.

"You promised me once, that for better or worse you'd stick by me." She sucked in a breath of cool air. "But you didn't. You ran. And you broke my heart."

"I know. That was a mistake. I see it now."

She nodded.

"We can start over." He took her hand in his. "We can make this work. I love you and Joseph."

She brushed a tear from her cheek. "When it really mattered, you didn't love us enough. Joseph deserves better. I deserve better."

Lauren returned to her mom's house, and without saying a word to her mom, went directly back to her bedroom. She gathered Joseph in her arms and held him close. The tears slid down her cheeks.

A knock sounded at her door. "Lauren, are you okay?"

She wiped at her face with the back of her sleeve. "Yes. I'm fine." She went to the door and opened it. "Paul is going back to Denver. Without us. He wants to be able to see Joseph when he's down this way and I told him that would be fine. I don't expect we'll see him much."

"Oh."

"There's something I need to do. Can you—"

"I'll stay with Joseph."

Lauren stepped out into the cold air and made her way down the street. Her heart thudded inside her with every step she took toward Ethan's house. Before she reached the house, she stopped and steadied her breathing. To her surprise, the front door opened and Ethan stood there, his gaze locked on hers. She took a few steps forward, and he closed the space between them.

"I know what I want," Lauren said.

Ethan said nothing, but kept his eyes on her.

"I want a man I can trust. A man who won't turn his back on me because life is rough. A man who can love my son despite his imperfections. I want a family."

"Paul?"

"I sent him back to Denver."

Ethan brushed her cheek with the backs of his fingers. "I love you." He paused. "And I love Joseph."

She rested her hands on his shoulders. "I love you too. But this won't be easy."

"I don't need easy. I need you." He leaned in and laid his lips across hers. He deepened the kiss, awakening every nerve in her body.

This was where she belonged.

In his arms.

chapter 47

Lauren sat next to Ethan at her mom's dinner table. Bethany and Matt sat across from them, with her mom at the head of the table.

"Kaylee, come sit down. We're ready for dinner," Bethany said. "You can play with your Christmas presents after we eat."

Jace dropped his silverware on the floor and giggled.

A browned turkey sat in the middle of the table, making Lauren's mouth water.

Joseph started to fuss, so Ethan rose and lifted the baby from his carrier.

"I can hold him," Lauren said, reaching for Joseph.

Ethan snuggled the baby closer to him and kissed him on the forehead. "No way. I'm holding my little man for dinner."

"You can't eat and hold him," she protested.

"Yes, I can. I'm getting really good at it. Isn't that right, J.J.?" Ethan cooed at Joseph, and Lauren's heart smiled. She'd never imagined she'd be sitting at Christmas dinner with Ethan at her side. Or that Ethan would assume the role of daddy so easily and effortlessly. A surge of pure joy enveloped her.

"Let's thank God for all that He's given us," her mom said.

Lauren was bursting with gratitude. She didn't know what the future held as far as Joseph's health or how the Down syndrome would affect him, but she had Ethan. Together they'd face whatever lay ahead.

Together.
Ethan loved her.
And he loved her perfectly imperfect son.
She finally had her happily-ever-after.

Coming Soon
Prejudice Meets Pride
by Rachael Anderson

After years of pinching pennies and struggling to get through art school, Emma Mackie's hard work finally pays off with the offer of a dream job. But when tragedy strikes, she has no choice but to make a cross-country move to Colorado Springs to take temporary custody of her two nieces. She has no money, no job prospects, and no idea how to be a mother to two little girls, but she isn't about to let that stop her. Nor is she about to accept the help of Kevin Grantham, her handsome new neighbor, who seems to think she's incapable of doing anything on her own.

Fun, compelling, and romantic, *Prejudice Meets Pride* is the story of a guy who thinks he has it all figured out and a girl who isn't afraid to show him that he doesn't. It's about learning what it means to trust, figuring out how to give and to take, and realizing that not everyone gets to pick the person they fall in love with. Sometimes, love picks them.

To learn more, see: RachaelReneeAnderson.com

Acknowledgments

So many people have helped me with this book and I am so thankful. I'd like to especially thank Rachael Anderson, Braden Bell, and Stephanie Fowers for their invaluable advice and encouragement. They are awesome critiquers and cheerleaders! And I want to thank Rachael for all of her extra help on this project.

I'd also like to thank the members of Indie Author Hub for answering questions and for much-needed support.

Most of all, I want to thank my amazing husband, Del, for his never-ending support, love, and encouragement. He is always there for me and continually lifts me up. Thank you to my kids who are always kind and supportive and who think I'm the "best author ever." I have a wonderful family and I am very grateful for each one of them.

Thank you to my readers! Without you, I'd have no reason to write these stories.

About the Author

Rebecca Talley grew up in Santa Barbara, CA. After high school graduation, she attended Brigham Young University. She graduated with a bachelor's degree in Communications. While at BYU, she met and married her sweetheart, Del. They are the proud parents of ten highly-creative, multi-talented children, including a son with Down syndrome. They also have the most adorable granddaughter in the world. Rebecca lives in Houston, TX with her husband and most of her children.

Rebecca is the author of *Grasshopper Pie* (WindRiver 2003), *Heaven Scent* (CFI 2008), *Altared Plans* (CFI 2009), *The Upside of Down* (CFI 2011), *Gabby's Secret* (DuBon Publishing 2011), *Hook Me: What to Include in Your First Chapter* (DuBon Publishing 2012), *Aura* (DuBon Publishing 2012), and numerous children's stories and articles for both online and print magazines.

When she isn't writing, Rebecca loves to date her husband, play with her kids, swim in the ocean, eat Dove dark chocolate, and dance to disco music while she cleans the house.

You can find Rebecca online at:

www.rebeccatalley.com
www.rebeccatalleywrites.blogspot.com